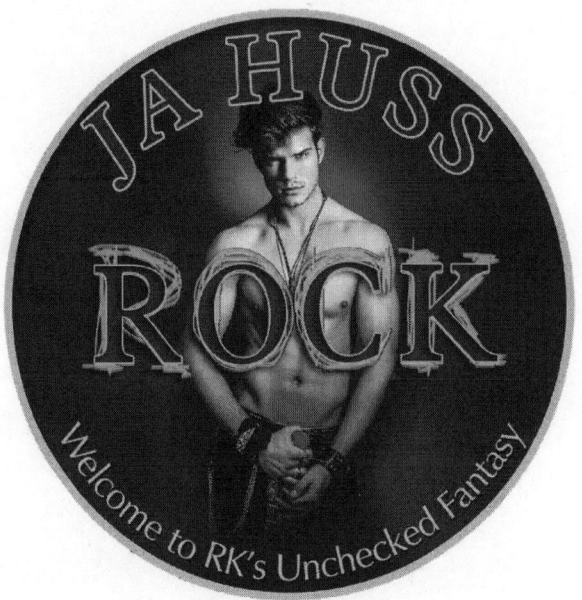

JA HUSS

ROCK

Welcome to RK's Unchecked Fantasy

A Rock Star Romantic Suspense
By J. A. Huss

ROCK

Copyright © 2016 by JA Huss
ISBN-978-1-944475-03-1

Edited by RJ Locksley
Cover Model: Robert Reider
Cover Photo: Luciana Varga
Cover Design: J. A. Huss

DEDICATION

To all the cool kids who keep taking risks even when they fail.

Prologue

Melissa Vetti's lips were softer than the down blankets on her bed and they were equally as warm. We lingered in the kiss longer than we should've. Longer than ever before, not moving, not tonguing each other, not seeking more with wandering hands trying to pick at the buttons on our jeans. Just connected.

"I love you," I whispered into her mouth.

"I know," she giggled into mine. She always said that when I pushed, but at least this time it didn't come with a litany of excuses. *We're too young. You're leaving in three months. We have our whole lives to fall in love.*

It was too late for me though, because I'd been in love with her since the sixth grade when we ditched the chaperones on the class camping trip in Rocky Mountain National Park in the middle of the night.

We both lived next to that park. We wandered into that forest so many times, the woods were our home. And the spot the school chose for the class trip was close by. Our town is not really rich, even though if you want to buy a decent house up here in Grand Lake these days, it's gonna cost you a million dollars. Our schools are not by any means well-equipped. Hell, most younger kids who live here, and there aren't many, go to school in Granby, the next town over. But a trip to the local woods was something everyone could afford.

I knew the way—hell, she knew the way too. And when the small waterfall came into view, the moon making the water in the pool shimmer silver, we both got sweaty hands and chills up our spines.

Missy Vetti and I had our first kiss that night and I loved every moment of it. The sound of the forest at night. The cool midnight breeze whipping past our skin making us shiver, even though it was July. The heat of her breath mixing with mine and the way my fingers found their way into her hair and pulled her close out of instinct.

That's all we did that night. Just one kiss in the dark. But it was enough for me to fall in love. And now that we were on the verge of college, it seemed like every moment had been wasted. Like I should've done so much more with her. Everything felt like a missed opportunity.

"You have to go before my dad gets up, RK."

"I know." I'd been sneaking into her house to sleep over for years. Not every night. And we didn't fuck or anything. Missy Vetti was as pure as the water rushing down the mountain and her dad spent every night sleeping like a bear in the winter, so we never got caught. Or maybe he knew and didn't care? Maybe he knew his daughter was perfect and would never let a boy spoil her with sex?

I reluctantly pulled away from our embrace and sat up in her bed, looking back over my shoulder. "Pick you up at eight?"

She smiled big. Big. Big. Big.

That's all I got—a smile.

And I have seen that smile in my nightmares for the past five years and asked myself the same question over and over again.

Why did I kill her?

Chapter One

There are no words perfect enough to describe my memory of the Vetti twins so I had to write a song. A nine-minute masterpiece that flowed from my heart, to my mind, and finally out through my fingertips as I picked and plucked each note on the antique baby grand we kept in front of the music room window overlooking the mountain.

My description might seem excessive, but every word is necessary.

The length—an indicator of my reluctance to finish the song. I still consider it incomplete and that's why I've never performed it in public, even though someone leaked the only video of it to *Metal Notes Magazine Online* and not a show goes by that they, the fans, don't chant for it from the dark, hiding behind their fake lighters projecting from their phones.

The flow of creativity—because it all came from my heart. Broken as it was, as I sat in front of Melissa's grave, tapping out the tempo on my leg, the rain pouring down on me in rivers. At the time I had no lyrics, only the melody, because the only words in my head were dark and I refused to give that darkness a place to live inside me forever. I refused to let Melissa be reduced to RK's pathetic darkness.

The imagery—because I could see their bedrooms from the music room in my house. The flick of their lights sent me signals all growing up, lights that will never flick again because there is no *them* anymore. I breathe deeply as I sit in my truck and look through the thick fog mixed with a light snow to find their house.

Not their house, RK. Her house.

And I hate that in my mind I still call myself RK instead of Rowan Kyle. Or Rock, for that matter. I'm Rock to the entire world, to everyone but me. When can I stop being RK or Rowan Kyle and just be Rock?

I am wordy and incoherent most of the time, I know this. My lyrics are nothing but run-on sentences broken up with the bass guitar and the beat of the drums as the lead plays with the tempo just enough to make you stop and say, *Yes. That's nice. Who is that? What is the name of that song?*

That's how we became mega-rock stars in the span of five years. That's how I pulled myself up from the darkness that surrounded me after Melissa died. That's what got me through.

But now that's gone too.

Because my band, Son of a Jack, the band I started when all five of us were penniless on the streets of

Hollywood, desperate for change and opportunity, is as dead as Melissa.

It's like my life is on song repeat when all I want is a shuffle.

I survived the crash that took Melissa and me over the edge of a mountain road five years ago, the night of our high-school prom. Melissa's twin sister, Melanie, survived that car crash with me. She was not there. But she was a survivor nonetheless. Because I broke them apart. I cut them in half. And she, like me, had to learn to live on.

I survived the crash that took Son of a Jack over the edge of a cliff on another mountain road as we were driving up to Winter Park to ski. My drummer, Kenner, survived the crash with me. He was there. So he earned his survivor badge honestly. I broke the band apart too. And he, like me, has to learn to live on.

That was eight weeks ago.

I've been in rehab up in Steamboat Springs ever since. Well, until today. My larynx was fractured. A group II fracture that was elevated to a group III after they tried to intubate me and fucked it up even worse. They repaired it with resorbable plates in Denver and then sent me somewhere pretty to recuperate. They say it's working now. That's what they say.

I have no idea if the operation was a success because I refuse to talk. And it's not because I don't want to talk or I don't remember so I have nothing to say. I remember every moment of the crash because I was not drunk. I was not high. I was not asleep. They said all those things about me afterward, but the blood tests came back clean, and I know I wasn't asleep because I relive every second of that crash in slow motion every time I close my eyes.

So fuck them. I wasn't asleep.

But the throat still hurts like hell, so I'm not gonna talk until that goes away. My thoughts are so crazy I'm almost afraid of what might come out if I do talk, so it's better this way.

I shut the truck off and let out a sigh.

Melanie's light is on. She lives alone now. Her sister is gone. Her father died of lung cancer two years ago. I never came for the funeral. I was in Bangkok getting sucked off after a show when I got the call.

And that night I *was* high and I *was* drunk, and the thought of traveling back to Colorado for a funeral, well, let's just say that bitch's mouth was a lot more enticing than a twenty-hour trip that would bring me right back to the place I ran from a few years earlier.

No. I missed it. On purpose.

I get out of the truck and turn away from Mel's house and then face mine.

And it *is* mine. My dad died last year, and no, I didn't come home for that either. He left the house to me and the bar to my brother, TJ.

Toby John, I correct myself, or Teej, as I like to call him. When will he stop being TJ and Teej and start being Toby John? When can we go back to the way things were?

I push the key in the door lock and it swings open with a creak. The alarm sounds and I key in the familiar numbers to silence it.

I killed this house too. I can feel death in here. It winds around me like a mist. A thick fog of putrid decay.

I walk past all the white sheet-covered furniture, into the living room, round the corner and through the kitchen, and keep walking until I see it.

The piano.

I told myself all the way here I would not sit down and play. And I won't. But I pull the sheet off and stare at it for a moment. It's still black, but the luster is gone. It's still big, but it feels smaller. I flick the lights on in this room and then turn around and walk to the door that leads to the garage.

The tools are all here, but the cars are gone. I have no idea if my father bequeathed me a car with the house, but I'm not looking for a car.

I'm looking for a sledgehammer.

I spy the handle sticking out from a pile of stacked tile and cut-up drywall. A remnant from years ago when my dad decided to remodel the master bath for my mom. She died before it was finished.

Like I said. Putrid decay.

If I can destroy everything tonight with this sledgehammer, I will. Just let me get that fucker in my hands, just let me get that motherfucker in my hands and this whole house is going down. This whole life, or what's left of it, is going down.

The sledgehammer is propped up against the back wall behind a stack of cinderblocks. I throw them into the center of the garage floor—breaking some of them, but who the fuck cares—and after a dozen of these tosses, when the parking pad is good and littered with cracked blocks, I wedge the sledgehammer out and let out a roar of victory before the pain shoots up my throat like fire.

I drop the sledgehammer and bend over to stop my head from spinning. The aftereffects of a serious injury combined with the memories of how I got that wound are pure agony.

Bending over really doesn't help, so I drop to my knees, my head bowed, to wait out the pain.

"RK?"

And that's how she finds me.

On my fucking knees. As broken as the litter of crumbling cinderblocks around me.

Her snow boots are dripping water because we are eight thousand feet up in the Rocky Mountains, and as ridiculous as it sounds, it snows here in May. That's all I see. Just her feet. Because I can't lift my head and look her in the eyes.

"I heard you were coming back. TJ told me you're not allowed to leave Grand County until the investigation is over, so I figured you'd show up here. I was—" She stops, then walks forward to stand in front of me and kneels down. "I was waiting for you. I have a lot of things I want to say to you."

Her last few words come out with a hitch and I know she's crying.

"Melanie," I say. My voice is that of a stranger—raspy and deep. I don't even recognize myself talking. And I want to say more, but the pain is so bad, I have to take a deep breath to stop my own tears. But I force the words out. I have to force the words out because they need to be said and they need to be said now or I'll never get through this night. I'll never make it if she stays.

So I become that guy you see on those tabloid TV shows. The dick.

"Get the fuck out of my house."

Chapter Two

There's a long silence that hangs in the air.
Not seconds, but minutes.

Her boots never move. The puddle just continues to grow beneath her feet. I watch the trickle of water as it makes its way to me and when it finally touches the faded blue jeans and seeps in to touch my knee, I can't take it anymore.

I look up.

She nods her head. "That's all I ever wanted from you, RK. Acknowledgment. That I matter in this. That what happened happened to all of us and not just you. You were not the only one confused. You were not the only one who was sad afterward. But you were the only one selfish enough to walk away from this town. From your friends. From your family. From me. And as much as I'd like to yell and scream at you right now, I'm not going to. I'm going to tell you something else instead. And I'm going to say it calmly."

I just stare at her. Because I don't even know this girl. I have no clue who she is. The girl standing in front of me is not Missy's sister. She's Melanie, but she's some Mel I've never met before. Her hair is long and dark. Darker than I remember. Her eyes are dark too. They are still blue, but the eyeliner is thick and black. Her jeans are ripped and her cropped biker jacket is leather.

She looks so much like... But why shouldn't she? They were identical.

"Feel free to get up and walk out," she continues when I say nothing. "I'm prepared for that, since you do it so often. I'll follow you. In this house, outside the house. If you get in your truck and drive off, I'll follow you. I've had something to say to you for five years and tonight's the night, Rock. Tonight is your night."

I stand up and walk out. If I'm forced to hear her out, I'm sure as fuck not going to do it kneeling at her feet. I have so much to say about what she just said, I can't keep still. I hate the fact that she called me Rock. Even though I want to be Rock, it feels like an insult coming from her. It feels like a badge I'd rather not wear. So I go back into the house. She follows like she said, and I make my way to the kitchen. I flick the lights on and pull open the fridge out of habit.

To my surprise, there's food in there. And beer.

I grab a beer and twist the top off, then take a seat at the bar and take a small sip.

It burns.

It burns like fuck. But it feels good at the same time. The burn and the cold. I take another sip and wait for

Melanie to join me. She stands in the archway that leads to the front hall and watches.

I stare back.

"You can thank TJ for the groceries." She waits for my response and when I don't say anything back, she shakes her head in disgust.

"Melanie," I say, wincing as the pain takes over. "I can't talk to you." I clutch my throat to help her understand and she narrows her eyes at me. "It fucking hurts. So just say what you have to say and leave."

Her chest rises and falls, like she just took a giant breath of air. Something necessary to deal with me tonight. Then she walks over to the connected family room, pulls the white sheet off the couch, and has a seat.

I take a big breath too. To ask myself to be patient with her. The less I piss her off, the faster she will talk, and the sooner I can get rid of her.

"It's a confession."

OK. I walk over to the family room with my beer and take a seat in the chair opposite her, not bothering to remove the white sheet. I wave my hand, a gesture that says, *Let's get this show on the road.*

"Back when we were kids—" She stares at me and her blue eyes sparkle as the corners of her mouth lift up into a smile.

I like the smile, it feels so very, very familiar, so I smile back.

"We were all at that summer camp that came to town, remember? The music one? Your dad had talked all those college kids from the Colorado Conservatory into coming up here for six weeks to turn us into musicians."

I smile bigger at that memory because it's a good one. Teej and me. Mel and Missy. And a bunch of other kids too, tourist kids. Not even town kids. It was a pretty big deal that summer. We were music freaks. I come from a family of music freaks. Mel and Missy too. And even if the twins didn't come from a family of music freaks, they were along for the ride because they were the only neighbors for six miles in any direction. Teej is two years older than me, Mel and Missy are my same age. The four of us were inseparable.

Until I broke the girls in half.

I lean over and massage my temple with a fingertip as Melanie talks.

"I was mad that summer because you wanted—"

"Melissa played the cello, and I needed a cello," I explain, before I remember I should not be talking. I wince and grab my throat, then take another small sip of the cold beer and the tears are knocking as that goes down, that's how bad it hurts. It feels like I've got sand or rocks in my throat and there's no way to get beyond it. If I drink, it hurts to use the muscles. If I don't drink, it hurts because it's dry.

"I know, RK. You always made decisions based on logic. My sister always thinks ahead too. She's a planner. Like you."

Melanie using the present tense to talk about her sister hurts more than my throat and I almost get up and walk out.

"She always knew what you needed before you knew you needed it, didn't she?"

And the switch to past tense makes it all hit home again.

"So poor, pathetic Melanie was the odd one out that summer. You and TJ on violin…" Melanie hesitates for a second. "Missy on cello and that little blonde summer girl on viola."

"You have to have a violist, Mel," I say, the rocks in my throat grinding together. I take another small sip. I'll never be able to drink enough alcohol to get drunk at this rate. I can barely swallow. "It wasn't like I—" *Jesus*. I take another sip and force it down.

Mel appears beside me with a glass of ice water. "I'm pretty sure the alcohol is making it worse."

I shake my head, but accept the ice water all the same and take a small sip. It still burns, but it's soothing too, so I take another sip and then guzzle the rest, hoping the cold will numb the pain a little. Melanie waits me out, so I try to get one last sentence past the agony. "I just wanted you to have a good group, and our group was not good for you. Your viola skills sucked, no offense, and your bass skills"—I look up at her— "rocked."

I think that was the longest sentence I've said since the accident and it requires a very deep breath for many reasons after I'm done.

But Mel is still chatty. "No, RK, you're misunderstanding me. I'm not telling you this so you feel sorry for me or so you can make me feel better with some bullshit compliment. I'm telling you this because that was the summer I realized something."

I look her straight in the eyes as she pauses.

"That was the day I realized you were always going to plow over me. Over us. Over everyone. I knew you wanted the best group. I knew you wanted to impress people with your skills. I knew that I was not what you were looking for. And I came to terms with it back then. When I was fourteen, I already knew. That summer was the best thing that ever happened to me."

I just stare at her, confused as to where this is going.

"Because you're the kind of guy who changes people, RK. You're the kind of guy girls fixate on and can't let go. You're the kind of guy who breaks up families, and drives drunk, and ruins lives. You ruin people, *Rock*. And I just wanted to come here tonight to thank you. For knocking that stupid crush I had on you right out of my head. Because if you were any less of an asshole, I might've actually liked you. And then *I* might've been the one you killed on prom night instead of my sister."

Chapter Three

I am stunned silent as she walks out. I watch her, and I'm silent because of the injury, but I'm stunned silent on the inside too.

I am blank. I am RK's blank mind.

And then, after the door slams shut with a bang, my thoughts are racing, my throat is killing me, and the house seems like the wrong place to be. Like wrong, man. Just wrong. I get up and follow Mel out the door. By the time I get to the driveway she's already inside her place and the lights are off. A signal, I guess. It speaks loud and clear to me. *Don't come here.*

I get in my truck and start it up, the tires spinning a little on the wet blacktop driveway, and then head down the hill and drive towards town. There is nothing going on in town. Less than five hundred people call Grand

Lake home year-round. No one wants to stick around for the dead-end life up here in the winter.

But in the summer it's overflowing with people. Tourists. Parties and boating and fishing and music and theatre. The place is alive during the summer.

It's May, so when I come around the mountain and see the streets down below it's clear we're not quite there yet. It's empty and dark tonight. As dark as it gets on a night with no moon and only the occasional street lamp. There's no twenty-four-hour drugstore here, but I got the next best thing.

The bar. Float's.

We have more than one—even in the winter we're not that small. But Float's is my dad's bar.

Was my dad's.

It's TJ's bar now and even though he's the last person I need to see and talk to at the moment, I need something for this pain and that place is my best bet.

And a drink would be nice too. Something stronger than beer that will help knock my ass out with a few swallows. Something that will take away the nightmares, and the crazy thoughts, and the confusion.

I drive down the twisted road to the town and the lake and pull into the dirt parking lot. I practically grew up in this parking lot and I've got so many memories rattling around in my head, I clear my throat to make the pain worse, just to keep them at bay.

Float's is a ramshackle wooden building made of graying barn wood. The large deck has umbrella tables in the summer, but none right now, and a small grassy lawn that is mostly covered in snow. The large dock out back that the place is named for has no canopy and no band playing since the outside shows don't start until Memorial Day weekend.

I pull open the door and there's a familiar scent and a familiar sound, but that's it. It's been remodeled inside—new gleaming stainless-steel bar, new stainless-steel tables that look like they belong down in some trendy LoDo bar in Denver. The booths are black leather with stainless-steel accents and the staff are all wearing black slacks, crisp white collared shirts, and black aprons. It's all very trendy and not at all my style.

Not TJ's style either.

I scan the room looking at the faces and realize I recognize way too many of them.

A few turn and look in my direction and that's when the whispering starts. Every head turns towards me. Every face is staring at me. And I just stand there like an idiot until TJ pushes his way out of a group of guys at a back booth and stands a few feet in front of me. He looks different too. His hair is short and styled, which matches his very conservative clothes—dark suit coat, dark slacks, and white shirt.

We are the same height, both over six foot, but that's pretty much where the similarities end. My hair is brushing against my shoulders, my black leather jacket jingles with the zippers on the sleeves and front, and even though I spent the better part of the last six weeks working out to take my mind off the injury and the accident, I'm nowhere near as big as he is.

Even under the clean-cut costume, one look into my brother's eyes tells me all I need to know. He is every bit the soldier he turned himself into five years ago when I left town.

The music cuts off and the whole place goes quiet. "She already called me," Teej says, like this silence was planned for dramatic effect. "Says you haven't changed."

He looks at me with that steely gaze, seeing me for what I am as well. The good-for-nothing rock star.

I don't think that's a fair assessment to be honest. Both the 'rock star' part I see in TJ's disgusted expression and the 'haven't changed' part Mel accused me of. Melanie was never going to give me a chance. She had her mind made up the second she saw me pull in the driveway.

"Says you're an asshole, says you were rude, says you're just as fucked up as ever."

I nod and sigh.

"She says you're pretending you can't talk, but she says you sounded just fine to her. Why the fuck are you here, RK? You've been gone five years and never once came home. Not for Dad, not for Mel's dad. Not for me, not for her. So why the fuck are you here?"

I pull the pen and paper out of my pocket and start writing, but Teej smacks the pad out of my hand and it goes flying across the room, hits the floor, and slides under the pool table.

"You'll talk to me, asshole. I deserve that much, you understand? I deserve the pain it takes for you to speak. So fuck you and your little pad of paper."

I don't know how to answer his question in a few words. That's like a fucking paragraph of words. And it's really two questions in one. Why am I in town? He knows why. I'm not allowed to leave the county until the sheriff clears me to go. And there's not a lot of towns in Grand County, Colorado. Winter Park is too close to Denver, too accessible and too many people, even though the ski slopes have been shut down for the year. Steamboat is in the next county over, so I can't even stay in rehab. Grand Lake is the only place I had to go unless I wanted to hide out in some seedy mountain hotel in

Fraser or Granby. And why the fuck should I? I own a four-bedroom house with a view of Rocky Mountain National Park on one side and Grand Lake on the other.

That is a no-brainer.

"Why the fuck did you come here tonight, RK?"

That's a more difficult one to explain. Especially with my history, so I start with something easy. "Thank you," I croak out. "For the fridge stuff."

"It wasn't my idea," he says back. "So save your thanks."

OK, I throw up my hands and turn to leave because I know when I can't win. I'm not getting any help here tonight.

"I know why you came," he calls after me.

If I was smart I'd keep walking, because I can see it coming. But I don't. I turn around and ask for it. "Why, Teej? If you're so smart, go ahead and tell me." I growl out the words past my damaged vocal cords and try my best to keep a straight face through the pain.

"Drugs," he says simply.

And I'd like to deny it, but I can't. Because it's true. So I just nod. "I'm in a lot of pain and they didn't give me a prescription when I checked out today, so—"

"They didn't give you a prescription because you're an addict, *Rock*."

I raise my hand in a goodbye because it's no use denying it. It's a waste of breath, or in my case, the pain required to get the words out.

He doesn't call out to me this time, just lets me go. I can hear the whole place erupt in talking before the front door closes behind me. Let them talk. They don't know shit. I don't need his fucking bar anyway. We have a liquor store on the edge of town, so I get back in my truck, drive over there, and go inside. There's one dude behind the counter strumming a decent Martin guitar. I give him a nod and head for the Scotch. They don't have much.

"You need something special?" the guy with the guitar asks me.

I was hoping I wouldn't have to talk to anyone, but I look past him and see the cheap good Scotch on a shelf behind his head, and then point to a bottle of Glenmorangie. He grabs it and puts it on the counter.

"Looking to get drunk, my friend?"

I shake my head. "Sleep," I croak out. And that's when he recognizes me.

"Rock?" he asks, even though he knows it's me. "Hey dude, how's it going?" He says it with sympathy and a wave of gratitude flows through me. Mel didn't ask. TJ didn't ask. But this guy, someone I don't even know, he asks.

"Could be better," I say as clearly as I can, because he deserves a few painful words.

He pulls a marijuana container from his pocket and holds it out. "You need some pain relief too?" He obviously reads the tabloids, which is more than I can say for my ex-friends and family.

"Thanks, but can't smoke," I say as I clutch my throat.

"I wish I had some oxy, dude, that'd do it. But I don't touch the shit."

"Don't worry about it," I tell him and throw down a hundred-dollar bill. "Keep the change." He puts the bottle into a paper bag and hands it over.

"Hey," he calls out just before I walk out the door. "My uncle is an ear, nose, throat doctor in Denver. But he has appointments at the medical offices in Granby one day a week. He's real good, maybe he'll give you a prescription? I'll tell him you'll stop by on Monday."

I give him a nod as the door closed behind me.

With any luck I can drink myself into a stupor and sleep right through Monday.

Chapter Four

I met Kenner before I met all the rest of the guys in the band. We were hanging out on Sunset Boulevard passing out flyers for a show, just a few blocks down from a local club. We were promoting this piece-of-shit band called EC Twist—stupid fucking name—and lamenting the lack of good rock music in the current LA scene as we talked ourselves up and generally beat on our chests like alphas. But the second he called himself a *percussionist* I knew he and I were going to do something together. Maybe just bang the drums for a while or maybe just fuck off and get drunk, but we were going to do something.

We tossed the flyers in the overflowing trash bin on the corner and walked the sixteen blocks back to his place, which was really nothing more than a three-hundred-square-foot room, with a decrepit hotplate acting as a kitchen, pretending to be an apartment. He had a hammock hanging from large rusty bolts on either wall as his only piece of real furniture, and all his clothes were stacked neatly in towers along the perimeter of a pile of sheet music, random magazines, and unopened mail.

But in the middle of the room sat a sweet drum kit, and wedged into a space that practically blocked the entrance to the bathroom was an upright studio piano with a sleek ebony finish.

"My prize possession," Kenner said, waving to the piano. "Saved up for two years to have it professionally moved out here from my parents' house back in Kentucky."

The minute I sat on the bench and he took the stool, it was over, man. That bitch had a tone I hadn't heard since I left Colorado. They keys were perfectly weighted and responsive and my fingers picked out Missy's death song as Kenner found a beat and joined in. We played like it was meant to be, like the heavens opened up, and the sadness poured out of me until I saw the look of success in Kenner's eyes and had to stop and tell him we would never play that song again, but I had hundreds of songs just like it. *They are locked inside my head*, I told him. *But they are there.*

And the rest, as they say, is history. None of my songs are anything like Missy's death song, but Kenner didn't care. They were rock and fucking roll, man. They were loud, and sick, and had beats that would raise the dead—as long as the dead weren't named Melissa Vetti.

I pull into my driveway and cut the engine, holding the paper-bagged bottle of Scotch by the neck, and get out. I look over at the Vetti house out of habit and that pain in my chest—that fucking pain I've been running from for five years—hits me so hard, I don't even have a word to describe it.

But then there's a movement in the dark window, a flutter of the sheer white curtains in Melissa's room, and I know she's watching me.

Elias and Ian came next. Both played guitar, Ian on lead and Elias on bass.

We added Mo a few months after we started getting noticed in the club scene, after that first demo that landed us in meetings with assholes and scammers—the general term we used to describe the underground music scene of the up-and-coming. That's when I decided I wanted to concentrate on singing and writing, and he took my place on the keys.

I wrote a new song every week that first year we were playing. We released them all online first, and when the big-shot assholes came knocking we had at least sixteen guaranteed hits on our hands. We exploded onto the scene, opening up for bands with millions of fans, millions of hits online, and millions of dollars backing their shit up.

The fans ate us up and we did the lather, rinse, repeat. One more year of weekly songs, not signing shit as far as contracts go, not making any promises to anyone other than ourselves, uploading direct until we had so many plays for the subscriptions service and a feature in all the stores at least once a month, the dollars came pouring in.

We signed our first recording contract with smug faces and know-it-all attitudes, flicking the middle finger at the very men who wanted to take us global until they loved to hate us because they needed our rising star to make them shine.

I walk up the snow-covered stone pavers leading to the house and realize I never locked the front door when I left. In fact, it's standing open about an inch. I go inside, slamming the dark mahogany monstrosity so loud, I hope Mel hears it from her house down the hill.

There's melted snow on the heated floor tiles that look so much like aged antique barn wood, you can't tell the difference unless you get down on your knees and touch the planks with your fingertips.

My eyes track the snow to my room, where I was not earlier.

Someone is here.

I walk down the hallway to my room, slide my hand around the side of the wall, and flick the light on as I raise the bottle, ready to slam it over the intruder's head.

Melanie is sitting on my bed. I squint at her because my fucking throat still hurts. She looks at the raised bottle and I let my arm drop to my side. I raise my hands in a shrug, asking her 'what the fuck?' in Rock sign language.

She shakes her head, and starts writing on a pad of paper in her hand. She scribbles furiously for a few seconds, and then lifts it up for me to see.

If you won't talk to me, then I won't talk to you.

"Get out," I grumble, the pain shooting through my whole body this time. I have to hold my breath and close my eyes to make it stop, and even then, it takes to the count of ten. I point to the front door. "Get. Out!" I scream the last part so loud, I taste the blood rising up from my throat. I turn and plow my way through the house, bouncing off white-sheeted furniture, until I make it to the kitchen and turn the cold tap on and douse my mouth with Grand Lake's finest icy mountain water.

I gulp until my throat is nothing but burning cold. I shut the tap off but stare down into the black drain of the sink. I can feel Melanie's eyes on my back. I give her a sidelong look over my shoulder and find her just a step or two behind me, her eyes filled with hate and loathing.

Fuck you, I mouth.

You'd like to, she mouths back.

I shake my head, a little stunned that she'd say something like that. After everything that happened, that she would *dare.* I turn all the way around and take her in. She shrugs the jacket off, letting the heavy leather slide down her arms and fall to a heap on the floor.

What the fuck?

Her fingertips whip her black Metallica t-shirt over her head and she lets that drop to the floor too.

"Mel—" But I stop when her bra comes off and she stands there, baring her breasts to me with downcast eyes. She takes my hand and places it on top of her peaked-up nipple, rubbing it, squeezing it—her hand over mine.

Then she's tugging on my jeans and breathing heavy in my ear. I see the past so clearly, I almost get dizzy.

"RK," she whispers, and I swear to God—I swear on all the things I've lost and all the things God owes me—she sounds so much like Missy, I let myself buy into the illusion.

She has my dick out before I can shake myself back to reality, and who the fuck wants reality when all it is is death?

Fuck reality. This girl is my girl. She is the exact image. The same voice. A precise copy of the only person I will ever love.

I flip the button on her jeans and rip the zipper down, my hands reaching between her legs, my fingertips sliding into the slick pool of wetness. She moans as I push her back down the hallway and into my room, both of us tripping over the rug covering the faux-antique barn wood planks.

She laughs as we fall, her head hitting the floor hard enough to make her wince. I breathe through the thumping of my heart and place my hand under her head to make sure she's OK.

She takes that opportunity to fist my cock. I tug her jeans down, backing off enough to drag them down to her knees, then flip her knees up to her chin and place my tongue over her pussy.

I kiss it. Thoroughly. Deeply. I lick and suck her clit until she's fisting my hair and bucking her hips.

"RK," she moans, gripping my shoulders, urging me to continue. But now all I can think about is how I never fucked Missy. How she got away and I never even fucked her. Why didn't I fuck her?

I move to Melanie's stomach, licking and biting my way up her body until I reach her neck and I bury my face into the scent of her hair as my cock buries itself inside her pussy.

She moans loudly this time. "Jesus," she says.

I rock into her, my hands cupping her face, my hips grinding against hers. Thrusting, harder, deeper, then slow and soft until she's urging me to go fast again. I rest my body on top of her chest, dip my head down and bite the sensitive skin of her breast as she cups it and pushes her nipple into my mouth.

Her other hand is on my back, her long fingernails digging into my flesh as I pump her harder and harder.

"I hate you," she says into my ear, her voice way too soft for the harsh words. "I hate you so much, RK. For leaving me. For leaving this town and never coming back. For being so talented and smart, and so willing to throw it all away."

But she's still moving with our shared rhythm as she talks.

"I hate you too," I croak back, thrusting deep inside her until she buckles underneath me, throws her head back, and comes all over my dick. "I hate you for not being…" I have to force the words out through the pain, because I need her to feel them. I need her to hurt with me. "For not being the one I want."

Her whole body goes still—and then she grips my shoulders, pushes me back, and manages to get her foot up against my chest even though her jeans are still around her knees.

She kicks and I go flying backwards, crashing my head against the tiled floor. She stands up, hiking her jeans back into place, buttons them. Then she stands over me, straddling my hips, and sinks down until she's sitting on my stomach.

Her face is nothing but sadness as she reaches for me, placing her warm palms against my cheeks. "You are a sick, sick, man, Rowan Kyle Saber. A very sick man."

"Melanie—" I croak.

"Fuck you." She slaps my face and stands back up. "Just fuck you. You should know me better."

I breathe in her contempt and hate as she walks out.

The front door slams just as I'm pulling my pants back up and I can't get to that bottle of Scotch fast enough. I find it hastily discarded on the front room couch as I rush through to the kitchen and twist the cap off.

I guzzle this time. I need it. I need this fucking whiskey like death needs darkness. And when I finally come up for air, my whole body is heating up and my head is spinning from the burn, and the pain, and the heartache.

Ian. Elias. Mo... Missy. Dad. Mom.

Why the fuck am I still alive when everyone I ever loved gets to enjoy that darkness?

Just why?

My phone buzzes in my pants and I whip it out and check the incoming call. Jayce. I tab accept and grunt into the phone.

"Rock," Jayce says on the other end. Her voice is strong but small, just like her. She's been our manager—*was* our manager—ever since we signed that first deal. "You were supposed to text me when you got home. I have to report you in if you don't want the sheriff issuing a warrant for your arrest."

"Mmm," I grunt again. I'm going to pay for that last yell. I can feel my vocal cords swelling as the seconds pass. I can taste the blood. My hand flies up to my neck and palms the skin over my Adam's apple. I close my eyes and wish this fucking night would just—

"OK, I'm going to take that as an I'm fine and let you get some rest." She pauses for a moment, breathing into the phone. "You're fine, right?"

I shake my head, because no, I'm so fucking far from fine.

"Kenner woke up," she blurts.

I swallow hard before I can stop myself and let out a small cry of pain.

"Rock?"

"Yeah." I try to talk. "Is he—"

"He doesn't remember anything. They're still assessing nerve damage, but the fractures have mostly healed while he was unconscious." She drops off for a few seconds before adding, "He *will* be OK, Rock. We just have to let him heal. We all have to heal, Rock. We just need a little time to get a grip on it, right?"

She waits for my answer but I can't even force myself to lie. "No," I say through the pain. "We're not going to heal, Jayce. We're never getting past this."

I end the call and the tears build in my eyes. From the pain, I tell myself. The throat. But that's not why I want to cry.

It's relief. It overwhelms me so thoroughly, I fall to my knees, just barely managing to keep a hold of the neck of the Scotch, and crawl over to the living room.

I drink the whole thing propped up on the floor between the coffee table and the couch, imagining all the ways life might get better. All the ways Kenner might get better. Both his arms are dislocated at the elbow, splinted from wrist to shoulder, and his hands are held together with pins and plates.

How long before he can pound on another drum?

How long before I can sing?

How long before we both realize we'll never do either of those things again and life isn't worth living?

I think I'm there.

Chapter Five

A knocking wakes me up. My eyelids flip open, then close again as the bright light of the sun blinds me.

"Sir?" a voice says outside my window. "Sir? Are you OK?" More knocking. "Can you open the door, sir?"

I shield my eyes from the sun and shake my head as I try to process what's happening. I try to talk, to ask where I am, how did I get here… but the pain in my throat comes back so acutely, I have to take a deep, deep breath and close my eyes again.

"Sir, do you need a doctor? I'm a doctor. Do you need help?"

I swallow, my hand flying up to my throat to try to ease the flash of agony, and then turn my head to see who's talking to me. A man, about thirty or so, wearing a nice suit and a concerned expression. He's got thin wire-rimmed glasses that he pushes up his nose while staring at me intently, trying to make an assessment.

I realize my truck is running, so I tab the window and gesture to my throat, making a scribbling motion with my other hand.

"You can't talk?" the genius asks.

I nod.

He fishes around inside his coat and comes out with a pen and a business card, handing it to me. "Can you write?"

I take the pen and scribble, *Throat injury. Accident two months ago. I need something.*

Something, meaning drugs, but also something more than drugs. Because I've had enough blackouts in the past several years to recognize what just happened.

The guy nods, sympathetic. "You're Rock, right? My nephew called me up yesterday and said you might come by. I'm William Chancer. *Dr.* William Chancer. Ear, nose, throat. I've read a little about your injury. What they had of it online. I'm not sure I'm the right guy to help you long term, but I'm probably the only guy up here in the mountains today. So come on inside and I'll see what I can do."

Finally, I sigh, a fucking break.

I tab the window until it's closed, then turn the truck off, pocket the keys, and get out, slamming the door behind me.

He skips up the snowy front steps, unlocks the medical building, and then holds the door open for me as I walk past him. I follow him down the hall and then wait as he unlocks his office door and waves me inside.

I stand at the counter while he begins flipping lights on and bringing the place to life.

"I usually get here first on Mondays," he says good-naturedly. "Actually, Pam took the day off since we're real slow today. Just one appointment in the afternoon. Figured I'd catch up on paperwork. And Dr. Patah, my partner, is taking advantage of the recent snow up in A-Basin before they shut the runs down for the summer."

I nod. Sure, sure. A-Basin is at thirteen thousand feet, so they still have plenty of snow up there to ski.

"So just…" He fumbles though a file cabinet for a clipboard and paperwork, and then places it on the counter in front of me. "Just fill these out the best you can while I get the coffee started. You want a cup?"

I think about this for a moment and then decide I do, and nod.

He disappears into a break room as I take a seat and start scribbling down information. I don't know any of the important stuff, like insurance, but I check my pants, realize I have my wallet, and then decide insurance doesn't matter. I have a gold card. I give him the number and expiration date instead.

The smell of freshly brewing coffee fills the office after a few minutes, and Chancer appears in a white coat looking official. "Come on back, Rock."

Is it weird that he calls me Rock? I decide it is. Mr. Saber is what professional people usually call me. Strangers sometimes call me Rowan, even though I have never answered to that name. They think Kyle is my middle name, but it's not. Friends call me RK and family switches off between RK and Rowan Kyle.

Fans call me Rock. Maybe he's a fan?

"Take a seat on the exam table in there. I'll grab the coffee. You like cream and sugar?" I shake my head and he says, "Me either," with a smile.

I take a seat on the edge of the table, paper crinkling under my jeans, and then shrug off my jacket since the heat is blasting in here. Chancer appears a few minutes later, two ceramic cups in hand. I take the one he offers me, stare at it dubiously, and decide I'm not quite ready to test out hot liquids.

"Yeah," Chancer says. "I imagine it hurts. I can see your throat is swollen from here. So hold off on the coffee for a moment and let me take a look first. It might go down fine, but it might not."

I nod. I kinda like Chancer. He's pretty good at one-way conversations.

"OK, I'll tell you what I think happened, you stop me when I get it wrong."

"'K," I manage to croak.

"Oh, definitely no talking yet. Just keep this handy," he says, taking my mug and offering me a pen and small notepad. "And stop me when you need to." He waits for my nod and then proceeds. "Some kind of incident up in the mountains about eight weeks ago?"

I nod. *Incident.* Nice.

"Some reports said group III fracture of the larynx. You ended up in Denver where they did surgery and made repairs. That was eight weeks ago, so…" Chancer's eyes wander up to the ceiling as his fingertips leave my throat and play with the two-day stubble of beard on his chin. "So technically you should've recovered." He stops talking to wait for my approval.

I shrug.

"Are you getting speech therapy?"

I scribble, *No. I had a therapist at rehab. But I don't want to talk yet.*

"OK, well, you should seriously consider doing that. But today, I'm guessing you're in pain."

I nod, then scribble, *It hurts, man. I'm not a wimp. I know they all think I'm after drugs, so they don't want to give them to me. But it fucking hurts.*

"Is it worse now than when they discharged you?"

I nod again. *I got home on Saturday night, saw some people, yelled a couple of times.*

Chancer nods sympathetically. "That's pretty indicative of a secondary flare-up. So I'm going to write you a prescription for an anti-inflammatory. As far as pain goes, I know all doctors have their own philosophy on addiction, but I firmly believe pain management takes precedent over past history. I also believe you, it's gotta hurt. The anti-inflammatory will help a little, but I'll give you a prescription for oxycodone too. Try not to use it. Don't fill it until you can't handle the pain. Are you really addicted to opiates?"

I nod, looking down at my feet, then scribble, *Been clean for eight months, though.*

Chancer smiles. "Just know that if you take the oxycodone your addiction will come back. The cravings, the shakes, the nausea. All the symptoms of withdrawal will have to be dealt with once you stop taking them. But you're a grown man, so I'm going to give you that option. It's up to you to decide."

Jesus, I could kiss this man.

"Give the coffee a try. See if it helps or hurts." He hands me the cup and I take it. "You are technically healed, Rock. They probably used resorbable plates to fix your fracture?"

I nod and write, *They did.* I'm really fucking afraid of how this coffee might go down, but I take a small sip. It's not hot. Like Chancer added cold water to the brew to spare me that shock. Just the right kind of warm. It goes down nice, actually. A small burn, but nothing like the alcohol.

"And your trach scar," Chancer says, pointing to the closed-up hole at the base of my throat, "looks like it healed well. So you are whole again." He gives me a sympathetic look. "On the outside. Well"—he chuckles—"inside too. But my point is, you're probably just afraid of the pain. Of not being able to manage it, and probably—" Chancer throws up his hands in a shrug. "Probably not all that interested in dealing with what really happened that night. The sad outcome."

I don't nod or scribble anything for that accusation.

"I'm sorry about that. I've always loved your music and I read about you in magazines. About your band. You guys were close, I think. And it's a shock to lose people like that. Especially after what happened to the Vetti girl back in high school."

Jesus fuck. It's time to go.

"But I'm glad you came by, OK?" Chancer sits down on a stool and starts scribbling prescriptions. He rips them off one at a time and then hands them over. "Just give the voice a rest for a few days. Pick up some liquid nutrition shakes from the pharmacy so the throat can heal again. And start thinking about speech therapy and…" He hesitates for a second. "Maybe even some regular therapy? Even if you just go through the motions, it helps, Rock. It does." He shuffles through a drawer until he comes up with a card. "Margie Sanderson is upstairs and she's nice in an old-fart kind of way. She won't judge you. She might not be the most professional therapist I've ever met," he says with a chuckle, "but she's good. And she knows you, so she'll want to help."

I'm never calling Margie Sanderson, but I take the card and stuff it into my wallet. I'm not interested in having that one-sided conversation with Chancer, regardless of how cool he's been about this.

"You're OK, Rock," Chancer says when I stand and shrug on my jacket. "And if you need to come back, I can ask for your medical files from the hospital. I just need your permission." He grabs a clipboard off the wall and hands it to me with a pen.

I sign. Whatever. Then I raise a hand in thanks and walk out of the building.

I get back in my car and the reality of what happened this past weekend hits me. Blackout. Again. This is Monday morning, so I lost all of Sunday. I stare out my window as the sun rises over the peak of the eastern mountains, wondering what I missed this time.

At least I'm not in jail.

And no one is dead.

Chapter Six

I take Chancer's advice and don't hand over the oxy prescription when I get to the City Market in Granby. Addiction is a fucked-up monkey and I really do not want to go through withdrawal again. Never. Beating that shit was the hardest thing I've ever done.

Well, it's high up on the list, anyway.

"Hey, RK," a girl says, coming up to me. I scan her face and come up with a name. Lizzy. "I heard you were back." She gives me a weak smile. Her brother was a friend of mine in junior high, but she looks just like him, so it's hard to make that memory disappear.

I grab my throat, hoping she'll understand I can't talk.

"Sorry," she says. "I know. I just wanted you to know I'm glad you're back. I'm glad you came home."

I don't bother telling her I was forced by the Grand County Sheriff, and she doesn't wait anyway. She just grips my upper arm as she passes me by, giving it a sympathetic squeeze, as a toddling little blonde girl of about four tags along behind her.

It's pretty sad when the town teen mom feels sorry for you. And you're a rock star. And she probably lives in the trailer park out off Highway 34.

I linger in the City Market, picking up some liquid nutrition like Chancer suggested, and a few other things I might need—shaving cream, toilet paper, soap, shit I haven't had to pick up in years because my house in LA has a whole staff of people to do that for me—until they finally call my name on the PA system. "Rock Saber, your prescription is ready. Rock Saber."

I roll my eyes at the Rock part. What the hell is wrong with these people? That prescription said Rowan Kyle.

If they did that shit in LA, I'd have a swarm rushing me for autographs and selfies. But there are only about eight people in the City Market, and none of them are interested in me. Not even Lizzy.

I wander back up to the counter and slap my gold card down.

"OK, RK," the overweight woman at the pharmacy register laughs. "Sounds funny. Rhymes, right? RK, OK." She laughs again. "Rowan Kyle, have you ever taken…"

I just nod yes as she babbles on about side effects. *Get me out of here.* I put my basket of shit up on the counter so I don't have to check out twice, and can't help thinking I could get used to this no-talking thing. It's nice, actually. I love not having to participate.

My phone buzzes in my pants as I walk back out to my truck. I throw my sack onto the passenger seat as I get in and then look at the message as I start the engine.

Kenner: dude help me man tell me what the fuck is happening

I'm still staring at his text when the next one comes in.

Kenner: what the hell is happening

Kenner: come see me

I hold my thumb over the letters on my screen, unsure what to say.

Rock: I can't I'm not allowed

Kenner: don't leave me here man they r telling me things rock I don't know what's happening

My phone rings. I decline and text back real fast.

Rock: i can't talk Kenner

Rock: my voice won't work

Rock: i can't talk

Rock: just texting OK

He never replies and I'm not sure what to do, so I pull out of the parking lot and head back to Grand Lake, wondering if it's going to warm up today. Even for the mountains, it's pretty late in the year to be so cold.

My phone buzzes just after I pass the bar and I check the message.

Jayce: Kenner is disoriented, Rock. Please don't talk to him until he has a few sessions with his therapist. He's in shock.

I throw the phone back onto the seat but she texts me seven more times trying to get an answer before I get to the house. I turn the truck off and pick up my phone to text back.

Rock: i was driving, sorry. and i can't talk anyway, so no worries there.

Jayce: No texting either. OK?

Why no texting?

Jayce: Rock?

Rock: why no texting? he's my best friend. i'd sure the fuck like to talk to him if the situation was reversed

A long pause from Jayce. The sun is starting to burn through the clouds over in the southeast, so I take that as a good sign.

Jayce: He's in shock. He needs professional help to deal with the deaths of Ian, Mo, and Elias.

The phone rings and I answer it on the truck's navigation panel, but don't say hello.

"You there, Rock?"

I grunt a little so Jayce knows I am.

"Just please don't communicate with him yet. He needs some time."

Well, no talking sucks when you want to argue. But I'm very interested in getting this pain under control, so I end the call and text back, *OK.*

Kenner. That's the only bright thing in my life right now. I still have Kenner.

I get out of the truck and immediately hear the music blaring from my house. I look over at the Vetti house, wondering if it's bothering Melanie, decide I don't give a fuck, and continue up the stone path leading to my front door.

I push it open and Son of a Jack's biggest hit, *Tell Me Something I Don't Know*, is so loud, I don't even hear the door when I slam it.

What the fuck? I guess my blackout is due to the one-man party I threw? I throw my keys down on the side table and notice all the furniture has been uncovered. The white sheets are nowhere in sight.

Since when do I tidy the house when I'm drinking? I have to laugh it off because what choice do I have?

The kitchen is nothing but empty beer bottles, the empty Scotch bottle, and a pizza box from Buzzard's, none of it eaten. I set my bag of things down on the counter, fish out the pills, and grab a glass. I take the two pills and decide I need a shower. And bed.

It's funny though, I think as I walk down the hallway to the bathroom. I don't have a hangover.

I start the shower and then walk across the hall to my room, flipping on the light as I go.

Melanie is sleeping in my bed. Her legs are bare and tangled up in the dark gray comforter, and she's topless.

I back out and walk to the bathroom, locking myself inside.

What the fuck? Did I sleep with her? What the fuck would possess her to want to sleep with me after that fight we had?

I know I do a lot of weird shit when I black out, but I don't think I've ever slept with a girl during one. I wake up hungover, dizzy, and still half-drunk. I'm typically confused, but not overly so. I might not remember everything, but most of the important shit comes back in a few minutes. A few hours at most. It's been a couple hours and I have no fucking memory of sleeping with Melanie.

I strip down and get into the shower as I think this through. Sometime in the middle of washing my hair, the music stops.

I freeze, waiting for Melanie's knock on the door.

It never comes.

I resume washing, finish up, and then wrap a towel around my waist, listening for any sound to give me a clue where she's at. Where she might be waiting to ambush me. Silence. I open the door and walk out into the hallway. "Mel?" I say, not loudly. I walk into the bedroom. Nothing. Then the kitchen. Just the mess I made.

Whew. OK, Rock. You have issues, man. Fucking your dead girlfriend's sister is not cool. Not. Fucking. Cool.

I throw on some jeans and a t-shirt, all shit left over from when I last lived here, and I'm just about to close the closet when I notice there's a pair of woman's shoes on the floor.

What the fuck? Why would Melanie leave a pair of shoes here?

I turn around and notice a lot of other things too. A gold necklace on the top of my dresser. A receipt from the local grocery store. I open a drawer and find girls' panties mixed in with my socks.

Did Missy keep things here before she died and I forgot?

No.

Then what the fuck?

I pull on my boots, grab a black hoodie, and make my way out of the house and down the driveway to Mel's.

Our fathers were best friends all growing up. Both semi-famous, washed-up rock stars for a gold-record hit their band had back in the nineties. Mel and I are both the products of trust funds for that little bit of success, although I've never touched mine. It's still sitting there in the bank where I left it five years ago.

The custom homes on the side of this mountain are part of that legacy. Mine sits a little higher up on a ridge than Mel's and that's why I always had such a good view of them growing up.

I knock on the thick hardwood door, then ring the doorbell for good measure. But I don't hear it inside, so maybe it's broken.

I try the handle, it turns, and I open the door a crack.

I should call out. Let her know I'm coming in. But I don't. I slip through and close the door quietly behind me. I want to see Missy's room and I want to do that alone.

I walk through the great room, empty of furniture, expecting to be caught any second, but there's no one in there. Just a pile of pillows and a blanket neatly folded and stacked on the floor. Hmmm. I continue down the hallway, all the doors are closed, and stop in front of Missy's room. My hand lingers on the doorknob. I know I should not do this. I should get the fuck out of this house right now. But I can't stop myself. I open it and look inside.

Empty.

Well, that sucks.

I go down the hall and try Mel's room.

Empty.

The master.

Empty.

In fact, once I circle my way back to the great room, I realize the entire house is empty. Just a few towels on the floor of the bathroom and the pillows and blankets on the floor.

"What are you doing here?" Melanie asks from behind me.

I turn and take her in. She's dressed in jeans and that same black leather jacket, her hair slicked back into a neat ponytail. Her boots have mud on them and her face is flushed from the cold morning.

I make a writing gesture and she shrugs. "I don't have any paper. Now why the fuck are you in my house?"

Thirty minutes ago I saw her sleeping in my bed, now she's acting like it never happened?

"You fuck me and then talk shit to make me walk out? You're sick, RK. I'm sorry to have to be the one to tell you, but you're sick and you need help."

"Were you in *my* house?" I croak. I need to understand what's happening.

"If you think that little display the other night will excuse the fact that you just broke into my place and were snooping around then—"

I walk out. Down her driveway, up mine, go inside, and slam the door.

I'm not in the mood to deal with Melanie Vetti's games. Really not in the mood. She fucked with my life so bad when we were kids, I can't go back to that.

Chapter Seven

Seven Years Ago

"Hey," Melanie says from the open garage door.
I'm working on my dirt bike, trying to get it ready for a weekend of off-road fun. It's hot as fuck today and sweat is dripping down my face with the grease and grime. Mel is dressed in those shortie-shorts she always wears, flashing the outline of her nipples through the thin white tank top.

"What's up?" I ask, barely giving her a look as I turn back to the bike.

"Do you mind if I tag along with you and Missy this weekend?"

I give her another quick glance. "What does Missy think about that?"

"She said whatever."

"Well," I say, mentally cursing Melissa for that, "we're just gonna have a date weekend."

"But all the guys are going."

"Yeah, but they all have girlfriends." I stop again and look over my shoulder. "You got a guy who wants to come? So you don't feel left out?"

"Forget it," she says, walking back down my driveway.

"Forgotten," I mutter to myself as I go back to work.

Thirty minutes later Missy walks up chattering about lunch. "Ham sandwich with chips or ham sandwich with chips?" She holds her hand up to shield her eyes from the sun, squinting her nose the way I think is so damn cute. She can't cook worth a shit, so I think I'll be eating cold sandwiches for the rest of my life.

I'm OK with that.

I laugh as I put down my tools, wipe my face with a clean rag, and stand up. Missy is wearing faded jeans. Her hair is hanging down her back in a braid and the promise ring I gave her is shining in the midday sun. I slip my hands around her waist, hoping I don't get her dirty, then plant a quick kiss on her nose. "Whatever you have is perfect."

She leans up and kisses me full on the mouth, her tongue slipping inside mine to tease me. I smile into her lips. "What's up with you?"

She kisses me harder, her hands reaching around my ass so her fingers can slip inside my back pockets. "I can't wait for this weekend."

"Me too," I say, opening my mouth to kiss her more thoroughly. One of her hands comes out of my pocket and reaches around to grab my dick.

I step back and push her away. "What are you—"

"RK?" Missy says from behind me. "What the hell, Melanie?" Her hair is all wet, like she just got out of the shower.

Fucking Melanie.

"Hey," Melanie says, all her Missy mannerisms gone. "Can't blame me for trying." She slips off Missy's promise ring, tossing it at her sister as she walks past.

We fought. Missy loved me, I know she did, but she loved her sister too. I went dirt-biking alone that weekend over that bullshit. It wasn't the first time Mel tricked me into thinking she was Missy. And it wasn't the last either.

Chapter Eight

I spend the entire next week alone, only venturing out in the evening to shop at the drug store in Granby. Melanie never comes back, although I find more and more of her shit stashed away in the house.

She's psycho, I remind myself. But it pisses me off that she's been in my house while I was away. I think she's been sleeping in my bed. What kind of freak does that? And I love how she accuses *me* of being sick. Shit. At least I'm not sneaking in her bedroom to sniff her sheets.

TJ came by once but I didn't answer the door. He stood out there calling me names for almost fifteen minutes before the sheriff showed up and yanked him back to his car.

I didn't call the sheriff, so maybe Melanie did that?

Kenner never called or texted back.

Jayce did. Does. She calls every morning and every evening to "check in with me". Like I have anywhere else to go. She also had about ten boxes of shit sent here. I only opened two of them, all clothes. So I guess I'm expected to just settle in. Why didn't they just put an ankle bracelet on me? Then I could ignore Jayce too.

My throat feels a hundred percent better. But no talking suits me. I might never talk again.

The piano taunts me from the front room. I walk by that thing ten times a day thinking I should smash it. I don't know why I blame it all on the piano, I just do.

And right now I'm sitting on the back deck, checking out the sunset over the mountains, feeling a little less sorry for myself than I did yesterday. I try not to go online to see what people are saying about the band, but I did log into Facebook once and there were so many sympathy notifications on my personal page, I just couldn't do it. I can't fucking look at those pictures of Elias, and Mo, and Ian. Not yet. Maybe not ever.

But each day I make progress. Maybe it's just getting out of bed before noon. Maybe it's being able to drink some ice water without clutching my throat in pain. Maybe it's almost enjoying a lukewarm cup of coffee. Maybe it's not reliving a play-by-play of the accident in my nightmares. Maybe it's hope that Kenner will play again.

I'll take all these maybes because they're all I have. This is RK's sad, empty life. This is RK's punishment for living. Twice. This is RK's bottom.

Well. No. RK's bottom happened a year and a half ago when they found me unconscious in an apartment bathtub I have no memory of entering, needle sticking out of my arm. I was missing for days and the papers pronounced me dead when people reported seeing me jump off the Santa Monica pier.

Tabloids.

But the truth was worse, right? People feel sorry for out-of-control depressed artists who try suicide. They don't feel sorry for addicts who throw their charmed life away on drugs and blow jobs from high-class prostitutes.

I never did that anyway. The prostitute thing. That girl who sucked me off in Bangkok was a friend.

I blacked out for two weeks after they took me to the hospital. I still don't remember all of it. Not the needles, not the party, not the cold—I was almost hypothermic when they finally did find me.

It was my lowest point, although the day Missy died and the day the band died, those points are up there with the lowest of the low too.

I probably should've died in that bathtub and they only found me after serving my phone company with a warrant and tracking me down using Find My iPhone.

After Jayce checked me out of the hospital she flew me to rehab somewhere in the Sierra Nevada Mountains. Six months of treatment to get me through the heroin withdrawals and another two to monitor my adherence to the new me, and I was free.

The band went into the studio, wrote ten new hits, released them old-school style on the internet along with a one-hour biopic video on how we rose to rock stardom so quickly, and planned a vacation before we went out on our second world tour.

We will never play that tour.

It hits me hard as I think about it.

We will *never* play that tour.

The world will never hear us play live again. I will never sing. Kenner will never drum. Ian will never do another solo and Elias will never find the rhythm. Mo will never pound keys.

Jayce will probably live on. She worked for us exclusively, but…

I'm gonna lose her too.

I'm gonna lose everything because of one stupid decision to take a vacation in the mountains. It's like those snow-capped peaks were just waiting for me to come back so they could finish the job.

But I miss it. I fucking miss it. I miss them. I miss us. I miss the energy on stage and the calm, contemplative creativity when we were in the studio.

I want RK's life back.

So it's only half a surprise when I go inside and don't get that feeling of hate and loathing when I walk by the piano. I try not to see myself playing at Missy's funeral or on stage with the Jacks. I try to make it become just a piano. Something I have loved longer than I can remember. Something that is so much a part of me, my heart aches for the feeling of perfectly weighted ivory keys. It's an old piano, one that has been in our family for almost a hundred years. One that has been sitting in this house, in front of this window with a stunning view of the Rocky Mountains, since before I was born.

It's a love affair. It's a deep longing. It's one of the many, many things I am now missing in my empty soul.

I sit down on the hard bench and feel a sense of wellbeing. I'm not going to play. Fuck no. I just want to sit. Try it out. Remember what it feels like to be at home. Because even though I am at home, and I've never had a real home other than this mountain-top house, it's been a while since I had the time to actually think about what being home *means*.

The night is here now, the last of the fading sunset nothing but an outline of pink and orange against the backdrop of jagged peaks. Melanie's light is on down the driveway. I can see her shadow walking around through the sheer curtains. I lean on the piano and watch her until the light goes out. A few minutes later her car backs out of the garage, the door closing behind her.

I wonder what she does all day? I wonder what kind of job she has? I wonder where she's going right now?

My stomach grumbles. I have not eaten real food since my last meal in Steamboat. That liquid nutrition was just fine while my throat was healing. But my stomach is getting pissed off at the lack of solid eats.

Grand Lake has about a dozen places that serve a burger, but some of them are lodges, and I don't feel like a lodge. I shrug on my leather jacket and get in the truck, my only aim to get some food. It's not too cold tonight. The weather has warmed up into the sixties during the day but the nights are always cool this high up in altitude.

I have every intention of going to Squeemie's for a burger, but my hands on the steering wheel have other things in mind. I weave down the mountain, making all the right turns until I'm on the main street heading into the trendy downtown district. Downtown is nothing but a few blocks of hotels and restaurants with a nice view of the lake.

The parking lot at Float's is packed and I have to parallel-park on the street and walk two blocks to the bar. Melanie's car is in the parking lot. So is TJ's Jeep.

I get a little nervous as I walk up to the front door, and then step back when it swings open just as I'm about to pull the handle. Live music blares from inside as tourists come bursting through, laughing and happy. The official kickoff to the summer season starts with live concerts outside on the stage dock, and that hasn't happened yet, but the lake starts jumping with fishermen the minute it thaws. Float's is the closest bar to the marina, so they tend to come here when they're done for the day.

I wait for the tourists to pass me, then catch the door before it closes and slip inside.

The place is jumping for not even being eight o'clock, but when I look up at the stage I understand why.

Melanie is up there with some local band and they are playing their hearts out. She's looking down at her guitar—not bass, which makes me pause, because she always preferred the bass—as she plucks out a slow tune and the back-up singer laments about some lost love.

Isn't that what we all write about? Love? I mean, look at most of the popular songs these days. Almost all of them are about a girl. Loving a girl, getting a girl, fucking a girl, losing a girl. Girls.

Nah, I think, wandering up to the bar to wait my turn for a drink. *Not girls. Love.*

Melanie sings the chorus, her voice loud and clear as she croons out the sad love song. She never liked to sing as a kid. She always left that to Missy and she sounds so much like her dead sister, I almost walk out.

Calm, RK, I tell myself as I move one person closer to a drink.

We do a lot of things these days we never said we'd do, don't we? TJ going into the fucking army is one of them. Jesus, I can't even with that. He never even liked to hunt when we were kids. I was the only one who hunted with my dad.

All I talked about growing up was Juilliard. How I was meant to be a musician. I play five instruments well.

Two extremely well. Juilliard was my destiny. I was all set to go when my life got ripped apart on prom night.

I was never meant to be a rock star. I was never wild as a kid. I was calm, and straight, and creative. I had everything going for me growing up. Good family with decent wealth. I never went hungry or worried about being cold in the winter. I never heard my parents fight over small things that set so many of my friends' families on the road to divorce. I was never hit, or belittled, or bullied by anyone other than my big brother, and even then, it was in a loving big-brother kind of way. Even my dad's shortcomings don't cancel out the life he provided for his family.

It was RK's charmed life back then.

No one respects a rock star. Rock stars are losers. Drug addicts. Egomaniacal assholes. Rock stars are selfish and lucky—not talented. Rock stars are freaks who drop out of school. Rock stars live on the edge of society because they don't belong anywhere else.

I guess I became all those things along the way to rock stardom. Or maybe I've always been all those things and it's got nothing to do with my lifestyle or my profession? Maybe it's just me.

Maybe I am RK's pathetic destiny? Maybe I am right where I'm supposed to be?

The guy in front of me shoves me out of the way once he gets his drinks and the bartender yells, "What can I—"

I turn to look at him, then try out the new voice. Not too loud though. "You got Sam Adams Summer yet?"

"RK," Doug yells over the din. "Hey, man," he yells again. "Sure, we got it in last week, just put it on tap a few days ago. You want me to tell Teej you're here?"

I shake my head. I can do without the welcome committee this time.

"Be right back," he says, taking off to grab my beer. And a few seconds later, every head at the bar slowly turns to look at me.

Maybe this was a mistake.

The music stops and I suddenly hear Missy—*Mel, Mel, Mel*—coming from the speakers. "We have a special guest tonight. It you're just up here for a visit, you might not know that RK Saber was born and raised in Grand Lake. His family owns this bar, in fact. He's not around much these days but this is the place he calls home, so let's give the hometown boy a round of applause."

"Rock!" someone yells. "Rock," another one screams. And then it's a chant. *Rock, Rock, Rock.*

I have been on stage in front of seventy thousand people when we packed the LA Coliseum and I can honestly say, this room of maybe three hundred makes me far more nervous.

It takes a minute to shake myself out of the panic, but I do manage it, raising a hand and flashing the sheepish grin that drives the girls wild when I'm on stage.

Teej appears in front of me, his face full of trouble and his eyes squinting down into slits. I'm expecting a sucker punch but instead he pulls me into a hug. "I'm glad you came back."

"Why?" I ask, surprised I'm so eager to talk. "So I can triple your receipts for tonight?"

"I'm gonna ignore that,'" he says, letting me go. "Look," he says, leaning down into my ear to gain some privacy in this very public place. "I'm sorry about the other night. Come back this way to my table."

He turns and leaves, so I follow him through the crowd, pushing my way past people who grab on to my jacket trying to start a conversation. We end up stage left at a group of tables that are all marked reserved. Each one is full, but TJ takes me to the back booth and some guy I don't know gets up when TJ points to him.

I slip into my assigned spot and then Doug is there with my beer.

"Hey, man, how you doing?" Sean Whimel asks to my left.

"Sorry I didn't get a chance to say hi last week," Gretchen Linnie says across the table. "TJ was acting like a royal asshole." She shoots him a warning look, like she will personally get up and kick his ass if he scares me away tonight.

I take a sip of beer to hide my grin. Fucking TJ has always had a thing for Gretchen. But I figured they never had a chance once she moved away for college and Teej went into the army.

I nod to each of them. "I'm OK," I say to Sean. And, "It's OK," to Gretchen. She shoots me a hesitant smile, like she's trying to feel me out. See how much I need to be coddled.

I'm not sure I even mind that too much. I appreciate her protectiveness, actually. Not many people on my side these days. I take another sip of beer, trying to pretend I'm too busy drinking to notice the awkward silence.

"Are you hungry, RK?" Lisa Gantry asks as she walks up, wearing the fancy uniform that does not say 'rock band playing tonight.' She's got her pen and pad ready to take my order.

"I am, actually," I say, almost not recognizing my voice. I have to close my eyes to shut out the image of me trying to sing with this raspy shit. "Just a cheeseburger. No onions."

"Coming up," she says with a smile.

I scrub my hand down my face as things go silent again. I've got a week's worth of stubble. I bet I look a lot worse than I feel. Maybe that's why they're being so nice to me? I probably look every bit the drug addict they've come to know.

"So," Sean says.

"So, how have you been?" I ask him. "Still working at the marina with your dad?"

He nods. "You know it. It's in my blood. We always knew where we'd end up, right?" Sean and I were pretty tight in high school. He was a jock and I was way into the music, but somehow it worked. "Me on the lake, you taking over the world."

"I'm not sure it worked out for me," I say back.

"It did," Melanie says, coming up on my right. She shoots me a sympathetic smile.

I look over at Teej, just to see if he's gonna throw me a bone. Give me some kind of clue as to what's happening here.

An intervention? A facing of facts? A reality check?

He shrugs. "To brothers," he says, raising his shot glass of something.

"Yeah," I say, raising my beer back. I'm regretting my impulse to come here tonight. I look up at Melanie, then scoot over and pat the seat, just so she won't loom over me and make me feel watched.

She accepts my offer with a smile as I take another sip, and then says, "You want to play a song with us tonight?"

I almost snort out my beer. "Fuck, no."

"Too good?" TJ starts in.

I stare him straight in the eyes. "I'm not too good, asshole. I'm fucking—" I almost say it. But being sad is, well, *sad*. So I don't. "I'm not ready to play yet," is where I leave it.

There's a long collective sigh from all five people in the booth. I stare into my beer.

"Hey, I'm sorry, man," Sean says. "I know you don't want to hear it, and I know it doesn't help. But I'm so fucking sorry this shit happened."

"We all went to the hospital," Gretchen says. She makes a circular motion at everyone in the booth. "But they said no visitors. The sheriff, you know."

I nod. Sure, sure.

"And then," she continues, "we heard you were transferred up to some private place in Steamboat where they have more armed guards than Fort Knox." Everyone laughs, even Teej and Melanie. "But we tried, RK. We did try. We wouldn't leave you hanging like that."

Like that. Like I did to them after Missy died. Jesus.

"Nice one, Gretchen," TJ says. "Nice bedside manner you got there."

"I didn't mean it that way," Gretchen explains.

I wave her off. "I know, Gretch. No worries. Thanks for trying."

"Your voice sounds better," Melanie says.

I nod. "Getting there, anyway. I'm not expecting much," I say, drawing a picture of an eighth note in the condensation on my glass.

"I saw a bunch of boxes being delivered the other day," Mel continues. "Does that mean you're staying?"

I shrug. "I have to stay. They won't let me leave until they figure out what happened that night." I glance up at TJ and I see all the questions on his face. What *did* happen that night? He wants to ask so bad. But it's rude, right? Even his meathead ass knows that.

Lisa Gantry comes with my food and sets my plate down. "Thanks," I mumble, adding the lettuce and tomato to the burger and taking the smallest bite I can manage.

They all watch me chew, like they've never seen it done before. I swallow with a grimace. "Hey, Lisa," I call out, just as she's about to turn away from the table next to us.

"Yeah, Rock?"

Rock. "I'm gonna take this to go."

She smiles and takes my plate back. "I'll wrap it up. Be right back."

I look at Teej. "Sorry, but this is the first time I've eaten anything solid in weeks and I just need…" What the fuck do I need? "Privacy," I finally say.

"We understand." Gretchen reaches over and takes my hand in both of hers. "We do, RK." She looks up at Mel, then to her right, where TJ sits. "Right, you guys?"

They all nod and I let out a breath. "So what do you do these days, Gretchen?"

"Oh, I'm just home on break from grad school. One more year and I have my master's in family counseling."

"That's nice. It suits you," I say. No wonder she's so understanding tonight. She's got my fucking number. I push on Mel's shoulder when I see Lisa coming with my box. She scoots out so I can stand, and then I give them all a wave. "Thanks for the conversation. See you guys around, right?"

"I got your bill," Teej says.

I just take my box from Lisa and push my way through the crowd again.

No one tries to start a conversation or grab my leather on the way out.

I drive home and click the opener I found in a kitchen drawer the other day so I can park in the garage instead of the driveway. That fucking sledgehammer is in the middle of the parking pad, surrounded by all the broken cinderblocks. I get out, leave the truck idling, and then spend the next twenty minutes cleaning that shit up before I can pull in, close the door, and feel satisfied that the world can't find me now.

Lesson learned tonight.

I'm not ready.

Chapter Nine

It takes me hours to eat that burger, but the thought of one more liquid nutrition shake is enough to spur me on to victory. My throat is sore as fuck by the time I'm done.

I pop my pills and crash on the couch. I haven't slept in my bedroom since I thought I saw Mel.

Did I see her? Was she really there? Or did I imagine it?

I can't tell. I was fucked up that day. But it freaks me out because of the way I used to sneak into Missy's bedroom window when I was a teenager.

I fall asleep watching a movie on HBO with no sound, wondering who the fuck has been paying my cable bill all these years.

A noise wakes me. Another movie is playing on the flatscreen, but the sound is still down. So that wasn't it.

More noise. This time I know it's coming from the bedrooms. I get up, wondering why I didn't set the alarm when I came in. It's stupid to think I'm safe up here. It's stupid to think I can just go out in public, tell people where I'm at, and be left alone.

I grab a fire poker and stalk my way down the hallway. The noise has stopped, but I'm pretty sure it came from my room. I take a deep breath and kick the door in. It swings wildly, banging against the wall before swinging back and hitting my foot.

Melanie is standing in the center of my room in her pajamas. She squeals, her hands up as she steps back.

"What the fuck are you doing here?" I say, still looking around for a threat.

"I thought you were out! Your truck!"

"Is in the garage," I growl. I stare at her for several seconds. She looks down at her clothes. She's only wearing a pair of shorts and one of those stupid see-through tank tops. Her jeans are in a heap in a pile near the bed. "You were here the other day, weren't you? I saw you and when I came out of the shower you were gone."

"RK, look—"

"Don't 'RK, look' me, you fucking bitch. What the hell are you doing in my house?"

She swallows hard and just watching her do that makes my own throat hurt.

"What?" I say again, raising my voice.

"I think we need to call TJ—"

"Fuck TJ. This is *my* house. And you need to explain or I'm calling the sheriff and pressing charges, Melanie."

She bites her lip. I almost die thinking about when Missy used to do that. Almost die right then and there. Why did the girl I love have to have an identical twin? Why?

"I live here," Melanie says, her hands out in front of her like she's warding me off. "I live here, RK. I moved in after your dad got sick. I've been living here in your room for almost two years."

I want to smash Melanie's face in with this poker. I want to make her different so I don't have to see Missy every time I look at her. I want to forget every moment of my life. Black out all twenty-three fucking years of it. Forget every goddamned second. Never be born. I should've jumped off the Santa Monica Pier that night. I wish I had. Let myself drown in RK's pre-determined end. I should've ended it poetically instead of pathetically. Because that's what I am now. Pathetic.

"Why do you hate me?" I ask her. "Why have you always hated me so much?"

"I don't—"

"You do. You said so the first night I came home. I'm the kind of guy who breaks hearts. Breaks families apart. I'm the kind of guy who runs people over. But I wasn't that guy when we were kids, Melanie. I was never mean to you and all you did was fuck with me."

She screws up her face. "What do you mean? I never—"

"Oh, fuck you. You never tricked me into kissing you?"

Her eyebrows furrow. "That time we were supposed to go dirt biking."

"Go—" Jesus Christ, she's delusional. "I never invited you, bitch. I invited Missy. And then you came outside dressed like her. Your hair all done up like her. Biting your fucking lip like her."

"RK, listen to me. You're misunderstanding things—"

I laugh so hard it hurts my throat. "I have a perfect grasp of the situation, thanks."

She stares at me, letting her arms drop to her sides now that my perceived threat moment has passed. "I—" She stops. "I don't know what to say to you."

"Just tell me why you hate me so bad. That's all. Tell me why you couldn't let me be happy. Why, Melanie? Why were you so fucking jealous? I never treated you bad. I was nothing but good to you until you couldn't accept the fact that I loved Missy, not you."

"RK, listen to me. That's not—"

"You tricked me over and over, Melanie. It got to the point where I couldn't even trust Missy. I never knew who I was talking to. You fucked with me, Melanie. You *fucked* with me."

"I have to go—"

I grab her wrist as she tries to get past me, pushing her up against the wall. She struggles, knocks me in the chest with her elbow, and then tries to bring a knee up between my legs. I press my hips against her so hard, she's pinned.

"Let go," she snarls.

"No," I say calmly. "You got to have your say that night I came home. When I was on my fucking knees in so much pain I couldn't think straight. Now I get to have mine."

"Why are you so messed up, RK? Why do you have to make everything so difficult?"

"You want easy?" I laugh. "Fuck easy and fuck you too."

Melanie stares at me. Bites her goddamned lip. I want to slap her. I want to slap the Missy right out of her. "I hate you," I say. "I hate you so much more than you hate me. I'm so out of your league in the hate department, Melanie. You have no idea the amount of loathing that burns through my blood when I look at your face. You don't deserve to live. She was the one who deserved to live."

"RK—"

I stop her with a kiss. I have no idea why. Because that hate is real.

She kisses me back, her tongue twisting with mine in a way that feels so familiar, the ache in my heart might split me in half.

"If I close my eyes," I say into her mouth. "I can pretend you're her."

"Close them," she pants back, her breathing kicked up, her chest heaving. "I am her."

I do close them, but it's from the pain, and I pull away before it goes too far again. Why do I let her get to me this way? Why do I—

But Melanie places her hands on my hips before I can make my escape, tucking her thumbs into my jeans the way Missy used to. She places her head on my chest the way Missy used to. She sighs deeply the way Missy used to. I picture Missy and me the afternoon of prom. How happy she was. How excited she was. How fucking beautiful she was.

Melanie is none of those things, but her touch is real and Missy isn't.

My hand goes looking for her breast, cupping around it, squeezing just enough to make Melanie hiss in a breath.

"RK," she says.

All I hear is Missy.

"RK," she says again.

I push her backward until she bumps into the bed and falls back. I reach for her shorts and pull them down her legs before I change my mind. Her fingers fumble at the button on my jeans, then the zipper. Her palm flattens against my cock, the warmth of her skin almost too much to bear.

A moment later I feel her breath. Her wet tongue licking my shaft. I reach down and pull her tank top up, twisting her nipple hard enough to make her cry out.

She sucks my tip, her tongue flattening out, and I want so badly to open my eyes, but I can't. I can't fucking look at her because if I see Melanie, I will die all over again. Just like I did out on that mountain on prom night. I will die.

If you do this, some unknown reasonable voice in my head declares, *you will die anyway, Rock. Because this isn't the girl you want her to be.*

I step back and saliva pours out of Melanie's mouth as my cock retreats. "What are you doing?" she asks, reaching for me again.

"No," I say, shaking my head. "No."

"No what?" Melanie asks, grabbing onto my jeans with a death grip. Like she's got me now and I'm never getting away. "Don't," she begs. "Don't—"

"I can't do this. You're not the one I love, Melanie. And even though I could give a fuck if I hurt you when I scream Missy's name when I come down your throat, if there's some kind of afterworld and Missy is looking down on me, I'd never want her to see this." I reach down and pick up her clothes, just as she stands up to make her case. But I tune it out and shove her shorts and tank top into her bare chest. "Get out."

"RK!" She's pleading. "RK, listen to me!"

I grab her by the arm and turn her around, giving her a push on her back. "Go home, Melanie."

"I'm not Melanie! RK, listen! I'm not Melanie! I'm Missy!"

I just stare at her. The balls on this woman. The fucking balls on this woman. I stare into her eyes as she repeats those words over and over again, and then I seethe. "I have never hit a woman in my life, but the next time you pull this on me, I'll beat the fucking shit out of you."

I yank her all the way down the hall, fling the front door open, and shove her outside, clutching her scant clothing to her naked body.

She screams it again. "I'm Missy! I'm *Missy*!"

It takes every ounce of willpower not to make good on my threat.

I slam the door, blocking out the tears and the pleading. Blocking out her face, her body, her eyes. Erasing her voice, and her hair, and her stolen mannerisms. And I walk to the back of the house, grab my phone and a pair of noise-canceling headphones, and play the fuck out of Son of a Jack.

I have more than a hundred recordings in my music library, and I start with number one and listen until the whole world goes silent.

Chapter Ten

Someone is kicking my front door. "Go the fuck away," I whisper into the couch pillow. It took me hours to fall asleep last night. Hours of Melanie's treachery running through my head. Hours of all the ways she fucked me over. All the little things she's been doing since I got here to lead up to that insane declaration last night.

The lip-biting. The singing on stage. The leather jacket and the ripped jeans. Sleeping in my bed, her shit stuffed into corners and crevices.

Hell, I was so goddamned confused last night, it took me until dawn to remember she admitted to living here.

Living here.

In my house. As if that's even legal. I'm so calling the sheriff today. I'm getting a restraining order for this bitch. I've had it. I've fucking had it.

The kicks to the front door are harder and come in quick succession.

I don't even bother answering. I'd have to yell to make whoever it is hear me, and no. No way am I gonna fuck up my voice again over some overzealous FedEx guy. Or TJ coming to call me a piece of shit for the way I treated Melanie last night.

You know what? Why doesn't TJ date her ass? Oh, I know why, she's crazy with a capital C. Insane. Blow-your-mind kind of crazy. And not in any of the ways that girls have blown my mind before. It's blow your mind like a nuclear test explosion out in the desert. Fake houses, filled with fake families, go flying apart in all directions so Melanie Vetti can see how much damage she can do with one strike.

I'm done. I sit up as the door kicking continues. I think I can hear voices. TJ. Maybe someone else. Some loud girl with him. I'd say it was Melanie, but I know she's not coming back over her to plead her case. I'd say it was Gretchen, but I can't imagine in a million years that sweet, understanding, family-counseling Gretchen has it in her.

I rub the stubble on my face and decide I really need to start shaving again. It's starting to itch. I get up, walk into the kitchen, the barn wood tiles warm on my feet because I turned the heat on last night and it radiates up from under the floor.

I was cold, man. It was only in the forties last night, but I couldn't shake it. The kind of cold that seeps into your bones and no matter how many blankets you wrap yourself into, that shit will just not go away until you take a shower. Or turn the fucking heat on even though it's almost June.

I wiggle my toes. Feels good right now.

The coffee pot is in the dishwasher, so I get it out and find a mug as I listen to the people outside my front door getting more and more pissed off.

My phone beeps an incoming text but it's all the way across the room, so that shit can wait until I've got my joe.

It rings. I ignore. Pings another text. Then two more calls. All ignored.

The kicking at the front door gets so loud, I almost think it will come crashing open. Let it. I've got a gun around here somewhere. There's probably a dozen of them down in the safe. I'll get one out, I decide. Get one out and take care of biz.

And I know damn well I set the alarm last night. Motherfuckers will set that shit off and then I *will* press charges.

And the more I think about Melanie being in my house all these years the more pissed off I get. I'm totally pressing charges if she comes back here. One hundred percent sure about—

The coffee maker dings as another call comes through on my phone. I pour me a mug and then walk over to the couch, flipping on the remote as I sit. My phone is lost in the blankets, so it takes me a good thirty pissed-off seconds to find it, and then I read the messages.

Jayce: I'm outside, you asshole. Open the door right now or I'll cut your balls off when I see you next.

Shit. I get up and set my coffee down on the bar as I half jog to the front of the house. I disarm the alarm and swing the door open. "Jayce! What the fuck are you doing here?"

I get a flat palm slapped to my bare chest as she pushes past me, all red-faced and angry. A vein sticks out of her temple. It pulsates to the beat of her heart.

"What the hell, Rock? Just what the hell?" She spins around and I realize she's crying.

"What?" I ask. Jesus. Now what happened? "What's wrong, Jayce?"

"I thought you were dead!" She screams it and the last bit comes out through a sob. "I thought you killed yourself. Overdosed—"

"Overdosed?" It hurts that she'd think I'd be back on the drugs.

"I've been texting you for hours! That little cunt! That little fucking cunt! I told her not to say a word to you unless I was here! But did she listen? No, Miss I-know-him-better-than-anyone had to go fuck things up. And I thought you were dead!"

I blink three times, then let out the breath I was holding. "What the fuck are you talking about?"

"She said she told you!" Jayce is hysterical. I have seen her many ways. I have seen her threaten a fifty-year-old fat-cat music executive and make him sweat. I have seen her point a finger in the face of groupies and make them cower in fear as the band walked by to get in a limo. I have seen her negotiate contracts and appearances with smug determination and cunning. But I have never seen this woman hysterical. Jayce is the glue that holds my world together. She is calm, she is collected, she is tolerant of all the crazy things lead singers of rock bands do.

She is not this person standing in front of me.

"Jayce, what the hell is going on?"

"We need to talk," TJ says from the front stoop.

I squint my eyes at him. Melanie stands down at the end of my driveway biting her nails. I point my finger past TJ to Melanie. "If it's about her, fuck off. I'm done here, Teej. I have been patient with that psycho for as long as I can. I'm sure she's still one of your good friends and all that bullshit, but I'm out, man. I'm fucking out. And if I find her in my house one more time, she's going to jail."

TJ looks over my shoulder at Jayce, and when I whirl around to see what's going on with that, Jayce is in the middle of a shrug.

I get the feeling we're not all on the same page here. "What did she tell you?" I flick my thumb out towards Melanie. "What the fuck did she say happened last night?"

I'm imagining rape, or bruises on her arm that she says came from me. Did I manhandle her last night? I don't think I grabbed her that hard. Jesus Christ, she might say I hit her or something.

"Look, whatever she told you guys, it's not true, OK?"

Jayce comes around from behind me and stands next to TJ. I'm getting a really bad feeling about this new partnership. Jayce is my friend, not his. I found her. She belongs to me, dammit. And if TJ thinks he's gonna get her to gang up on me and take his side in whatever the fuck this is, well—

"Rock," Jayce says, coming towards me and wrapping her arms around my middle.

She's short and tiny and has big fucking tits for that little body. She squishes them up against my chest and it's so ridiculous to be thinking about her tits, I laugh. "What are you doing?"

She backs off just enough to wipe the snot from her face and then she says, "Can you at least put a shirt on so I'm not distracted by your abs?"

TJ lets off a grunt but I smile big and roll my eyes. "You've seen my cock plenty of times, I'm sure you can handle some abs, midget."

"Yeah, but you were pissing, or yanking yourself when you were stoned. I just need to focus, Rock. Shirt, please."

"Fucking women," I grumble, walking off to the back of the house to find yesterday's t-shirt. I tug it on and by this time, TJ and Jayce have made their way to the kitchen bar. "Now what the fuck is the emergency?" A horrible thought occurs to me. "It's not Kenner, is it?"

"No, no, no," Jayce quickly says. "No. It's…" Her gaze wanders to the front door, which is still standing open, and which still frames a view of Melanie Vetti standing at the end of my driveway.

"Don't believe her, Jayce. She's a pathological liar. She's been that way her whole fucking life. You have no idea the things she used to lie to me about when we were kids."

"RK," TJ says. "What did she tell you last night?"

I squint my eyes at him. "What did she tell *you*?"

Just then a car comes screeching into the driveway. I walk to the front of the house again and Gretchen Linnie bolts out of her pea-green hybrid car and runs over to Melanie. They hug for a second, and then Gretchen holds her at arm's length before looking over her shoulder.

"Gretchen?" I say as loud as I can without straining my voice.

She turns back to Melanie and nods her head a few times before whirling around and walking up the driveway towards the house.

"What the fuck is happening?" I turn, find Jayce and TJ behind me. "What the hell did Melanie tell you guys? Because whatever it was, it's not true, man. I never touched her. I pushed her out of the house, but I never hurt her."

Gretchen comes in the house before TJ or Jayce can answer, and then she closes the door softly and says, "I think you need to take a seat, RK. We have something we need to tell you."

My heart starts racing with possibilities. What the hell is happening? "Nah," I say, as calmly as I can manage. "I'm not taking a seat. I'm just fine standing. And you guys are freaking me out. I don't like to be ambushed, you should know me better than that. So say whatever you have to say or I'm calling the sheriff and having all of you thrown out of my house."

"Please," Jayce says, taking my hand and leading me over to the couch. "Just sit, Rock. It's not as bad—" But she can't even finish her sentence.

She pushes on my chest until I walk backwards and take a seat on the couch. I rest my elbows on my knees and hold my head in my hands, distracted again with the week-old stubble on my chin and how I really need to shave.

"Whatever it is, you guys. Just say it." My words come out like a man defeated. I don't know what's going on, but it's bad. It's bad if Jayce is here. If TJ is here and he's not calling me names and being a dick. If Gretchen, the family counselor, is here to make sure whatever it is they have to say to me goes over without violence or screaming.

"Melanie," Jayce starts.

I look up at her and she frowns so big, she might start crying again. I hold my hand out to her and she takes it, sitting so close to me on the couch, we meld into each other. "Spit it out, Jayce. You're killing me with this sadness, chick. You're killing me."

"Melanie was telling the truth last night, RK." Gretchen is the one who says it.

"Which fucking part?" I ask, pissed off that all this is about that cunt.

"The part when she told you she was Missy," TJ says.

Chapter Eleven

A tap on my truck window jolts me awake.
"Rock?"

I shake my head and open my eyes to pine trees.

"Rock?" the voice asks again. I look to my left and see Dr. Chancer squinting down at me, trying to shield his eyes from the sun. "Everything OK?"

I tab the window button and croak, "Yeah," but my voice is raspy and the pain is back.

"Ah," Chancer says. "Hurt it again, huh?"

Well, I'm assuming so. Since it hurts. But... I glance around and have no idea how I got to the parking lot again.

"Are early Monday morning visits going to be the norm for you?" Chancer chuckles. "Come on in. I have a full day today, and I got stuck on the highway from a rockslide they were clearing, but I can take a quick look. I'm betting you just strained it again."

I leave the window down because it's getting hot. I feel sticky from old sweat. I get out and follow Chancer into his offices.

He waves me into a room as the front desk people, and the full room of patients, eye me with curiosity. "So, lose your temper?" Chancer says, setting his briefcase down and snapping on a pair of gloves. He palpitates my throat while I think that question over.

I decide, "Probably," is a safe, and likely true, answer.

"You need to stop doing that," he replies. "Say 'ah.'" He looks down my throat, nods for me to close my trap, and then takes his gloves off and throws them into the trash can. "Rock, you're fine. It's a slight abrasion, probably from all that yelling."

"What do you know about my yelling?"

He picks up a phone on the wall and presses a few buttons. "Yeah, this is Dr. Chancer downstairs. I have Rock in my office." He pauses. Then, "Mmm-hmm." He looks at me and smiles. "Sure, sure."

What the fuck is he doing?

Chancer smiles at me, but he's listening to the person on the other end of that line. He chuckles. "Yeah, yeah. OK. I'll send him up." He puts the phone receiver back in place on the wall and picks up his briefcase. "Go upstairs and talk to Margie, Rock. She's the best person to help you today."

Chancer opens the exam room door and walks out, leaving me sitting there.

I let out a big breath and get down from the table, feeling pretty stupid for showing up here again. What the fuck did I do now?

I walk past everyone in the waiting room and front desk and push my way into the little vestibule area where the stairs meet the front door. I'm heading straight through them when someone calls my name from above.

"RK. Do not walk out on me. I just ditched my eight o'clock to accommodate you."

I turn around and look up. This must be— "Margie?"

"Get up here. I heard all about this weekend and today is your come-to-Jesus moment, Rowan Kyle. And it's about time. These little Rock Hunts are over."

Then she turns away and walks out of my line of sight.

I follow her, more out of dumbfounded curiosity than anything else. A door swings closed to an office down the hallway and I stop to read the plaque. *Dr. Margie Sanderson, PhD, LP.* Dammit. The counselor Chancer told me about last week.

The door swings open again and Margie peeks her head out. "Get in here, Mr. Saber. I'm not in a good mood today so I have very little patience for your bullshit."

The door closes again.

I pull on the handle and walk inside to a minimalist waiting room. Two uncomfortable-looking chairs, a window, no reception, a door that leads into another office. Margie is in there, already sitting at her desk, shuffling through a thick file folder of papers. "Sit," she barks at me, pointing to one of two chairs in front of her desk.

I look warily around, decide I'm happy she didn't ask me to lie on the couch, and take a seat.

"Rock climbing, huh?" Margie says, still looking at the papers in the folder.

"What?"

She peeks at me over her thin-wire-framed glasses. "The outfit, Rowan Kyle." She points a pen at my clothes.

I glance down and realize I look like a model in a Patagonia catalog. Oak-brown rock pants, trail shirt, and multicolored climbing shoes on my feet. "Yeah…"

"Well, after TJ and Missy called me on Saturday morning—"

"Missy?" I laugh. "Are you kidding me? She told you she thinks she's Missy?"

"Rock," Margie says, this time taking her wire-framed glasses off and holding them by the temple. "We went over this years ago. Melanie is the Vetti twin who died. Missy is the Vetti twin who lived. I'm not rehashing, I'm not going to coddle you, and I'm done playing games. So repeat after me. Melanie Vetti died five years ago on prom night."

I just stare at her.

"Say it."

I shake my head. "You guys have gone crazy."

"No, Rowan Kyle, *you* have gone crazy. And frankly, I'm surprised you lasted this long living in that delusional world of yours. We're getting to the bottom of this, and we're going to start that process today. But in order to do that, I need you to accept the facts, RK. Melissa Vetti did not go to prom with you that night five years ago. Melanie Vetti did. We talked about this before you took off to Hollywood and turned yourself into a rock star. But how fitting, right?"

"Fitting?" My mind is spinning. Nothing is fitting right now.

"A rock star?" Margie says, like that explains it all.

I shake my head.

"Missy is upset. TJ is mad as hell. Gretchen, who I should not have let lead this intervention, is blaming herself for your erratic behavior. And it's not fair, RK. It's not fair that you've got the whole town twisted up again. Missy Vetti is alive and you need to come to terms with that."

I swallow hard, not even wincing at the pain in my throat.

"Do you remember rock climbing yesterday?"

I look down at my shoes. "I don't even know where these clothes came from. I'm not a rock climber."

"Well"—Margie sighs impatiently—"you had better knock that shit off then. If you don't want to fall off the side of a mountain, that is."

"I don't understand what's happening."

"You have selective dissociative amnesia."

I actually laugh. Like loud. "Get the fuck out of here. I don't have amnesia."

Margie leans back in her chair. It makes a sickening squeaking sound that grinds around in my brain. She chews on the tip of her glasses. "Then how do you explain your blackouts?"

"I got drunk."

"You got drunk?" She laughs. "OK, you got drunk. Did you drive drunk down to the Patagonia in Boulder to shop for gear too? Which by the way, violates the terms of your release. Then drive back up into the mountains, climb Route 3 in the Upper Herd basin, fuck around all day with strangers who posted selfies on Facebook—tagging you, I might add. Which gives a very poor public appearance when Mo, Elias, and Ian have been dead less than three months. Jayce assured me she could keep you under control, but that's a topic for another day. And then you drove back to the clinic parking lot to sleep before an unscheduled appointment with Chancer." She shoots me a half-serious sneer. "I don't think you were drunk, RK. Do you feel hungover?"

I don't, actually. No. Not one bit.

"The only thing you black out from, Rowan Kyle, is the memory of Melanie Vetti's death. And we need to get to the bottom of this, do you understand me?"

Chapter Twelve

I'm living the dream. That's how the song starts. Four minutes, sixteen seconds. Piano-driven, soft drums, slow rhythm, acoustic guitar most of the time, but we have a rock-and-roll version as well.

I wrote this song while I was on the bus from Denver to LA. In one of those fifty-cent essay notebooks that have that godawful black and white design on them and that huge-ass crease down the middle of the book where the manufacturer practically stapled the pages together so it never lies flat when you set it down. It only bulges open.

I had thick tan rubber bands around it for that reason.

Am I living the dream? Or is the dream living me?

That's what that song is about.

I guess I have my answer.

Two hours later I pull into my driveway. TJ's car is there. Gretchen's piece-of-shit hybrid is there. And Missy Vetti opens the door before I even get up the walkway.

I stop and look at her. Really, *really* look at her. She bites her lip and shrugs. "I told you so many times, but you never believed me."

"How could you let this happen?"

"I'm sorry, RK. There is a very logical explanation for everything, but you wouldn't listen to me. You refused to listen to me."

"Why did I take Melanie to prom?" I have searched and searched my memory for the past two hours for this answer. I asked Margie over and over again, but she said this needed to be worked out in person with Missy. That she was the only one who could convince me of the truth I refused to see.

"You didn't," Missy says. "At least you thought you didn't. You thought you took me, which explains why it was so confusing, RK. It's normal, OK?"

"Normal?" I look down at the rock shoes I don't remember buying. There are so many cuts on my hands from whatever I was doing yesterday, I can't count them. One of my fingernails is ripped open past the quick, dried blood caked on it. Presumably from trying to haul my body up and over rocks I have no business climbing. "There is nothing normal about losing time, Mel—" I look her in the eyes and try out her new name. "Missy."

It hits me then. The pain is raw and open. My chest feels like it might split in two. I look down at my feet and shake my head.

"You OK, RK?" TJ says, standing behind Missy.

"How the fuck did I get this way?" I ask them. "How the fuck?"

"Rock," Gretchen says. "You just need time to put the pieces together, that's all. You just need to go back and remember. We all told you it was Melanie, not Missy who died. But you had it in your head—"

"She fucking tricked me so many times." I stare at Missy, daring her to break the facade and prove to everyone that this is just another one of Melanie's lies.

"I know," Missy says. "I realize it probably happened a lot more than I thought. And I know that's why you didn't believe me. But I swear to God, RK, I'm Missy. I'm alive. And I'm sorry that what happened that night fucked you up so bad."

Anger floods through me. "What did you do? Why was Melanie in my car? Do you have any idea what she told me? Did you know? Did you tell her to say those things?"

"What things?" Jayce says, pushing her way past TJ and Gretchen. She walks up to me and throws her arms around my neck, so high up on her tiptoes she might actually be off the ground. "What things did she tell you, Rock? I don't know anything about this shit, OK?" She sinks back down onto her heels and takes my face in both her hands. "I don't have a history. I have no horse in this race. I don't care which of those lying twin bitches is dead or alive. We just need to get to the bottom of it so we can move forward." She stares at me, her eyes darting back and forth as she searches inside of me for understanding.

"Just…" I look at each of them as they plead with their eyes. "Just give me a day to figure this shit out, OK? Leave," I say firmly. "Everyone leave. I don't want to talk to any of you right now."

I push past them all and go into the house. I see three purses on the side table next to the door and toss them outside just before I slam the door and set the alarm.

Leaving is the easy part, I sing the lyrics from another song in my head. *Leaving is easy when you've got nothing left to lose.*

I don't bother to see if they leave. They won't come back inside. I just go to the fridge and open it up, pulling out an orange and a beer that I take over to the counter. I cut the orange, pour the beer into a glass, and drop the fruit pieces in.

I like summer beer. It's almost always a wheat beer. Light and sunny, like the days. I take my beer outside and sip it slowly on the back deck, wondering how the hell all the pieces of this puzzle fit together in my head.

Missy.

She's alive? I'm still trying to wrap my mind around that one. I've dreamed about this miracle for five fucking years and now that it's happened, I feel... nothing.

Not one thing. I am RK's empty heart.

What the fuck is wrong with me?

I finish my beer pondering that, but I have no answers, none that make me feel better anyway. I'm crazy, that's for sure. I lost my shit a while back and I have no idea where that happened.

Melanie was a cunt. A total cunt. That bitch tricked me into believing she was Missy so many times. I almost fucked her once. I almost *fucked* her once.

That hurts. Because I was saving myself for Missy. I never dated anyone but Missy. But Melanie was always there. Inserting herself into my life, my head. She tried to steal every milestone memory I only wanted to make with Missy. And she probably succeeded more times than I'd care to admit.

I *almost* fucked her.

I was a goddamned virgin the night I rolled into Hollywood. A sweet guy who always tried to do the right thing. Saving myself for the girl I wanted to marry. We had a hotel picked out for after prom. A nice cabin down in Frisco. Right on the lake because we were lake people. We understood mountain lakes and the towns that surrounded them.

But things got weird.

I gulp down my beer and go back inside. I'm sitting at the piano before I even have time to second-guess it, and then my fingertips find the keys and fly into the melody.

The music flows out and I close my eyes. I see it. Not the images from the song, although I see those too, but the notes. They dance in my mind as I find each combination of keys to make the sound I'm looking for.

This is that song I wrote for Missy. The one I played at her funeral. The nine-minute masterpiece that I never played in public again, but had to endure listening to over and over, because someone from the funeral recorded it and leaked it online.

I don't want to see the images that go with the dozens of verses I've written to go with the music over the years. It's all dark. It's all wrong. So I see better times instead. I see myself. Lying down in a mountain meadow with Missy. Her head resting on my thigh as I play with her hair. She's twisting the stem of an orange wildflower and then she places it between her teeth and smiles.

She's wearing a black tank top that says *Devil Child*, the makeshift rock band we'd put together the summer after eleventh grade. We had one song and it was nonsense. Nothing but rock and roll. Nothing but fun. But my dad let us play Float's on festival day and people loved it.

But my unfinished song isn't a rock anthem. It's an ode. A three-part epic that declares my love for a girl with an evil twin.

I am poetic when I want to be. I'm not all flannel shirts and biker boots. Not always just a bare chest with perfect abs and too-long hair. Not always a leather jacket with jangling zippers. No only silver rings on my fingers.

I'm more than that. And I wrote this song as a declaration of love and hate for a girl with two sides.

Melanie, the mastermind of lies and deceit.

And Melissa, the transcendence of love into pure light.

I don't sing the dark lyrics out loud, there's no way I can force the sadness out of my heart to manage that. But I hear them in my head. I sway with the music as my fingers pick out each part of my lyrical composition until I reach the end.

I open my eyes and look out the window.

Missy Vetti is standing less than three feet from me on the other side, tears running down her face, eyes red, face flushed, hands pressed up against the glass, begging me to let her back in. Begging me to go looking for the hidden past I refuse to see. Pleading with me to see her. To believe her. To hear her.

"RK," she says on the other side of the window.

I say nothing.

"Please," she says. "Please, just give me ten minutes. Every story has two sides. Please give me a chance to explain."

I get up and walk out of the front room. I open the front door and she's already there, wringing her hands and taking deep breaths. "I only have one question for you, Missy."

"Anything," she says through a sob. "I'll tell you anything."

So would Melanie. She would say anything to make me believe her. "Did you tell your sister to break up with me for you that night?"

Chapter Thirteen

Melissa's face goes blank. Not a smile, not a frown. No denial or confirmation. Just blank.

"Because," I continue, "a lot of that stuff Melanie said that night sounded like it came right out of your mouth. It was bits and pieces of conversations we started to have. Things we both knew we'd need to say eventually, but never had the nerve."

"RK—"

A shake of my head is enough to stop her words. "I heard so many variations of it, Missy, I don't need your explanation."

She steels her gaze on me. "Well, I think I get to have one anyway."

"I'm not so sure about that. I'm really not."

"Do you remember that night?"

I shrug, taking in a deep breath. "Not the part about the lies." I don't. I don't understand any of this. I don't understand how this can be the girl I loved. The girl who visited me in my nightmares. The girl who died that night and then who didn't. "Maybe I am sick. Maybe I have blocked things out. But whose fault is that?"

"I never lied to you, RK. That was Melanie."

"Sure. Sure, I know that. But if what everyone is saying is true—"

"What do you mean *if*? You think I'm Melanie?" She snorts. "You need to come to terms with reality, RK. That's why you're here. That's the only reason you're back in Grand Lake."

"If Melanie died, then how the fuck did she get in my car wearing your dress? Wearing your jewelry? How the fuck did she become my prom date? And more importantly, why the fuck didn't I know? You got to have your say but I never get to have mine? Is that how this works?"

"Rock—"

"Don't call me that," I snap. "Do not. You don't get to call me Rock. You know why?" I stare her down with the building rage. Rage is a weakness and I've got enough weaknesses going right now, so I ratchet my anger down about a dozen notches and force myself to be calm. "Because fans call me Rock and you're not a fan, are you?"

She stays silent.

"You've never been a fan, have you? Never on my side. Never by my side. I thought you were, but if all this shit is true and I blocked out the days and weeks after the accident, and you—everyone—is insisting that I come to terms with reality, then that's the coldest one, I think. The fact that you were never on my side. Because if you were Melanie would not have been in the car with me that night. Melanie would not have said those things to me. Make me question our love. Our *plans*."

Her eyes start to water and she swallows hard. "We were going in very different directions, RK, you know—"

"Were we?" I interrupt. "That's funny, because we ended up in the same place, Melissa."

She closes her open mouth, crosses her arms in front of her like she's suddenly cold, and looks down at her black combat boots.

"I never asked you to change your plans for me," I say.

"You were going to Juilliard."

"And you weren't. So what? You just wanted to move on with your life? I can understand that. Even now, as fucked up as I am, I can understand that. But I never asked you to wait."

"Than what kind of admission are you trying to get from me?" She's defensive now. Whatever emotion drove her up my driveway to my front door is melting away before my eyes.

"How did Melanie get in my car that night and become my prom date?"

She inhales deep. Bracing herself for something. "Do you really want to know?"

"Of course I want to fucking know!" My shout startles her. Makes her take a step back.

"She was very sick—"

"Fuck off!" I shake my head as the story just gets more and more incredible.

"She was, RK! Don't laugh!"

I slam the door in her face but her black combat boot stops it, makes it bounce back. "You don't know what's true," she says, the anger building. "You are the last person to lecture me about reality, Rowan Kyle Saber. You have no idea. Melanie was sick her entire life. She had—"

"Mental issues," I say. "Yeah, I figured that out early."

"Childhood schizophrenia, RK. You don't even know what that really means."

"Give me a little credit, Melissa. I'm not as stupid as I look. I knew you two your whole lives. You think I didn't know she saw a therapist? Please. My parents talked about it all the time, even if you didn't. But that doesn't answer my question. Why was she in my car?"

Melissa hesitates.

"Say it, Missy. I need to know I wasn't crazy. So say it. If you ever felt anything for me, then fucking say it."

"She was your girlfriend at least half of the time, RK. She used to pretend—"

I slam the door and this time her boot doesn't stop it.

Fuck this, fuck that, fuck all of it. I'm out.

I walk back inside and fling the fridge door open, find a beer, twist the cap off and draw that shit down my throat like it's the answer I'm looking for. I guzzle half the bottle and then come up for air as Melissa's last words echo around in my head.

No.

No. I might be crazy, I admit that. I've done some fucked-up shit in the past few years, but no. No, this is too much.

I grind my teeth as all the memories come flooding in. The summers we spent hiking. All the fucking music lessons. The band we had in high school. The trips into

Denver, and skiing, and watching Melissa cheer for the football games.

Which memories were real?

I grab my leather jacket, my keys, and an old cowboy hat my dad used to wear that's sitting on the same peg he probably hung it on years ago before he died. I go out into the garage and get in my truck. Fuck this shit. I start the engine, press the garage door opener, and then start backing out.

A blaring horn makes me step on the brake automatically and when I look in the rear-view, I see Jayce's cream-colored Mercedes behind me.

I put the truck in park and watch her walk up towards me in the side-view, then reluctantly tab the window.

"What?" I ask.

Jayce opens her mouth to speak, can't find the words, and then closes it.

"What the fuck am I supposed to believe, Jayce? Tell me. Because I'm not sure any of this is real anymore."

"Come on, Rock. Turn your truck off, get in my car, and we'll go find a bar. Not your brother's bar, not any bar in this Mayberry town or even in these godforsaken mountains. Somewhere far, OK? Somewhere no one knows you."

My eyes drift up to her face and see the pity. "Don't do that, Jayce. Just don't, OK? I'm fine. Fuck these girls. Especially that girl," I say, nodding to the Vetti house. "Whoever she is. And I don't want to be with you tonight either, so—"

"No, no, no, Rock. You're not leaving alone. I will follow you. I'm not letting you out of my sight. If you think you're going to disappear for a few days, you can forget it."

I look back down at my dashboard.

"I'm not moving my car, so you're going to have to mow it over, Rock. I'm not kidding."

I turn the truck off and just sit there. "What the fuck is wrong with these people?"

Jayce is silent, and then I see her shrug from the corner of my eye.

"Melissa just told me that I was dating Melanie. But not the whole time, Jayce." I laugh because it's ridiculous. "What the fuck does that mean? Not the whole time? Which parts were her and which parts were Melanie?"

"Does it matter?"

"Fuck yeah, it matters!" I yell. "I loved her, Jayce. Missy, not Melanie. Melanie was a freak. A lying, schizo freak!" I open the door, making Jayce step out of my way, and then pocket my keys and go back inside. "I don't want to get drunk. I don't want to go find some anonymous bar and pretend that conversation I just had with a dead girl who I obviously never knew at all didn't just happen."

"Rock," Jayce says, following me into the house. "You're here to recover, OK? Let's just focus on that until that judge gets his head out of his ass and says you can leave. I mean, I see why you left. I do. I had a fucked-up childhood and got the hell out of Dodge as soon as I could too. And if I had a major traumatic incident and was forced to go back to my hometown to sort things out, I'd slit my fucking wrists. Or kill someone. Probably kill someone. But you're too nice to kill people, so you just need to keep it all in perspective, Rock. Temp-or-ary," she says, stressing each syllable.

I get my phone out and dial the landline at the Vetti house. Missy picks up on the first ring. "Tell me," I bark. "Tell me which parts of us were real."

"Is that manager person there?" Missy asks.

I look over at Jayce, cover the phone, and say, "Take off, OK? I'll be fine."

"Rock—"

"Go," I say. "Out. I'm not joking, Jayce."

She nods, squeezes my shoulder, and then walks back to the garage and disappears.

"She's gone," I tell Melissa. "Now tell me, which parts of our relationship were real? And why the fuck did you let her do that to me? I mean, do you have any idea how fucked up that is?"

"We were kids, RK."

"The fuck we were! Eighteen is old enough to know better, Missy. Hell, ten is old enough to know better. Who was the girl I kissed on the sixth-grade trip? Just tell me, OK. I need to know that at least."

"Me," she whispers.

"And that afternoon before prom? Who was I with that day?"

"Me," she says again. "Me both times."

"Then what the fuck, Missy?" I'm so relieved. I'm so fucking relieved my anger dies and the next few words come out in a whisper. "How could you fuck with me like that?"

"Can I come over?"

"Hell the fuck no, you can't come over. I don't ever want to see you again. Ever, Missy. Ever. I'm done."

"I just… we just… drifted apart, RK. You were going one way and I was going another. I wanted to leave Grand Lake, but not—"

Her words drift off, but I hear them in my head anyway. *But not with you.* She wanted to leave, she just didn't want to leave with me.

"I never thought I wanted to get married or settle down, RK. I wanted to play in a band and just drift. Find my place in the world."

"Drift," I say flatly. "Well, isn't it ironic? That I'm the one who drifted and you're the one who stayed anchored."

"And then all that shit happened."

"All that shit? Like Melanie trying to kill me? That shit?"

"What?"

"Oh, yeah, I guess you weren't there." I laugh. "Well, the irony is thick tonight. Because you know what really happened that night we crashed?"

Silence.

I try to say what's in my head, but I lose track. I don't remember. It scares me for a second, but I recover with another accusation. "Why did you guys trick me?" She says nothing. Like her head just went blank too. "Why did you hate me? What did I ever do to you?"

"Why did you leave?" she says, her turn to change the subject.

I don't know why. It was just… the end of the line for me. The edge of my sanity. I had this overwhelming urge.

"I'm sorry," Missy says.

"I bet you are," I say. "I bet I could write a book about this shit, call it a true story, and no one would believe me."

"So much has happened since you left. Not one day has gone by that I didn't wish things were different. We've been through so much."

"Yeah," I say softly, my anger fading into bleak nothingness. "We have. And you know the really sad part, Missy?" I wait for her to ask, but she doesn't. "The really sad part is that we could've done all that stuff together instead of alone. And now it's too late."

I end the call and turn my phone off, throwing it against the wall as I grab my keys again, walk back to my truck, and back out. Jayce is gone, probably figuring I'd spend the night letting Melissa Vetti sweet-talk me into not doing anything crazy.

But Jayce should know me better.

I don't go through town. I head higher up into the mountains, take the very twisted road all the way into Estes Park, and then wind my way back south down to a bar I know.

It takes me almost three hours to get there, and by that time it's prime time. But I'm not here to drink, I'm here to listen. Just chill, forget, and be nobody.

The band on the stage out on the edge of the Poudre River was what gave my dad the idea to open Float's all those years ago. It's legendary, this bar in the middle of nowhere. I put the cowboy hat on before I get out of my truck, pay the cover, and find a seat inside, in the back. I can still hear the music well enough from inside.

That's the only thing I have left, I guess. The music. Not my music. I'm pretty sure my music is gone for good. But other people's music is better than nothing.

So I sit, nursing a beer, until the set ends and people flock inside for drinks as the next band sets up.

The hat is the only attempt I make to hide, but no one thinks RK Saber is going to be hanging out at the Mish, so no one looks too close. No one sees me at all.

I'm just some guy in a tattered flannel, ripped jeans, and a cowboy hat. I could be anyone.

I am RK's anonymous body.

No more, no less.

Chapter Fourteen

TJ and Melissa appear in front of my table a few
hours later, but I've got a little buzz going from the
beers, and the smile on my face doesn't even break as I
ignore them and enjoy the fourth band on stage since I
got here.

"If you're hiding, brother," Teej says, all sarcastic
like he does, "this is the wrong place to go." He eyes me
for a minute. "Unless you wanted us to find you."

That makes me laugh. "I don't need a babysitter." TJ
pulls up a chair at my table and motions for Missy to sit.
She does, not looking me in the eye. Teej sits next to her,
almost across from me, and mostly blocking my view of
the show outside. "And if I was hiding, believe me"—I
look at him to make sure he knows I'm serious—"you
would not find me."

"Well, maybe you haven't noticed, but you're in Larimer County, bro. Out of bounds. So we're gonna need to go."

"Nah," I say. "I really don't mind jail. At least I can be sure you assholes won't follow me there."

"None of this is what you think, RK."

"Is that so?" I glare at him. What kind of brother is he? I have no idea anymore. Who are these people?

"That's so," Melissa says. "It's a long fucking story, RK."

"Yeah?" I say, looking over at Melissa. "How long of a story, Missy? When did you start lying to me?"

"We're not having that conversation in public," TJ says.

"No? OK." I stand up and throw down a twenty for the waitress, pushing past the crowd until I find the front door and walk right out.

Gretchen is waiting at my truck. She giggles as I walk up. "I knew you'd make a break for it!"

I tap a finger on her blonde head. "Can't get nothing past you, Gretch." I grab both her shoulders, gently move her aside, and then unlock my truck.

"Wait," Gretchen says, as TJ and Missy walk up behind her. "Just let Melissa explain, RK. Seriously, it's a story you need to hear. I'm on your side, OK? I am. But you need to hear her out."

Missy is avoiding my gaze, not looking me in the eye when she finds her voice. "One drive home, RK. That's all I want. One drive home and I get to talk and you get to listen. And if you want me to disappear when we get back to your house, then I will. I'll never bother you again."

"I'm very fucking sure, no matter what you say, I'll never want to talk to you again when I get home. I'm calling my lawyer, getting this ridiculous county arrest thing lifted, and I'm outta here. I'm going back to LA to piss away all my money and make the most of whatever life I have left."

I almost feel the hurt coursing through Missy's body as my words sink in. A pang of guilt strikes me in the heart and I'm about to apologize when she nods and whispers, "Deal. If that's what you need, RK, then that's what you need. All I want is a chance to set things right with you."

I wave her towards the passenger side of the truck and get in, ignoring TJ and Gretchen completely. We slam our doors at the same time and then Missy says, "Are you OK to drive?"

I huff out a breath as I start the truck. "I had two beers over the course of six hours, Melissa. Give me a little fucking credit. I get that everyone up here thinks I'm the biggest fuck-up in history, but I'm not."

"I was just asking—"

"Sure. Sure." I flip the headlights on, wait for a lonely car to pass me on the highway, and then pull onto the road. I don't look back at TJ and Gretchen, but I'm sure they're already in his Jeep and they'll be following us the whole way back. We sit in silence as I navigate the mountain road and honestly, I can't blame her for not trusting me to get her home safe. It's a twisty road, it's dark, and there are few cars and no lights up here. Not even a moon tonight. Just the cone of illumination coming from my truck and then total blackout on either side.

"How the fuck did this happen?" I finally ask, getting sick of the tension and the emptiness. I glance over at her, huddled against the door like she can't put enough distance between us. Her head rests on the window and her face is glowing with a bluish haze from the dashboard lights. She's wearing a black shirt under her jacket—probably a tank top, if I had to guess. She likes the tanks. The jacket is the same black leather one I saw her in that first night at my house. And faded blue jeans with so many rips, I can see a good portion of her thigh.

I should've known she wasn't Melanie. She morphed into this dark girl about halfway through our junior year. Black eye makeup and red lips. Piercings and even a few tattoos. And that was about the same time Melanie morphed into a girl who wore dresses and no makeup. Then they both cut their hair. First Missy, I think. Then Mel.

Did they mean to do that switch? How do I know this is really Missy? How can anyone be so sure?

Her hair is long and dark, pulled back into a ponytail tonight, but long whips of it hang down, fluttering against her face from the vents. And she's got those black combat boots on again. Docs or something similar.

She's the one who looks like a rock star tonight. Like she was meant to be one and I'm the fake.

I never wanted to be a rock star. That was Melissa's dream all growing up, not mine. *RK*, she used to say. *Can you imagine how great it would be to play in stadiums in front of thousands of people?*

"I'm not sure where to start," Missy says, answering my forgotten question. "I just need to gather my thoughts for a minute."

"So you can get your lies straight?" I glance over as I say it, expecting a reaction, but she just bites her lip and looks worried.

I don't think Melissa had any idea how many people actually fit into a stadium. They are incredibly big. And while every stadium show I've ever played was exhilarating, almost inciting panic in me, I actually prefer the smaller venues. Stadiums sound horrible. I know the fans don't care. They just want a shot to be there in the fray. Hear the music at its loudest. Be part of it.

My dad once told me about how he managed to get front row at a Metallica show in LA once. There was sort of a mini-riot. The band had to stop playing because they had chairs on the stadium floor and too many people. Fans rushed the stage and suddenly the chairs weren't chairs, but obstacles. Floods of people were trying to get closer, chairs got knocked over, people got knocked over, until they had start lifting the chairs up and passing them up to the band to dispose of.

They called it a riot, but it wasn't. It was an experience for those people. That's what they came for. Not to hear Metallica—but to be part of them.

I don't mind being part of a big dramatic experience like that, but I prefer the small shows. I prefer five hundred people to fifty thousand. I prefer venues with amazing acoustics instead of the echo of the stadium.

I never wanted to go big, I wanted to stay small.

Irony gets you every time.

"The first time she did it we were six."

"Did what?" I ask, pulling myself back to the present.

"Pretended to be me."

"Ah." I laugh. So this is where we're going.

"She woke up that day and said, 'I'm Missy.' And I of course said, 'No, I'm Missy.' But she insisted and insisted. She walked out to breakfast and told our dad that Melanie was lying and pretending to be Missy."

"What did you say?" I am caught up in that scene because I can totally picture it. Like one hundred percent of it. I can picture their room the way it looked when they were six. Pink bunk beds, two white desks, pictures of horses and kittens on the walls.

"I tried to tell him, but he really didn't care. And Mel winked at me. This stupid exaggerated wink that a six-year-old thinks is so sly. So I figured it was a joke, right?" She stops talking and when I glance over she's looking straight at me, like she's waiting for an answer.

I say nothing.

"It was a harmless joke. 'That's what twins do,' she said as we walked into school. 'They fool the adults. Let's fool the adults today. You be me and I'll be you.'"

"So you went along."

I catch her reflection nodding in the windshield.

"And no one could tell you apart?"

"She had me down, Rock—"

"Don't call me Rock. I'm fucking RK to you. Don't call me Rock."

I glance over at Missy as she pulls back a little. Like my request is ridiculous. "OK," she says. And then she lets that go and continues. "It's like she was studying me. She knew all my little mannerisms. The way I tilted my head when I was thinking. The way I chewed on my cheek and bit my lip when I was conflicted. The way I stayed quiet when she would get loud. She was practicing, RK. She was *practicing*."

Missy stops for a few moments as I deal with a particularly hairy part of the drive. It's a series of switchbacks and ninety-degree turns that wind up the mountain. I can tell the edge of the cliff makes her nervous. Hell, it makes me nervous. I have not missed the mountain roads while I've been away, I can say that for sure.

My dad used to make fun of me when I was little and got nervous when we drove in the mountains. One time he said, "You know why they put that guardrail on the side of the road, RK?"

And I said, "To keep people safe."

He laughed. Like a really big guffaw. "No," he explained, like this was a fact of life I needed to learn. "No. They don't put them there to keep people safe. They put them there to make people feel safe. There's a big difference, RK. If you hit that guard rail you're going off the side of the mountain, son. It's over. They don't keep you safe, they only make you *feel* safe."

It was a conversation I never forgot and I couldn't have been more than eight. It was the first harsh reality I ever had to face in my life.

You're never safe.

I shrug that memory off and go back to thinking about my current drive, and once we clear the switchbacks and are making a not-so-serious descent, Missy resumes. "I didn't think much about it back then because it was only every once in a while, you know? Did you ever hear of that phrase 'boil the frog?'"

"Sure. You put a frog in cold water and turn up the heat. The temperature increases so slowly that the frog doesn't notice that it's getting hotter and hotter until it's too late. The water is boiling and the frog is dead."

"Well, looking back, that's how I felt, RK. Melanie was practicing to be me because one day she was going to *turn into* me. And I'd never notice because she put me in a pot of cold water and turned up the heat."

Just the thought sends a shiver up my spine. "How many times did she do it?'

"Oh," Missy says, like she's considering my question. "A few times that year, for sure. At least three."

"And no one noticed?"

"Did you notice?"

"I was six too."

"But you never noticed?"

"Not until later. I mean, obviously I had my own issues with her delusions. She tricked me a lot, Missy. But if you're saying she made a habit of it all growing up, then yeah, she probably got me more than I realized."

"She did," Missy spits. "She did, RK. And I caught her so many times. And you know what?" Her voice is loud now, like she's angry as fuck. "It pissed me off to no end that you didn't know. I'd get so angry at you for not being able to tell. It was like you didn't even know me."

"How the fuck was I supposed to know, Melissa? You two are fucking identical. You share the same DNA. You have the same voice, the same hair color, eyes, skin, body. All of it was identical."

"*Not* identical, RK. Because we are not the same person."

"No? Well, then you're right, I guess. I didn't notice."

She huffs out some air and chews on that for a few seconds. "Not identical. She was sick and I was not. She was mean and I was nice. She was devious and I was honest. So no, RK, we were not identical. Not even close."

I shake my head in disgust. "Is that all you have to say then? Not identical? I should've known better and the fact that I didn't catch on early enough, or often enough, is grounds for lying about who and what you were to me? I fucking loved you, Melissa. Loved. You. Not her, you."

"That's not what I'm saying. I'm saying at first I thought it was funny. I thought tricking people was funny. A joke we were playing. But as we got older I caught her doing it all the time. When we'd go shopping she purposefully chose outfits that I'd never wear. Outfits that said Melanie. She'd do her makeup different. She'd style her hair different. She'd even talk different. But then I'd catch her wearing my clothes, using my makeup, styling her hair the way I did mine. Talking like me, acting like me… being *me*, RK." She sighs, like she's trying to calm herself down. "But the main point of that is that she didn't *tell me first* like she did when we were six. She just morphed into Melissa and left Melanie behind."

"Is that why you cut your hair in high school?" I remember that day, actually. I loved Missy's long hair. It always smelled so fucking good. And then one day it was short.

"Yeah, I even did it myself. But she cried and cried to my dad until he took us both to the salon. They said my hair was choppy and needed to be fixed. And while we were there Melanie got hers cut the same way. People saw us as the twins. They never knew we were so different."

"How could your dad not know?"

"I don't know," Missy says. I can hear the stress in her voice. Like this hurts her the same way me not knowing did. "How could he not know?"

"Maybe he did know?" I'm sorta thinking out loud now, getting caught up in her story.

"Yeah, I thought that too. He knew, RK. I think he knew she was sick and didn't want to admit it was serious. So he ignored the whole thing. *It's a joke*, he probably thought. It's a phase all twins go through, he was probably told. But it wasn't a joke. Not to me. I lost myself to her, RK. And that day I was supposed to go to prom with you, Melanie caught me talking on the phone to Gretchen that morning. I was talking about you. How I was afraid that you'd ask me to go away to Juilliard with you and then make me return to this town after you were done. I was afraid you'd crush me, RK. Steal my dreams and I'd end up being nothing but RK's little wife. And it wasn't like that would be so bad. One day. But right out of high school?" She shakes her head and hesitates. "I just didn't know. I just maybe wanted to be…"

"A rock star," I finish for her. "You wanted the life I have now. Don't you love that fucking irony?" She says nothing. "Then what happened?" I prod her to continue.

"I hung up with Gretchen and Mel was there as soon as I ended the call. And she said she wanted to go to prom with you."

"What'd you say?" I feel the anger building in me. "'Sure, he's all yours? I don't want him anyway?'"

"No," Missy says, her own anger building. "Of course not. I said fuck no. I might not've wanted all the things you were offering me right then, but I loved you, RK. I loved you back."

"So how the fuck did she end up in *your* dress, in *my* car, as *my* date?"

"She locked me in the basement bathroom, RK. My dad was gone that evening. Some show down in Denver, remember? Your dad went too. She punched me in the face, knocked me back so hard, I hit my head on the counter and passed out. When I came to the door was locked. I screamed until my voice was gone, RK. I screamed. But who was going to hear me? I was afraid of her. She was truly messing with my life. She applied to colleges using my name. I think she was going to kill me and then pretend she was me."

I run that scenario through my head for a long time. A long fucking time. Missy keeps talking...

"Melanie was jealous of us, RK. She got asked to the prom. It wasn't like she didn't get asked, you know? Jason Cartney and Mike Grenshaw both asked her to prom and she said no. You why she said no?"

I look over at Missy and shrug. I'm lost.

"So no one would notice when Melanie didn't show up at prom. She planned that night, RK. Very thoroughly. Every bit of it was planned ahead of time. She's the one who told our dad he should play that show in Denver that night. She's the reason he was gone. The reason your dad was gone. The reason why no one could hear me screaming for help."

I have to admit; it sounds like something Melanie would do.

"Why do I have to have the crazy twin sister? Why? All my life people have told me how lucky I am to be an identical twin. Do I look lucky to you, RK?"

I glance over at her, see the tears, and look back to the road. What am I supposed to say to all this?

"Why did she hate me? You asked me that earlier. Why did I hate you? I never hated you. I never even hated Melanie. She hated us, RK. She hated us because we were in love. So she became me. That's what happened."

I look straight ahead and sigh as we pass through Estes Park and make the final leg of the drive back to Grand Lake. It takes a few more minutes to work up the nerve to finally ask what's on my mind.

"What if..." I say, looking over at Missy through the corner of my eye. "What if she really did that? What if that was Missy out on that mountain and she did die?

And you're really Melanie trying to convince me that you're Missy?"

Missy starts crying. Softly, but sobs all the same. She says nothing until we're almost home and she starts trying to pull herself together, probably thinking Gretchen and TJ will see how upset she is if they follow us all the way back to the house.

"Who are you?" I ask as I pull the truck into the garage and close it up behind us. "Look at me, Melissa. Who are you? Just say it and I'll believe you, OK? If you say Missy, I'll believe you and we'll stop talking about this. Because I don't like it any more than you do. I feel used, I feel lied to, I feel dirty, man. Dirty. So you have one chance to tell me who you are and that's who you're going to stay."

Her tears start rolling again. Long streams down her face. "I'm Melissa, RK. I swear on everything. I am Melissa. It just hurts me so bad that you'd fall for it. It hurts. She stole everything from me that night. Everything."

I let out a long breath of air and sit in the dark quiet of the garage.

"Do you want me to leave and never come back?" she asks.

"Where will you go?"

"TJ's, I guess. Gretchen's. I can't live in that house, RK. I can't. That's why I moved in with your dad when he was sick. I sold everything and never went back until I found out you were coming home and then I grabbed some blankets and a pillow, tried to stash all my shit in TJ's room so you didn't find out how pathetic and sad my life was, and moved back home. But it's not my home. It's where I met the monster who looked exactly like me. I want to wipe her away, RK. Forget all about her. Just look forward and never look back. These past few years have been the worst in my life. And when I saw you on TV, that very first time you were on TV, and I realized you were living my dream, well…" She stops.

Two years. I was gone two years before the first TV appearance.

Missy's breath hitches with her crying. "Well, I was lost, RK. Lost. I wanted you back so bad. And I knew it was wrong to need you when I was at my lowest. It was wrong to need you. So I tried to put everything back together, RK. And living with your dad was the first step."

"It took you two years to miss me?" It hurts, I admit. Two fucking years.

"That's what you heard? From all that I just said? Are you kidding me? I missed you the moment I guessed what was happening in that bathroom. I missed you after the incident and at the funeral. I missed you the second you left, RK. Because you walked out, only you thought you were leaving Melanie. So she wins, right? She wins after all. Even though you know I'm alive and she's dead, she wins. And that's all I have to say, RK. That's my story and you can believe it or not, but that's my story and I'll get out of your life now." She reaches over, presses the garage door opener, gets out of the car, and walks away.

I sit in the truck, rolling the past few hours over in my head. It's like a goddamned movie. I'm living some freaky, fucked-up Quentin Tarantino movie.

What the hell am I supposed to believe? This girl just admitted that her twin practiced being her for more than a decade. Fooled everyone, from teachers, to friends, and maybe even her father. And now she says she's the girl I thought was dead.

What the fuck am I supposed to believe?

I don't know. But I guess there's only one way to find out what's true and what's not.

Be with her. Test her memories. See if she's real, see if she's not.

So I get out of the truck, walk down the driveway, walk straight into her house without knocking, and find her sitting on the blankets in her empty house.

"OK," I say. "I believe you, Missy. I believe you and if you want to be part of my life, then…" I walk over and extend my hand. She stares at it, then up at me. "Then come home with me and we'll work it out."

She takes my hand with a smile and I pull her to her feet.

I'm just not sure what that smile means. Is she proud of her lie? Or is she happy we get a second chance at love?

I just don't know yet, but I'm going to figure it out.

Chapter Fifteen

"Sorry I took over your room," Missy says as we stand in the kitchen. "Most of my stuff is in TJ's room now, so I'll sleep in there."

I wave a hand at her as I shrug off my leather jacket. She does the same and we both drape them over dining room chairs like we've made a habit of doing that over the years. "Forget it. I'm not interested in sleeping in that room. Or TJ's for that matter. I'm fine on the couch."

She nods with a slight smile. "OK. Well." We stare at each other for a few awkward seconds.

"Well," I say. "I'll see you in the morning then. We can take things from there."

She nods and walks off, disappearing down the hallway that leads to the bedrooms. I grab a glass of water and take it into the living room, taking a long gulp and setting it down on the coffee table as I drop into the cushions of the wide sectional couch and sink back with a sigh.

What a fucking day. I have to let out a laugh at that. What a fucking month. Hell, months, I guess. How long ago was the accident? I lost track of time.

I flick on the TV out of habit, then flick it off again and fish my phone out of my pocket. It's been a long time since I fell asleep to music and I miss it. That was a nightly ritual no matter where I was in the world. I slide the lock screen open and pull up my playlist. Sleep, it's called.

A smile widens on my face because I've always found that funny. I write beautiful, poetic lyrics and my playlists are named Sleep, Writing, Driving, and Fucking. They have numbers and little descriptors after the titles to differentiate the types of sleep, or writing, or driving, or fucking music. Descriptors like Sleep Soft, Driving Coastline, Writing Love Songs, and Fucking Hard.

I'm about to choose Fucking Hard just for the memories, but... I look over my shoulder at the dark hallway. Fucking Hard music is too loud. Besides, I'm not really interested in reliving those memories. I use the Fucking category to wipe away the girls, their faces, their lies. They all lie. *Oh, Rock*, I hear them say in my mind. *Oh, God, I love you so much.*

All lies.

They want to fuck a rock star. They want to say they did it. Tell their friends, brag about it. They want to feel important and I guess being with a rock star does that for them. Lies. When was the last time someone loved me? Not me, Rock. Me, Rowan Kyle.

This is RK's lie of a life.

But here's the thing about being a rock star. I'm not allowed to have problems because I have money. People think fame and fortune wipes away problems but in my experience it just causes more. Problems like the logistics of flying from London to Singapore to make the next show. Problems like the piano is out of tune for the finale and makes me sound like shit. Problems like a hundred girls throwing themselves at me as I try to exit the building and get in a limo.

No one gives a fuck about those problems. I'm not allowed to complain about logistics, or music quality while playing a show, or trying to choose a girl to fuck, just because I need to feel something that doesn't come with withdrawal sickness the next day.

Problems are things like no rent money, losing a house to the bank, kids getting sick the day you get laid off. Those are real problems.

Who cares if I have no friends left? No voice? Not one that people will recognize, anyway. Who cares if I am basically on house arrest up in what amounts to a beautiful national park in Colorado? No one, that's who.

I sigh and choose Sleep Soft as my playlist, then kick my boots off as Beethoven's Für Elise begins. I do a much better rendition of this than Beethoven does himself. I actually chuckle at that thought as I rip my shirt over my head, unbutton my pants, and slip my jeans off.

I leave the boxers on because of Missy.

I play Für Elise slow. I think Beethoven did it wrong. It loses its feeling when you play it at his tempo. Everything loses its feeling when you play it too fast. That's why most of the Jack songs are fast. Rock and roll, man. Rock and fucking roll. Meaningless noise.

But sometimes I fuck around and do an acoustic version of a song. We include those as bonus tracks on full albums or release them on the internet. Most of the guys don't join in my fascination with slow. Kenner did, of course. Because Kenner is… well, Kenner. A musician, like me. Not a rock star.

When I play Für Elise I play it like there's a baby sleeping in the next room. The music *is* sleep. *Is* calm. *Is* dreams. My fingers barely touch the piano keys. My head bows low and my shoulders slump like I'd fall asleep while playing if the notes weren't so motherfucking beautiful they'd haunt me in my nightmares.

Now I tap it out on my leg, my head falling back against the cushions, my eyes closing as I hear it in my mind. I let the notes drag on like I don't want them to end. Like finishing this song will kill me and I'll either have to start it again and play it on repeat until I collapse from exhaustion, or die just from the emptiness the end of the song makes me feel.

Beethoven does that to me. Drives me mad from the inside out. I glance towards the front room. Towards the piano. I wouldn't mind playing right now, but not with Missy in the house. No. I decided weeks ago I'm never playing in front of an audience again. My rock star days are over and I can't even begin to explain how happy I am about it.

I wish I could take back that moment when Missy caught me playing. It sends the wrong message. I still want to listen to music, but my band days ended with Ian, Elias, and Mo. I don't know what Kenner's gonna do, obviously. I haven't talked to him. Hell, maybe his arms and hands will heal well enough for pounding on things again. And if he wants to get another band together, more power to him.

But not me.

I've got enough money. I'll still get royalties from songs. Jayce said that sales of all songs are through the fucking roof. I'll get paid on that shit for a while. And I can still write. That's my real talent anyway. Singing isn't my superpower, writing lyrics is.

Just like my dad.

I wonder, if Missy is for real, if we'll fall in love and have kids. Teach them to play, and write, and love music like our dads did with us.

Nah.

Missy's not into the domestic life.

I sigh and lie back, pulling on the crumpled quilt that made its home over the back of the couch in the weeks I've been here.

What will I do if she really is Missy? Will I love her the way I used to? Will she make me happy? Will she bury this creeping sadness inside me, put it in a vault and keep the key in her heart? Will she make me sane again?

What will I do if she's really Mel? Will I hate her? Or forgive her? Will I give in? Or give up and let go of the one or two things that are holding me together these days?

I don't know. I just don't know.

Chapter Sixteen

The smell of coffee wakes me. I sit up, rubbing the nightmares away as I run my hand through my hair and get it off my face.

"Sorry," Missy says from the kitchen. "I'm an early bird."

I nod, recalling all the mornings she woke me up with a text. That makes everything better for like, oh, three seconds. And then I remember why she's here.

"If you sleep in one of the bedrooms I won't wake you."

"Doesn't matter," I say, standing up and pulling my jeans on. I wave her off as I make my way into the front bathroom to piss. I splash water on my face after I wash my hands and steal a look in the mirror.

It surprises me every time. The same sandy brown hair hanging over my face. The same wheat-colored eyes. The same mouth, and nose, and scruffy chin.

How can I possibly look the same on the outside when everything has changed on the inside?

I let out a long breath and grab a towel, letting it go. Because what's the point of dwelling on shit that makes no sense?

Missy has the TV on when I get back to the kitchen and grab a mug. I pour and take a sip, even though it's hot. It burns a little going down but nothing like it did last week.

I guess time does heal all things.

Well.

"Hey?" Missy calls from the living room. "I gotta work today. Wanna come with me?"

I stare at her. "Where do you work?"

She laughs. "Float's."

"Oh," I say, taking another sip of coffee.

"I'm not just a pretty voice, Rowan Kyle."

Her using my full name makes me smile. I walk past her and open the door to the back deck. The sun is just coming up over the mountains in the east. "What time is it?"

"Five fifteen."

"What?" I ask, turning back to look at her. "Why the fuck are you up so early to work at Float's?"

"We do breakfast on the weekends in the summer, RK. Have for years. And I make enough tips during breakfast to pay the cable and my phone bill."

"Ah, fuck. I'll take care of that shit, Missy. I can't believe you've been paying my bills."

"Well, it's not like you've been here." It comes out kinda snotty and I go still for a few seconds. "Sorry," she says under her breath. "I didn't mean anything by that comment."

"Sure," I say. "Sure." I walk out onto the deck, enjoying how the wood feels on my bare feet. "I'm gonna decline your offer."

"Why?" she pushes, following me out onto the deck. "You have plans today? Or you just want to avoid the bar?"

"Does it matter?" My retort comes out just as snide as her comment. I can almost feel her cringe behind me.

"Well, yeah. You gotta eat, right? We have really good food there now. Not like you remember."

"Not much about that place is like I remember."

"Maybe that's good," she says. "Maybe that's bad. But it's your home. This town is still your home. People care about you, RK. Love you. They want you to get better. Be happy and live on."

Live on. God, that fucking hurts. It hits me in the chest like a brick.

"I can't say anything right this morning. Forget I mentioned it." She turns to go, but I catch her by the wrist.

"Wait," I say. "Sorry. I don't mean to be dramatic, OK? It's just…" I shake my head. "Ian, and Mo, and Elias. And Kenner, too. He's alive, he'll live, like me. But live *on*, Missy? How the fuck do we live on? How the fuck do we put our shitty lives back together?"

She sighs deeply and places a hand on my bare shoulder. It sends a chill up my arm. Little pinpricks of emotion. "Just one day at a time, RK. One moment at a time. You wake up, you drink coffee, you shoot the shit with me. We eat breakfast, and go to work, and come home. And it still hurts. Maybe every moment of that day hurts. But you do it anyway because you have to take these little teeny-tiny baby steps before anything big can happen."

I stare into her blue eyes. The dark makeup she was wearing last night is smudged and black. And she's got a major case of bedhead. That thick, fabulous, mahogany hair is all tousled, and dramatic, and sexy as fuck. "Is that how it's done?" I whisper.

She nods. "It is, RK. That's how it's done." She swallows hard and my eyes dart down to her neck, then her nipples peaking through her white t-shirt. Her legs are bare. Maybe she has shorts on, maybe not. I can't tell because the shirt is big and hangs down to the top of her thighs.

I let go of her wrist and she removes her hand from my shoulder. "OK, then," I say.

"OK?"

"Yeah. OK. I'll come with."

She smiles big. Big. Big. Big. And all I see is Missy. She can't possibly be Melanie. She can't possibly. I know that smile. I'd swear on my own life. I know that smile and it's not the smile of her devious, lying cunt of a sister. It's that same smile she gave me the day of prom. "Let me shower and then we'll go," she says, taking off into the house. I walk over to the hanging curtains, pull them aside, and watch her ass until it disappears into the hallway.

I down the coffee and follow a few minutes later, veering off towards the front room where all the boxes of shit Jayce sent are still stacked. I rummage through them, find an old, ripped Anthrax t-shirt, a pair of ripped jeans to match, and boxers. But then I see one that says *gear*.

Gear? What kind of gear? Music gear? I walk over to the box and rip the tape holding it closed. Inside is, well, lots of shit I don't recognize. Carabiners and things that look like clamps. Some rope and...

Fuck.

It's climbing gear, I realize.

I look over my shoulder real fast, like this stuff is a secret and I need to make sure Missy doesn't catch me looking at it. I go into the kitchen, look through half a dozen drawers until I find packing tape, and then seal it back up.

Secret, RK.

I let out a long breath, then grab my clothes and go into the front bathroom and shower, skip the shave, and still get done before Missy does.

I wait patiently as she blow-dries her hair and then walks into the kitchen where I'm fucking around playing a game on my phone.

"Ready," she says with a smile. She's wearing a proper waitress uniform. Crisp white shirt, black slacks, and some fancy black leather flats. But she still looks like a rock star even though that wild mane is pulled back into a tame ponytail. Her eyes are darked up with her signature eyeliner and thick lashes, but her lips are clear gloss.

"Me going out makes you happy?" I ask, not able to stop looking at her. Suddenly overcome by how fucking beautiful she is. Suddenly remembering why I fell in love with her.

"Very," she says. "Want me to drive?"

"Nah. I got it."

We walk out to the garage and I open her door for her, then close it up after she slides in and goes for her seatbelt. Maybe coming home isn't such a bad idea after all? Maybe, I think as I get in and start the truck up, coming home and finding the girl I thought was gone forever is still here will be the best thing that ever happened to me?

The lake air is warmer than it was up on our part of the mountain, but it's still cool when Missy and I get out of the truck and walk up to the front of the bar. I open the door for her and she smiles over her shoulder at me as she walks inside.

It's a flurry of commotion and people inside and all the tables are set with white linen cloth and a vase with one fresh rose. Nothing like the bar I was in the other night. The stage has a piano now, and some guy I don't know fucks around with sheet music as he talks to Teej.

"What the fuck is this?" I mumble. Missy wanders off towards the back and I make my way over to TJ. "Hey," I say, eyeing the pianist.

TJ cocks his head at me like he's got lots of questions, but then turns back to his conversation and says, "Yeah, that's gonna work, Richie. We'll do that playlist." He jumps down off the stage and claps me on the back. "So, you and Missy work things out last night?" He nods towards the back of the bar where there's a sliver of her in view behind the pick-up counter for the kitchen.

"Not really. But I'm willing to listen."

"Where'd she sleep last night?"

"My room. But before you get any ideas, I slept on the couch."

He shoots me a dubious look and then grabs me by the t-shirt. "Come on, you can eat at my table."

I follow him to the back where we were sitting the other night and slide into the booth. Teej takes the side opposite me. "So what's going on here?" I ask. "You do fancy breakfast now?"

"Have for years, RK. Only in the summer though. We close brunch at eleven and then it's just bar food again. You gonna be here next weekend for Festival Day?"

He's talking about the first show Float's puts on out by the lake at the beginning of summer. "Sure, probably."

"Not gonna call that lawyer today and get the fuck out of town? Go back to LA and spend all your money like a petulant asshole?"

I shrug. "Might. Might not. Depends on how things go, I guess."

"With Missy?"

"With everything. I still haven't seen Kenner. So I'd like to at least drive down to Denver and make sure he's OK. The only reason I haven't been down that way already is because Jayce asked me not to. I guess he's confused or something."

"Hmmm," Teej says. "Understandable. He was in a coma for what? A month?"

"Eight weeks?" I say, thinking back. "I don't even know what the date is."

"June second."

"Kinda late for the dock shows to start, isn't it?"

"Yeah, well. Things got complicated when you came home. I didn't have time to worry about it."

"But now you do?" I look at him with narrow eyes. It feels like he's leaving things out.

"You're getting better, right? Improving. I'm not as worried as I was."

"You were worried?" I huff out a laugh. "Could've fooled me that first night I came into town."

"You came here looking for drugs, RK. You know you did."

"I was in a lot of fucking pain that night, asshole. You'd have been looking for relief too."

"Maybe. But I wouldn't have to worry about the aftereffects of my meds."

"You want to go there?" I snarl. "Because we can. I've been clean for a while now and you're hardly the Rock expert you once were."

"Right," he says, snarling back at me. Teej is a huge guy these days. Muscles press against his white dress shirt under his suit jacket. His short hair still makes him look military, even if it is styled when he's at work. And his eyes seem to say, *Fuck with me and I'll kill you.* I realize I don't know this version of Toby John Saber.

"I see the Army did good things for your disposition."

"You don't know me either, Rock."

"Don't call me Rock, OK? I don't like it."

He shrugs. "Everyone calls you Rock, what's the difference?"

"The difference is it's not my name. Fans call me Rock. Reporters call me Rock. Jayce calls me Rock. You, and Missy, and everyone else in this town who knows me do not call me Rock. So if that's a message that needs to get around, make sure it spreads. I don't fucking like it."

The front door opens and a crowd comes in, chattering like their lives are not in shambles. I envy them. Then the piano starts and Beethoven's Adagio Pirouette fills the room. I frown at the guy on the piano and then look at Teej. "A little dramatic for breakfast, don't you think?"

TJ shrugs. "You don't like it, play something else." And then he gets up and walks off, calling, "I'll send Missy over with a menu. It's on the house."

So that's what this is about. I stare at the guy on piano and critique him. He's not very good. I mean, yeah, he hits all the notes, but he's amateur hour. If TJ thinks he can stick me in a room with a piano and a subpar player and think that will be enough for me to take over the guy's job, he's got issues.

Missy comes by with a menu a few minutes later and the tables are starting to fill up. "The orange-ginger pancakes are good. So's the bacon and cheddar strata."

"Fancy shit," I say, looking over my choices. "Where'd Teej develop such a swanky palate? Iraq?"

"Don't be a dick, RK. We have a chef in the summer. It's his menu. And it's good food, so pick something. I've got tables."

"Relax," I say. "I'm just fucking around. And I'll have the BLT strata. I had that in London once and it was delicious." Missy stares at me for a moment, her face blank. "What?" I ask.

"Nothing," she says, waving a hand at me and taking the menu. "It's just I forget who you are sometimes. It's hard for me to think of you as this famous world traveler. I'll be right back with some coffee. Want juice too?"

"Sure," I say. I watch her ass as she walks off to put my order in. She sounded a little regretful. Maybe even jealous she got stuck here in this small-town life and I went out and saw everything she didn't.

The piano guy transitions into the worst rendition of Für Elise I've ever heard. He plays extra fast, like he knows I play it extra slow and he's doing it on purpose to piss me off. I actually wonder if Teej told him to do that.

Another waitress brings me coffee and juice, not Missy. I don't know this girl and she just seems nervous. "Thanks," I say, looking up at her smiling face, her blonde hair and blue eyes looking perfectly Scandinavian against her tan skin.

"Um," she starts. "I don't want to bother you, Rock, but..." She pulls a ticket stub out of her apron pocket and places it on the table in front of me. "I've been carrying this around hoping you'd come in. I've been waiting for weeks."

Weeks? Have I been here weeks already?

"I was at that show."

I pick up the stub and read it. Boston. Last year. "Yeah? I hope I wasn't too fucked up and ruined it for you."

"No." She laughs. "No, you were awesome. Best show I've ever heard. You know, usually when you see a band in concert they don't sound anything like their studio productions. But you guys..." She sighs. "You guys always sound better live. Can you please sign this for me?" She pulls out a Sharpie and I uncap it and scribble my name.

"Alice," Teej barks from a few empty tables over. "Leave him the fuck alone. I warned you about that."

"Sorry," Alice says, snatching up her ticket stub and smiling as she backs away, her crystal-blue eyes never leaving mine.

"Don't worry about it," I call.

It's nice, I think. It's nice to know people loved us. And maybe Son of a Jack is gone forever, but we left something behind.

Something worthwhile and beautiful. Something that will keep my lost friends alive forever, even though they're dead.

Chapter Seventeen

By the time I get done eating my BLT strata, which I have to admit was fucking fabulous, every table is full and neither Teej or Missy have time to visit. So I make my way outside towards the dock.

I hear Sean Whimel shouting commands and threats at the various dock workers as they shore up the rigging for the upcoming shows. The dock has to be inspected every year by the county before Float's can put on shows. The area down by the lake has been built up over the years. Bars, restaurants, boutique hotels... they all have to obey the town noise ordinance. But Float's was grandfathered in a long time ago when my dad's friend was the mayor, so no matter how much people complain, the show will go on.

The back of the bar facing the lake is an expansive deck filled with umbrella tables and directly on the other side of the railing is a lawn of equal proportions for general admission seating. If you want to sit front row for a show, you get a rock. Boulder, actually. I'm not sure who flattened down the tops of the boulders that line the lake in front of Float's like stadium seating, or when it was done, but that someone was a genius.

The boulders all require tickets. Capacity of thirty, thirty-five if we have a rash of small girlfriends. Our little corner of the VIP market.

No one is standing guard over the boulders right now so I jump from one to another as I follow Sean Whimel's shouts.

"Goddamn it," Sean says to a worker I don't recognize. "Not like that, asshole. You want the fucking band to fall in the water? You want the inspector to shut us down on opening day?" Sean snatches a tool from the guy, who is rolling his eyes at Sean's theatrics, and then turns and smiles when he notices me. "Hey, RK. What's up, man? Come to help with the rigging?"

"I'll help." I did it enough growing up to know what needs to be done. Might as well waste time until Missy gets off work.

What will we do then?

I think about it as I let Sean boss me around and bark orders about shit I know better than he does. But I'm not even remotely interested in running this project, so I help where he needs it and spend the time zoning out, thinking about Missy.

My paranoia about the whole Melissa-Melanie thing is waning. I know Missy. I *know* Missy. And even though Melanie was a psychopathic liar, I know Missy.

This girl I've found myself living with is Missy. I feel it in my heart. Mel wasn't ever that good. I mean, sure, she got me a few times with her tricks. But in my defense, and regardless of Melissa's protests to the contrary last night, they are fucking identical. Right down to the moles on their legs, their equally thick eyelashes, and the shape of their toes.

I've seen both bodies. I'm not proud that Mel almost got me to fuck her. I'm ashamed of that fact, actually. But I figured it out before it got to that point.

Melanie was too eager. She was too aggressive. She was too mean.

Missy isn't any of those things.

But...

There is one little niggling thought that bothers me. That first night I came back, when Mel—*Missy*—found me on my knees in the garage. Why did she say those things? She was mean that night. She acted exactly how Melanie would act.

But TJ was mean that night too. And now he's not.

I don't know, so I decide to drop it.

Missy calls my name from the boulders sometime around noon. The sun is high overhead, blazing down on the water. All us dock workers lost our shirts about an hour ago, so I pick mine up and call over to Sean. "Taking off, man. See you around."

"Thanks for the help, RK. And come by on Wednesday for the launch party."

"What launch party?" I ask back. But Missy is behind me, poking my bare shoulder. "Ow."

"You're sunburned," she says.

"What launch party? I'm not playing in that fucking show next weekend, so why would I come to a launch party?"

"Of course you're not playing," Missy says. "None of those bands want you there upstaging them. It's their day, not yours. We have a party for the opening bands and this year it's next Wednesday night. Private and everything, so you won't be mugged by fangirls if you come." She smiles. "You wanna come? You can be my date. I have an extra ticket."

"I need a ticket?"

"Of course, you're no one special. Just Rowan Kyle Saber. Retired percussionist." She winks and grabs my arm. "Can you drive me home? I smell like food and want to shower."

I slip my shirt on and follow her up the rocks to the parking lot, then unlock her door and open it for her. She slides in and I give it a shove, then walk around and get in my side.

"What are you going to do the rest of the day?"

I start the truck up and shrug. "I dunno. Haven't thought much about it." I've thought a lot about it, actually. Trying to anticipate the empty silence Missy and I might encounter if we stay home all day. All the questions, the poking and prying. "What do you normally do on Saturday afternoons?"

"Sleep."

"Oh."

"Watch TV and stuff. I stay home mostly."

"So who do you hang with these days?" I pull the truck onto the highway that wraps up around the mountain we live on. "Gretchen?"

"When she's in town. She's not usually in town. She's only here…" Missy's words drift off.

"Oh, school's out, right? In between semesters?"

"Right," Missy says.

"Hey, that reminds me. I talked to that therapist out in Granby last week after... last Monday, I guess. And she said Gretchen was here for me. Said she shouldn't have let her take the lead or some shit. What the fuck does that mean?"

"Well, we had a little family meeting when they told us you were going to have to come home—"

"Who told you?"

"Um, well, you know, the sheriff's department. You remember Angelo Marzetti? He's a deputy now. He came into Float's before you were released from that rehab place and said you'd have to stay in Grand County until they completed their investigation. So we figured, you know, we wanted you to understand I was alive, not Melanie. And you said some weird shit right before you left, RK. After Mel's funeral. So we talked to Gretchen and she said she wasn't allowed to be like, your therapist or anything. But she could do volunteer work for Dr. Sanderson and help you out. So, you know. Gretchen is a friend and you deserve to have support from friends."

I suddenly remember a little quirk of Melissa's when she was a teenager. She says 'you know' a lot when she's nervous. Why is she nervous?

The truck climbs a hill as I weave around the side of the mountain, looking hesitantly at the guard rail. I always hated the fact that my house was built on a cliff. "Hmm," I say, rolling all that bullshit about Dr. Margie Sanderson and Gretchen around in my head. Maybe my driving makes Missy nervous? I can't blame her under the circumstances. I have been in two car accidents on these mountain roads. People died. Hell, maybe she thinks I'll kill her too?

"You don't have to babysit me, RK. If you want to go fishing with Sean or something. I'm a homebody now. I can keep myself busy."

"When did that happen?" I ask.

"What?"

"This homebody business? You were never a homebody when we were kids. You were always on the run if you weren't playing music. Hiking, biking, swimming, skiing."

"People change, RK. I've changed a lot." She shoots me a sidelong glance out of the corner of her eye. "So have you."

"Not all my changes were bad."

"Mine either," she quips. "Like I said, I can find plenty of ways to pass an afternoon."

"What's going on tonight?"

"I'm playing tonight. At Float's."

"Oh." Goddammit. Everything in the town revolves around the bar. The stage. The music.

"You don't have to come watch, either. Probably cramp my style. Probably bitch about how I play, or sing, or try to critique me the way you did that pianist this morning."

"I didn't—"

"You did." She laughs. "I saw the look on your face when he played Für Elise."

"He murdered that song."

"Anyway, I have fanboys. So you can stay home and do what reclusive rock stars do."

"You got a boyfriend?" I ask, picturing her fanboys.

"Do you think I'd be living in your bedroom if I did?"

I shrug as I pull the truck into the long driveway that leads up to our houses and then park in the garage when

I get there. We get out and I stare at the place where she grew up down the driveway. "Why don't you just sell that house if you don't want to live there? It's got to be worth, what? Two million by now?"

"I can't," she sighs. And then she goes inside the house, clicking the garage door shut. She leaves me there, watching her house disappear.

I follow her inside, drop my keys off on the kitchen counter, and then go for a beer. Missy already has the shower going.

I take a swig and wander down the bedroom hallway, calling out, "Wanna beer?" to let her know I'm coming, just in case she's undressing. I find her stripping out of her clothes in my room. She's not shy these days because she unbuttons her formerly crisp, white shirt and unleashes the bra on me. "Why can't you sell?" I ask, watching her slide the shirt off. Then I glance to her fingers as she unbuttons her pants. My eyes linger on her flat stomach. That belly button I've dreamed about kissing more times than I can remember. Those hip bones that always felt like the right place to put my hands when we were slow dancing.

"I just don't want to lose what I have left." She stares into my eyes as she unzips her pants and then shimmies, dropping them to her ankles.

"What do you mean?"

She steps out of her pants and reaches around behind her back to unclasp her bra. It falls forward, freeing her breasts. "Well," she says softly. "That's all *we* have left, right? Those memories of living next door to each other. I know they're not all good ones, but enough of them are for me to want to cling to it." She lets the bra fall to the floor and stands there naked. "Do you want to take a shower with me, RK? You smell like the lake."

"Is the lake a bad smell?" I ask, watching her closely.

"No," she says. "Not at all. I just want to be the one to wash it off you."

She slips by me, her fingertips flitting along my arm as she passes, sending a chill through my body.

Chapter Eighteen

I take my shirt off as I walk across the hallway, throwing it down on the floor. Missy is standing with her back to me, testing the temperature of the shower. She peeks over her shoulder and smiles. "I know you probably hear this all this time, but damn, Rowan Kyle. You should never take that shirt off in public again."

I go for my pants, unbuttoning them, unzipping them. She watches every move. And then I kick off my boots and fling them into the hallway with the shirt. She turns all the way around now and I feel myself getting hard as she presses her palm against my cock, squeezing it through my pants.

"If I knew you were coming back I'd have waited for you."

God, that hurts.

"I just…" She stops, her sad eyes lingering on mine. "I just didn't think you would. Come back, I mean."

"I'm sorry," I say. And I mean it. I'm so fucking sorry I wasn't her first.

"It's OK. We get to skip all that awkward fumbling, right?" She swallows hard and I know she's sorry too. She was the only girl I dreamed about. The only girl I ever wanted. Even after all my rock-star nights, Melissa Vetti is still the only girl I want.

I place both my hands on her cheeks and lean down to kiss her mouth. Her lips part, her tongue seeking out mine. It's soft, and slow, and short. Way, way too short.

She pulls away, taking her hand off my cock, and turns, stepping into the shower. I let my pants fall to the floor and toss them in the hallway. The shower has a clear glass surround and I watch her as she stands under the water, her fingers massaging it into her hair.

I step in with her and place my hands on her shoulders so I can turn her towards me. "Melissa—"

"Shh," she says. "I don't want to talk about it right now. I just want to enjoy this." She picks up the soap and starts to lather me up, massaging the bubbles along my arms. Over my chest. Up and down my back.

I grab the bottle of shampoo and squeeze some into my palm, then rub my hands together and begin working it through her long, dark, hair as I study her face. The makeup is smearing as I watch. It makes her look like she's crying.

"I feel like this is a dream," she says, her soapy hands moving to my front. "I feel like I've been granted some wish but it's all fake and you're just going to disappear again. Leave me here alone. Lonely. You want to know why I stay home, RK?"

No. No, I really don't.

"Because I'm lonely. Because you were my life. And I know I was having doubts back when we were about to graduate, but they were small doubts. Growing-up doubts. Not-knowing-what-I-wanted doubts. But I was never going to break up with you, RK. Never. And I was certainly never going to walk away from us."

Fuck. I guess I haven't looked at it from her point of view very much. "I walked away."

"You walked away." Her frown is so deep it hurts my heart.

"I'm sorry. I don't even know why—"

"Shh," she says again. "Later."

Her hand slides up and down my cock as she looks me in the eyes. It's a very intimate moment. Probably the most intimate moment I've had in years.

"Rinse," I say.

Missy turns away, and I swear, I know what she's feeling. Every time she does that I think she will never turn back to me again. I hate when she turns away. I watch as she rinses the shampoo out of her hair. The water streams down her face like that waterfall where we had our first kiss.

She's not Melanie. How could I ever think she was Melanie?

"Can I make you dinner tonight? Before the show?" she asks when she turns back. The relief that she's still here is real, as irrational as it is.

"Dinner?" I say, trying to wrap my head around the change of subject. I was about to attack her, lift her up, press her back against the wall, and fuck the shit out of her and now she's talking about dinner.

"Yeah. Do you still like lemon pasta? Like your mom used to make?"

"Jesus," I say. "The angel hair with the white wine sauce? I haven't thought about that in years."

"Yeah. Remember when I made that for you on your seventeenth birthday?" She laughs. It was a fun night. A really fun night. The kind of fun you only have with the girl of your dreams before you turn to drugs and need alcohol and sex to force the fun. "I fucked it all up," she says through a giggle.

I grin as I picture her attempt to cook me something. "I'm not sure how anyone can fuck that recipe up, but yeah. You did." She bites her lip and I almost die. "It was perfect though. Because you made it. And you made it special for me."

"You ate every bite."

"There was no chance in hell I wouldn't, Missy. Not after you went to all that trouble. So sure. I'm not gonna complain about a trip down memory lane with you tonight."

"Good," Missy sighs. "Good." And then she grabs the conditioner and the possibility of sex fades away.

I'm actually glad it fades. I'm glad she changed the subject. Turned us in a different direction. I know I hate-fucked her when I first got back into town, and I'm sorry about that. I'd like to take it back and get a do-over. I'd rather wait. Like we did when we were kids. I'd rather wait until we know for sure this is real, and special, and maybe even permanent.

I'd like to take my time with Melissa Vetti.

Chapter Nineteen

We finish up in the shower, get out, and go our separate ways. Her to the bedrooms where she's got her clothes stashed in various places. Me to the living room where my former life is boxed up in cardboard. I grab my usual jeans and a t-shirt—this one is a once black, now faded gray, Something Corporate tour shirt from 2003 that I found in a record store where Son of a Jack did a promo appearance right after the first album launched. It's been worn and washed so many times, there's a two-inch rip near my right hip and the sleeves are frayed. Fucking love this shirt.

I don't bother with the shoes, just finger-comb my hair back and make my way into the kitchen where Missy is already busy. "So," I say, coming up behind her as she puts a pot of water on to boil. "What kind of songs do you play, Miss? Covers? Originals?"

She shoots me a look over her shoulder, one eyebrow raised. "Covers? Please. I'm an artist, RK. I outgrew covers a while back."

"I know you're an artist. I'm just asking. I'm out of the loop. I kinda want to know if you're my competition."

"Shit." She laughs. "You can write the fuck out of a song, Rowan Kyle. I'm not sure there's anyone alive who comes close to your talent."

"Yeah," I say, backing up. "He's dead, I guess."

Missy sighs but doesn't turn around. "I know why you didn't come back for the funeral. So if you think I'm judging you for that"—she shoots me another look over her shoulder—"I'm not. Your dad was a dick. Hell, my dad was a dick too. They were a couple of old, washed-out, rock-star dicks. You don't get to choose your parents."

She whirls around and starts rummaging through the fridge for lemons, sets them on the counter, and then goes for a bottle of wine in the wine fridge under the counter.

"So why'd you move in and help him out?" I ask. "When he got sick?"

She shrugs her shoulders at me, still busy with food preparation. "I wanted to root through your room. I'd been dying to do it since you took off. So I figured, two birds, right? Keep that bitter old man happy as he wasted away from lung cancer and obsessively pine over my long-lost love at the same time."

I laugh.

"Besides, he was never an asshole to me. Just you and Teej."

"I guess TJ was pretty pissed off when I never showed up."

"He got over it. And I wouldn't call it pissed, not really. More like disappointed."

"Hmm," I grunt.

"Not because of your dad. Mostly because we all thought you'd come back. We were *hoping* you'd come back," she corrects. "We were looking forward to seeing you and when the day passed and you never showed, well. That's when it all became real. You were gone." She turns around and faces me, one half of a lemon clutched in each hand. "We just missed you, RK. That's all. No one's mad. No one's holding any grudges. No one wants you to leave again." She sighs deeply, staring into my eyes. Silent, like she's waiting for an answer.

"Well…" I stall for time. "I do have another life, you know. There's not much left of it right now, but it's still there. So eventually I'm going to have to deal with that."

"I know," Missy says with a small smile. "But not tonight. We can deal later. Not tonight."

And then she goes back to her cooking.

"Wanna hear some music?" I ask, watching the way her body moves. The small, feminine muscles of her back peeking through the tank top. The curve of her ass in the loose-fitting ripped jeans. Her red-painted toes as she scoots along the counter doing this and that.

"Your music?" she asks with a smile over her shoulder.

"Well, that's not what I was thinking. No."

"That song you wrote for me? The one you played at Mel's funeral?"

"Fuck, no," I say, trying to laugh but not quite making it.

"I love that song."

"Everyone does. They never stop asking for it. They scream it out at every show. It doesn't even have a fucking name. They just chant, 'The song, the song, the song,' over and over again. It drives me nuts."

"Does it have lyrics? You didn't sing that day."

"No," I say, my thoughts stuck on *that day*.

"You didn't write lyrics? Or you just don't sing lyrics?"

I see the words in my head. I've been writing lyrics for that song for years. Every once in a while I'll just stop everything because another verse comes to mind and I have to think about it. "Never wrote them," I lie.

"Why not? It's unusual for you, right? Maybe you're different these days but you wrote that song back when I knew you. And you always wrote the lyrics before the beats."

"I guess I changed the day I wrote that one."

"I don't believe you," she says, looking over her shoulder again. "But I'm not gonna push it. You're entitled to your private thoughts. Besides, I've rummaged through most of them while I've been staying here. I can't complain."

I smile big. I can't help it. "God, I missed you, Melissa Vetti."

"Ditto, Rowan Kyle Saber. You've been gone way too long."

I'm silent after that. Both of us are. For a few minutes, at least. I just watch her, wondering why I let the past dictate my future the way I did.

"Are you happy?" she asks, washing her hands and drying them on a dish towel. The wine sauce is simmering in a pan on the massive six-burner stove and the whole kitchen smells like lemons and white wine.

Like the past. Like it did when things were good, back before my mom got sick.

"Happy?" I repeat. "No. Not even close."

Missy leans back against the counter, studying me from top to bottom. "You look good. Considering what's happening. Was the rock-star life not what you imagined?"

"I never wanted to be a rock star, Missy. That was you."

"Ironic, isn't it?"

"Very."

"So what's it like? Tell me about it. Let me live vicariously through you."

I walk into the living room and slump down onto the couch. The pillows are all askew, kind of like my life. And the quilt I've been using is bunched up in one corner. Missy sits down next to me, pulling her feet in underneath her.

"And start from the beginning," she says. "I don't want to miss a thing."

"The beginning." I think about it for a few seconds.

"Your dad hired a private investigator. We knew you went to LA."

"Yeah. I still had his credit card back then. I needed it to escape. So I guess that part was easy."

"You got rid of it though. And then we lost you. Never got a job?"

"Not a real one. No. Everything was cash. I was sort of promoter for a few local clubs in Hollywood back then. I met Kenner first, we bonded, you know."

"He's an amazing musician."

"Yeah," I say, some of the sadness creeping back in. "He was."

"He's going to be OK, right?"

"I guess. If he can ever drum again he will."

"Why wouldn't he drum again? I don't know what all his injuries were exactly, but they... he... he'll recover."

I run all those words back in my head, trying to make sense of them, but then I decide none of this makes sense. "Same reason I'll probably never sing again."

"It hurts too much?" she asks.

"Well," I say, my hand automatically going to my throat. "Not too bad these days. It's getting better."

"I think he'll drum again. And I think you'll sing again too."

"Well, I think you're naively optimistic."

She laughs. "So you got to LA and became some kind of club promoter. Met Kenner. And then what happened?"

"We just..." I let out a long sigh. "We just got manic, you know? Fucking manic. Like sixteen-hour days writing songs. And we recorded a few, just us two playing whatever it was we needed. Him on drums, since he rocks the skins much better than I do. Me on guitar and piano. Sometimes I played bass, but mostly Kenner did that too, and we just mixed the tracks together to make songs. We got our hands on a violin and a cello. No one was making music like we were making music, you know? We just found something new. Something real. Something people wanted, but never knew they wanted it until they heard us."

I smile, remembering how much fun it was. "Life faded away, Missy. It all just faded away that first year. We got odd jobs doing this or that for the clubs just to pay the thousand-dollar-a-month rent on Kenner's shitty closet of a studio apartment. And we wrote." I look at her and shrug. "We just wrote."

"You had a lot to say, I guess."

I nod. "Yeah. We both did. Ian and Elias came next. A couple months into the whole project. And then Mo. It was fucking magic. Destiny."

"What was it like, RK? When you figured out things were changing. You were a hit and people knew who you were?"

"What was it like to realize I was famous?" I chuckle.

"Yeah. That." She leans forward. So, so, so interested in what I made of my life.

"Surreal, I guess. Once the money started flowing and people started calling we moved up, of course. Got a nice house in the hills and tricked out a studio so we could make the music right. Took conference calls with execs who wanted a piece of our pie. And then the offer to be opening act for Rage. I was barely twenty years old and I was on a world tour with the most famous rock band on the planet. Jayce was there, of course. She was managing another local Hollywood band when we met her, but we offered her more money to jump ship. She's amazing too."

"I think she's kind of a cunt, myself," Missy says.

I laugh. "Well, you're not alone. She is a cunt, but she's a damn effective one. Daddy's little rich girl. Graduated summa cum laude in marketing from Berkeley. She can talk circles around anyone, so don't get her started. She's relentless when it comes to promotion and public relations. Shit, she got people talking about us and never once had to mention my father to do it. It took them a long time to figure out who I was because I never told anyone my last name. I just morphed into… Rock."

"That's when I saw you on TV. You looked a little stunned when they brought up Jack."

"Son of a Jack," I say with a smile. "They ambushed me, for sure. But by then, I was over it. Fuck him, was all I kept thinking on that show. Fuck him."

"And then…" Missy hesitates. "Then the drugs?"

I nod, the excitement of reliving my path to success over.

"Why, RK? You knew what happened to your dad. I don't understand that part."

"I just forgot, I guess." I shrug. "I just forgot things. Forgot who I was, why I left."

"You don't forget those kinds of things, Rowan Kyle. It's not possible."

"It's a figure of speech, Miss. Time passes, wounds heal, life goes on, and sometimes the lessons you thought you learned don't stick."

"And last year? When they found you passed out in a bathtub with a needle sticking out of your arm? That was when you started to remember?"

"I didn't really have a choice," I say softly. Kind of ashamed. Kind of embarrassed. Kind of sad. "Kenner and Mo said they'd quit if I didn't go into rehab. And fuck, I didn't want to lose them, you know? I'd lost so much. Kenner and I were tight, but Mo and I were close too. He was our pianist. He and Kenner both played piano and that's always been my thing. So when Mo and Kenner said they were out unless I went all in…" I sigh. "I had to go all in."

"Do you love me?" Missy asks, her eyes darting wildly as she searches mine for my soul.

"Of course I do." It comes out as a whisper. "I've always loved you, Missy."

"Then you need to go all in for me too, Rowan Kyle. Or I'm out." She stares hard at me, like she really means this. "I don't want to be out. I'm sure Kenner and Mo were praying to whatever God they believe in that you'd do as they asked, because you're bigger than life, Rock." I cringe when she calls me that. "You're bigger than life and people are drawn to you like fireflies to the night. I don't want to be out. But I need you to be all in for me too."

I stare at my hands for a moment, wondering what it means to her. What does *all in* mean to her? For Kenner and Mo it was rehab. But I'm clean now. I have a fucking prescription for oxycodone somewhere in this house and I have no desire to fill that thing. No desire to shoot up or go looking for the high. The cravings are gone. I'm better now. That lesson stuck.

So I ask. Because I want her. I want her more than anything. I want her to be real, I want us to be together, I want the past to go away and leave me alone. "What does it mean to be all in, Miss?"

She smiles and scoots her body over to mine, wrapping her hands around my bicep and resting her cheek on my chest. "Just the truth, Rowan Kyle. Nothing more, nothing less. Just the truth."

"I don't think I've ever been a liar, Missy." I rest my head against hers, inhaling the sweet smell of her shampoo. "If I lied to you, I didn't mean it."

"I know, RK."

We sit still for a while, just breathing. Relaxing. Enjoying the moment. And then Missy jumps up and says, "Shit!" as she runs to the kitchen and starts fucking around with the wine sauce on the stove. It sizzles and she says, "Shit!" again.

"Don't worry." I laugh from the couch. "I'll eat it this time too."

She chuckles. "Fuck you, Rowan Kyle."

But it's a good fuck you. It's a friendly fuck you. It's a fuck you that says this second chance might actually be real. Even after all the bad shit that's happened, I might finally find something real.

Chapter Twenty

"You know,"* I say, after scarfing down her lemon pasta—which was perfect, even if she did burn the wine a little—"you're gonna miss your own show if we don't leave in like ten minutes." I stand in the hall bathroom doorway, leaning up against the doorjamb, watching her put on her makeup.

She rolls her eyes in the mirror as she applies some tan shit to her face with a sponge. "I'll be ready, don't worry."

I turn and look into TJ's room, which is directly across the hall from the bathroom. He's got one of those camp chairs pushed up against the wall, so I wander in, not bothering to flip on the lights, and take a seat.

There are seven guitars lined up in stands. Three bass, two acoustic, and two electric. I pick up the one within arm's reach, an old acoustic I recognize from when we were kids, and give it a strum.

"Play me a song, RK." Missy looks over at me and smiles.

"This fucker's so out of tune. When's the last time he played it?" I start twisting knobs as I strum, trying to make it sound decent.

"Oh, hell," Missy says, fluffing powder over her cheeks. "I have no clue. Long time, I think. He doesn't play at the bar. Not even to fuck around."

"Well, the strings aren't that old. He must've been in here doing something."

"Hmm," Missy says, applying something dark to her eyelids. "I play them every once in a while. I guess I must've put new strings on it."

I keep tuning as I watch her. She's wearing tight jeans now, and the curve of her ass is driving me crazy. The jeans are blue like a summer sky and have thin rips going up the whole length of her thighs. All the frayed strands are white, like she's been wearing them for years and they've been washed a million times. I can see her skin peek through when she moves just the right way.

"That sounds right," she says absently as I strum all the strings. "Play something. I'm your girlfriend. I deserve to have a song played for me."

I smile. Big. "You're my girlfriend, huh," I say, starting to pluck the strings out of habit.

She stops what she's doing to look over at me. "Aren't I?"

"You are if you want to be."

"That's not a very nice answer, Rowan Kyle."

"Did I ever tell you about how nervous I was when I kissed you that first time?"

She goes back to her makeup, satisfied with my rebuttal. "No. But go on."

"Do you remember it?" I ask, looking down at the fingerboard.

"Sixth grade camping trip." She laughs. "You did some funky interview in *Metal Notes* for Valentine's Day a couple years ago. Remember that?"

"Of course," I say.

"And the question was about the best kiss of your life." She stops with her makeup and looks over at me, squinting her eyes like she's trying to make me out in the dark. "Our first kiss was the best you ever had?" She cocks an eyebrow.

"Man," I say with a small laugh. "My fucking hands were sweating, my heart was racing, my mind was spinning. I'd imagined in my head so many times. What would it feel like? What would you do? Would you slap me?"

"Slap you? Ha!" She laughs. "You took forever to kiss me, RK. That whole year was torture as I waited." She stops with the makeup again and stares at me. "And I was so afraid Melanie would trick you and get that first kiss instead of me."

"Fuck that," I say. "Fuck her. I know she was your sister but—"

"Hey," she interrupts. "I can't defend her sickness. I'm not saying people are always responsible for their actions when they are mentally ill, but she was. She knew she was hurting me. *Us*, RK. She did it on purpose to hurt *us*. So I'm with you on that. Fuck her."

"Well," I say, realizing I'm playing the song, "she didn't win. Because you were the first girl I ever kissed, Melissa Vetti. And no one can ever take that away from us."

"I'm glad it was you," she says, drawing dark lines around her eyes. I watch her as my fingers do their rock-star thing, creating music that is almost as pretty as the girl in front of me. "I love that song, RK. I've played that video they have online about a thousand times." She sighs. "One day you'll sing me those lyrics I know you wrote and my life will be complete."

"Hmm," I say, closing my eyes to see what I feel in my mind's eye. "If I ever do, you will be the first to hear them. I wrote this song for you, you know. Not Melanie." I open my eyes. "I don't know why I thought you were the one who died, Miss. I really don't understand it."

"It's OK," she whispers. "We don't have to talk about that tonight." And then she pinks up her cheeks with blush, smacks on some matching lipstick, and turns to face me. "I'm ready."

I keep playing as I take her in. She's got some high-heeled boots on—black leather, of course—an old black tank top that has probably been around the same amount of time as the Something Corporate shirt I have on, and too many leather cuffs on her wrists to count. Her mahogany hair is straight and shiny, flowing across her shoulders and down her back. "You look like a rock star, Miss. And if I catch any of your fanboys getting fresh, Teej might have to kick my ass out for roughing them up."

She laughs as she turns off the bathroom light. "You're the only fanboy I need, RK. Come on, I gotta get to the show." She walks into the bedroom and holds her hand out to me. I set the guitar back down in the stand and take her hand, letting her pull me to my feet.

She turns to walk off, but I keep hold and pull her back into the dark room. "Missy," I say, letting go of her hand so I can dip my fingers under her hair and place my palms against her neck.

"Don't smear my lipstick." She giggles.

I place my lips on her throat and she tips her head back to give me access. "Lips aren't the only things that need kissing," I say, brushing against her skin so softly, it sends a shudder through her body. "You're the only girl I ever wanted. Ever. So yes," I whisper, gently nibbling her earlobe. "I want to give this another try. I want you to be my girlfriend. I need this second chance."

She places both her hands on mine and squeezes. "I feel like I'm living a dream, RK. Like all of this is fake and it's going to disappear any second."

"Welcome to my world," I say back. We bump foreheads and stare into each other's eyes for a moment. And then I pull back. "Come on. I'm ridiculously excited about watching you play tonight."

We get in the truck and drive down to the main road. The two sheriff's vehicles flank each side of the intersection. Missy waves to them as we drive off, one tailing us, one remaining there, standing sentry.

"Jesus Christ," I mumble. "Don't they have better things to do than watch me? This whole county has what? Five cops total?"

"Ten." Missy laughs. "It's not Hicksville, RK. And they're only here to protect you."

"I don't need protecting. Jayce is paranoid."

"Well, I think it's a good idea. We're isolated out here. People could come right up the road and knock on the damn door. So if Deputy Angelo Marzetti and friends want to stand guard, I'm not gonna complain. I even took them sodas and cookies the other day."

I grin at that, because that isn't something I could ever picture Melanie doing. Missy might be a terrible cook, but she tries hard. And baking the cops cookies is sweet. I slow down as a truck comes at us when I approach the twisty part of the drive down.

"You don't have to go so slow, RK. He's not gonna pull you over for speeding."

"I'm trying to be careful, Miss. I don't need another car going off the side of the mountain."

"What?" she asks. I look over at her puzzled face. "What's that got to do with anything?"

"My track record is pretty bad, right?" I sigh. "I'm just saying. I'm trying to drive safely."

"Hmm," she says, turning her body a little to look out the window.

"What's your band's name?" I ask, just to change the subject.

"House band," she says, turning back to me with a smile. Not a big one, but it's a smile. "I'm a solo act, RK."

"Melissa Vetti, rock star? Or Missy Vetti, singer-songwriter?"

"Either or, I guess." Her smile grows and I make a mental note not to bring up driving off a mountain again. "Or maybe both. I don't have any deep messages in my songs like you do."

"What are they about?" I'm dying to hear her.

"Love."

I laugh. "Aren't they all?"

"It's funny, you know? When I was a teen I'd try to write songs about the world. How I felt about it. What people were doing. Trends and stuff. But the harder I tried to get a message across, the dumber the song ended up being. So I gave up and just wrote things from my heart. How I felt about life instead of how I felt about what was happening in life. Most of that feeling comes from love for me. I write about you a lot. Growing up with you, loving you, losing you. Some are hard, some are soft. But they all come back to you, RK."

I'm silent for a few seconds. "I think if you look carefully you'll find that all my songs are about you as well."

"And you write them because you care about me. And your fans care about you, so that's why they like the songs?"

"That's the secret sauce," I say. "I can write a pop hit. I'm sure I could pull out any old notebook and make a pop hit out of something. But I don't want to. I think my fans would know my heart wasn't in it. So I don't do it. I only release songs that speak to me. Falling in love, being in love, losing love, and everything before, after, and in between. Kenner writes some fun shit, but we don't do too many of those or people stop taking you seriously."

"You don't do it for the money," she says. And it's not a question.

"I don't." I look over at her for a moment as we get to the outskirts of town. "I don't need a lot of it. Just enough. And I was raised up with just enough. It's not like I ever lacked anything. I don't need a bigger house, a better view, or a faster car. I don't mind where I came from. I had more than most. I like where I'm at. It's more than enough."

"You're not really gonna quit, are you?"

"Afraid you'll miss out on my rock-star lifestyle?" I wink at her, so she knows I'm joking.

"Nah, I'm just afraid you'll never hit your stride, RK. You've done a lot with the past five years but you've got so much more to do with that talent. I don't want you to quit because you're not done yet."

I nod. "Well, thanks. I appreciate that, Miss. And I'm sorry shit's fucked up at the moment. I'll figure it out eventually."

"I know you will," Missy says, sending me a smile that says she's at peace with what I'm going through. With my weird behavior. My struggles. The sheriff following me everywhere. "I have complete faith in you. And I'm not in a rush."

I park the truck on the street, since the dirt parking lot is full at this time of night, and take Missy's hand as we walk over to the bar. The sheriff's car that was behind us just pulls in front of Float's and parks right in the no-parking zone. A boisterous crowd of people have to move aside to accommodate him and they go eerily silent when they recognize me approaching.

"Hey, Rock," one guy says.

"What's up, man?" I say, pulling the door open for Missy.

"You playing tonight?" another guy asks.

"Nah," I say, looking over my shoulder just as someone's phone takes a flash picture. "Tonight belongs to singer-songwriter Missy Vetti, my future wife."

Missy lets out a gasp and then punches me in the arm. "What was that for?"

I shrug as we enter into the fray of people and waitresses. "Just trying to start the rumor early, that's all. Let everyone know I'm officially off the market. We're gonna have to watch TV tomorrow to see who reports it first."

"You're crazy," she says, but she leans up on her tiptoes and kisses me on the lips, forgetting all about her lipstick. "I'll see you after, OK?"

"I'll be here." I watch her ass as she walks off and shake my head with a sigh. Fucking girl is beautiful.

"Hey," Teej says, grasping my shoulder and leaning into my ear. "I'm gonna take you to the back so people don't bother you."

"I don't mind it," I say. "It's the hometown crowd."

"No," TJ says, raising his voice to be heard over the music. "The place is packed with townies tonight. I guess word got out you've been in here a few times. I called in security." He points to the back where two more fucking sheriff's deputies are standing at attention. Their eyes flick across the crowd.

"Why the fuck did you do that?" I ask.

He's pulling me along with him now, so I have to go with. "Jayce called earlier today. Said we need to have armed security in here at all times and since there's no private firms up here in the goddamned mountains, I asked the sheriff to help out this week. Just until I get our own guys."

"Jesus Christ. Someone is going to rob the bank tonight and I'm going to get blamed because all the cops are either here at Float's or at my house."

"I got a call in to some former military guys out in Denver," Teej says, clapping me on the back and pointing to his booth. "It's just for a couple more days." Gretchen and Sean are already there, talking, and smiling, and laughing.

"Hey," they both say at the same time.

But I'm still thinking about the words *former military guys*, so I just shoot them a wave as I lean back into TJ's ear. "Tell me again why we need former military guys for security?"

But TJ doesn't hear my question, or maybe he's just ignoring me, because he points to a guy a few tables away and walks over to do the clap-on-the-back greeting he just gave me.

"Take a shot, RK!" Sean pulls on my arm, scooting over into the interior of the half-moon-shaped booth to give me room. There are at least ten shot glasses on the table, but only four of them are full.

"Getting started early tonight, ladies?" I ask.

Gretchen shakes her head and then yells over the noise. "I'm driver. So drink all you want. I'll take you home tonight."

"Two for you!" Sean says. "And two for me!"

"Shit, I don't—"

"Fuck you, pussy," Sean says, cutting me off. "You're doing these shots or Gretchen will hold you down and pour them in."

Gretchen rolls her eyes at me. "Children, all of you."

I shrug. I might be a drug addict but I'm not an alcoholic. I down one, then the other, slamming both on the table the same time as Sean. "Damn," I say. "That was fucking smooth. What is that?" I grab the bottle and turn it towards me.

"Auchentoshan," Sean says. "Sixteen-year-old, limited-edition. You a Scotch man, Rock?"

I squint my eyes at him and say, "RK. And yeah, I've been known to buy a bottle or two. I have Auchentoshan 1957 at home in LA. Once this shit blows over, you need to come visit my theatre room bar."

"Dude." Sean's eyes are wide. "I'm gonna take you up on that. But until then"—he pours four more shots—"bottoms the fuck up!"

I'm just about to do another shot when I hear the squeak of the amp and the shuffling of the mic.

"Yeah, baby!" someone yells. I look around for the owner of the voice. It sounded like a fanboy.

But then the guitar starts, then the beat. The bass joins in and the stage lights come on, highlighting my girl like a… like a fucking rock star.

She leans into the guitar, her fingers dancing along the neck and even though I've seen her bite her goddamned lip many times in the past couple weeks, this is why I love it so much. That little tongue that darts out when she hits the high notes. The way she sucks that lip in and grimaces when her fingers have to do something tricky. She has always played this way. Her posture hasn't changed, the bend of her legs, the crook of her arm, the length of the strap, the way she never looks at the crowd unless she's singing. Like all the music is in her head and the audience is an accident.

She takes a deep breath as the music softens and then leans into the mic.

I stand up.

That fucking voice, man.

I push past some people in the aisle, making my way forward.

Can't get enough of it.

The deputies stop me, one guy leaning into my face, barking orders for me to go sit back down.

I ignore him. I see nothing. I hear nothing. Except Melissa fucking Vetti up there on stage.

I realize I recognize the melody. One she wrote a long, long time ago back when we were kids. But the words are different. Back then they were about war, and politics, and shit everyone wanted to forget.

But tonight they are about yearning, and craving, and fucking.

Just like she said on the drive down.

And when the song ends, in that fraction of a moment of silence before the crowd rewards her with noise, she looks me straight in the eyes and whispers into the mic, "Fuck the past, this is the future."

She doesn't wait for the crowd, just dives right into another song, this one harder, angrier, and sexy as fuck. Her long hair sticks to her face, no free hands to brush it aside. Her back arches and my eyes are trained on her breasts. Her mouth twists as she eases back and lets the bass and drums take over.

I'm mesmerized.

The deputies still block my way but they stop demanding that I go sit down. Eventually TJ appears, probably knowing that her set is just about done, and urges me back to the table. I get there just as she finishes.

"Um," Sean says as the music dies off. "You want me to introduce you, RK? I've got an in with the band."

I flip him the finger. "Fuck off. I can't help it. I haven't seen her play in years. She's so goddamned good, right?"

My eyes go back to Missy, taking her bow on stage as the people cheer. Not nearly enough cheers for my Missy. Not nearly enough cheers for what she just gave them.

Sean shoves a shot glass over towards me, his already in hand. "To being too goddamned good to play Float's in Grand Lake."

I drink to that.

Chapter Twenty-One

Missy shows up at the table just as Sean is pouring more shots of Auchentoshan, still doubling us all up. She downs them like a pro, and I watch, laughing, before downing mine. "Fucking good," I say again.

"Yeah, RK likes the expensive shit," Sean says. "I was hoping this might make you happy." He pours two more for both Missy and I, and then takes his attention to Gretchen, taunting her about being DD tonight.

I look up at Miss and take her hand, pulling her into my lap, since the booth is packed now that Teej is sitting across from me. She sinks down and I slip my hand up her shirt, enjoying the way her back feels. All sweaty and slick from her stage time. I fucking love it. She smells good too.

"So," she says, leaning into my ear so I can hear her over the music. "What'd you think?"

"Hmmm." I lean into her neck. "I think... I think it's a good thing those cops were here, because I was about to drag you offstage and make you fuck me like a rock star in the men's bathroom."

Her eyebrows go up and her eyes go wide. But she laughs. "Do you make a habit of that, Mr. Rock Star?"

"Nah," I say, gently grabbing her lip with my teeth. "Never. You're my first rock star, Melissa Vetti."

"You're my first too." And then she twists a little, making my dick get hard, and kisses my mouth. Her tongue tastes sweet, but the salt on her lips from her exertion on stage is tangy.

"I want to taste you," I whisper as we kiss.

"You are," she says back, our lips still touching.

"Not these lips," I say. "I want to eat your pussy until you scream."

She takes a deep breath, then stands, grabs my hand, and drags me to the back of the bar. She stops at a door marked *employees only*, looking over her shoulder with a smile.

I cock my head at her, but she just smiles bigger, pushes the door open, and pulls me inside. She doesn't stop and we pass the private restrooms and go all the way back to the employee break room. This time I push it open and whirl her inside, pushing her back against the door. "Is there a lock?"

"What fun is a lock?" she quips.

I love this fucking girl. I slip my hands up her shirt, squeezing her tits through her bra. She rests her head back against the door and moans. I pull her bra down, making her tits pop up, and then whip the tank top over her head.

I look down at her nipples, all pink and peaked up. I can't get my mouth on them fast enough. I bite, maybe a little too hard, and she gasps, arching her back and sliding her thigh between my legs. She rubs against my dick and I go for the button on her jeans. I rip it apart, drag her zipper down, and then grab the waist of her jeans and yank them down her legs as I go to my knees.

My tongue can't lick her fast enough. I tickle her clit and she grabs my hair with both hands, thrusting her hips outward, trying to give me access in this impossible position, with her damn pants still on.

"RK," she whispers. "God, please make tonight the night we do it right."

I laugh, squeezing her legs.

"I'm not even kidding!"

I pull back and slip a finger between her folds, easing it back and forth, getting her so wet, I almost can't handle it. I stand back up, keeping my hand in place, gently massaging her clit. I kiss her, then bring my wet fingers up and place them inside her mouth. She sucks on them, looking me in the eyes as she unbuttons my jeans and tugs the zipper down. Her hand is warm and soft as she reaches for my cock. Her fist is small, but her grip is tight as she pumps me, still staring into me, like she's searching for my soul.

"Like a rock star," I say, whispering as my eyes go half-mast. I take my finger from her mouth and ease it back between her legs, pushing up inside her. She squeals and I say, "I want to fuck you like a rock star."

"Please," she says, just as I grab her under her thighs, pushing her back against the door, and lift her legs up.

I have to look down between her legs. I can't stop myself. Her pussy is slightly open, the wetness I created with my finger beckoning my cock as I ease forward and press the tip against her opening.

"Yes," she says. "Yes, keep going."

I ease in, making her groan so loud, I consider cupping my hand over her mouth to shush her up. But the music is still loud enough. And even though I can hear people coming and going in the hallway outside, they are using the restrooms, not coming back here.

I pull away, looking at her face. I watch as her mouth opens and she takes deep, gasping breaths. And then I thrust inside her. Hard. Back out, thrust again. Harder.

"RK," she moans.

"Melissa," I say back.

"Fuck me. Fuck me."

I pound her, slamming her ass against the door, making it creak and rattle. But I don't care. I pound her harder, holding her legs up, the underside of her knees perfectly nestled into the crook of my arms.

She wraps her hands around my neck, holding me close, her fast breath gasping into my ear. Her pulse is going so fast, I can feel her wildly beating heart in my palms as I grip the inside of her legs.

"Come," I tell her. "Right fucking now."

Her pussy squeezes my dick and then I explode. I have a split second of concern over not using protection, but the pleasure wipes my mind of everything but how good she feels.

"Hey!" a voice says, knocking hard on the door.

"Gretchen!" Missy says.

"Get a fucking room, you two!"

"Shit!" Missy laughs. I release her legs, letting her feet settle on the ground again, and hold onto her arm as she reaches over and grabs a paper towel above the employee sink. She cleans up real fast, and I drag her jeans up her legs and fasten the button.

She smiles, doing the same for me.

"We're not done," I growl, grabbing her by the hair and pulling her towards me for a kiss. It starts rough, but she melds her breasts into my chest and wraps her arms around my neck. This gentles me like nobody's business. I kiss her a few times.

"You guys!" Gretchen says. "Come on, I'll drive you home."

"Coming!" Missy says, giving me one more peck before opening up a locker and checking her hair and makeup in the little mirror inside the door.

"We're not done, Melissa Vetti."

"Not even close," she says, winking at me as she pulls the door open to a waiting Gretchen.

"Oh, my God, you guys are disgusting. Who has sex in a break room?"

Missy giggles, then grabs my arm as if to cling to me. Her grin is wild and wide, her eyes are dancing as they look up at me, and when she leans into me, resting her head on my shoulder for a brief moment, just as I open the back passenger door to Gretchen's stupid hybrid car, I sigh.

It's long and deep. But everything about it is good.

"Get in," I tell Missy. She does, searching for her seatbelt as I close the door and walk over to the other side.

"You're not sitting in back, RK," Gretchen says.

"The fuck I'm not," I mumble, getting in next to Missy. Her hands are all over me as Gretchen huffs about not being a chauffeur and some other bullshit that I can't be bothered to listen to.

I put my arm around Miss and she leans into my chest. One hand tucked behind my back, one lifting my shirt up, a fraction at a time. And even though I just came inside her five minutes ago, I'm ready for more.

Gretchen talks the entire ride but I don't understand a word she says. Melissa's mouth is on mine, then biting my shoulder, then she's scooting back and lowering her face to my stomach, still lifting my shirt up with that one hand.

When Gretchen stops in my driveway, Missy and I give off half-hearted waves as I push her up against the front door and stare down into her blue eyes. "You know what?" I slur the words just a little.

"What?" She laughs back.

I have so many thoughts in my head at the moment. About her, her music, the bar, this town. What it felt like to come home after five years. How alone I felt. What it felt like to go to her show tonight. To be included. Part of something again.

"I missed you," I say.

"I missed you too."

"No," I say. "I mean I *missed* you." I place my hands on each of her cheeks and bump my forehead against hers. "I missed how you started that band. I missed how you worked out those songs. I missed all the mistakes, and all the triumphs. I missed the stressing out over money. I missed the conversation you had to have with Teej to get a spot. I missed picking out the guitar you play, the strap, the picks. I missed you making a decision about what you'd wear on stage. I missed you squealing to whoever is your best friend these days about your first show. I missed the applause, I missed TJ's proud face afterward, I missed the first blown amp, the first time someone said, *Hey, are you the chick who plays at Float's?* I missed everything, Melissa Vetti, rock star. And I'm so fucking sorry. Because life would've been so much better if we'd done it together."

She pouts her lips and nods her head. I can see a little gleam of light in her eyes as she tries not to cry. "I missed your life too."

"Yeah," I whisper. "It just would've been so much better if we'd done it together."

She looks up at me and smiles. "We're together now, RK. And that's all that matters."

I lean down and take her lip in my teeth, not biting hard, but just enough to make her squeal. One hand palms her breast while the other fucks with the door lock. It swings open and she goes tumbling backward, but I catch her around the waist, walk up forward, and kick the door closed. I get the alarm wrong twice, and I'm ready to panic that the sheriff will fuck up our sex plans, so I key it in very slowly to stop the frantic beeping.

Missy is laughing hard now, the mood back to the fun we were anticipating. I lead her into the family room.

I don't turn on the lights but I don't need to. The moon is bright and it shines right through the wall-sized windows leading to the deck. I take her over there, stand her in the silver shadow, and kiss her as I unbutton her pants. I bite her lip again and then drop to one knee. "Put your hand here," I say, placing it on my shoulder. "And give me your foot."

She does as I ask and we grin at each other as I slip her boot off. "Next one," I say. And we repeat that. I tug her pants down, bringing the strip of fabric she's calling underwear with them, and then say, "Step out."

She steps.

I stand back up and lift the tank top over her head, then palm both breasts before letting my hands slip under her arms, around her back, and undoing the bra clasps. I slide the straps over her shoulders and let it fall to the floor.

And then I step back and look at her. "You," I say, taking my shirt off and tossing it aside. She swallows hard and stares at my chest. I kick off my boots and undo my jeans, take them off, my boxer briefs with them, and stand there as naked as she is.

"You," she says back.

I reach for her face again, letting my knuckles caress her cheek. "Us."

She nods. "Us."

"Come here," I whisper, taking her hand and leading her over to the polished wood coffee table in front of the couch. "Sit here," I tell her softly. She sits on the coffee table and I sit on the couch a few inches in front of her.

I lean back into the cushions and wrap my fist around my dick. She shoots me a questioning look. "Open your legs," I say, beginning to pump my hand up and down my shaft. I can tell she blushes at my request, even in the dim light. "Do it," I urge quietly.

Missy takes a deep breath and closes her eyes as her thighs spread open. She smiles, but bows her head, like she's embarrassed.

I reach forward and tip her chin back up. "Look at me."

She does. "RK—"

"Shhh," I say. "Just look at me. We missed a lot in the past five years. I don't want to miss this. Not one moment of it. So just look at me and don't stop. I just need to see you, Melissa. I just need to see that you're real."

She nods, her eyes and her attention only on me.

"Now reach down between your legs and touch yourself." I get the lip-chewing over that one. We both smile. "Do it," I say. She bows her head again, but I'm there to tip her chin up. "Don't look away. Just look at me and I'll look at you."

We stare at each other, our eyes melding us together as she reaches down and begins to stroke herself. I don't watch that. I don't need to see that. And when I pump my cock a little harder, she doesn't watch what I'm doing either.

We only see what's behind our eyes.

"I love you," I say, scooting forward a little so my free hand can reach between her legs. We bump against each other. Our knees, our hands. And then I slip a finger inside her. She closes her eyes and opens her mouth, but then remembers the rules and meets my gaze again. Her free hand caresses my thigh and she scoots forward a little, scissoring our legs together, hers outside of mine, opening herself up to me.

She slides her hand to the inside of my thigh as I pump her, and me, just a little harder, and stretches her arm out until she's cupping my balls.

"Fuck," I say.

She opens her mouth like she wants to say something too, but she shakes her head just the tiniest bit. "What are we doing?"

"Loving," I say. "Not fucking. Loving."

"I want to climb into your lap and never leave," she says.

"Do it."

She lifts her knee, placing it on the couch next to my leg, then does it again with her other one. My hands go to her hips, gripping that spot where they fit so well for slow dancing. Her hands press down on my shoulders as she hovers over my lap.

And then she sits down. My cock finds her entrance easily. It's wet and open. Ready for me to fill her up. She bites her lip again and I know she wants to close her eyes and just moan because that's my first reaction too. Just let the pleasure take over. Just close off the world and sink into the ecstasy.

But we don't. Because we've missed enough and we're not going to miss this. So we watch each other. She moves. Up and down, her breath getting louder. Her body getting warmer. Her eyes getting heavier.

And I play with her hair. And kiss her chin. And bite her lip.

But our eyes do not wander. Our bond does not waver.

I come inside her. She comes all over me.

And we see every second of it. Our reflection in each other's eyes.

Chapter Twenty-Two

The tapping on my window wakes me up. I open my eyes and look out at the rising sun. The air conditioning is blaring in my face as I turn.

Dr. Chancer smiles at me as he takes a sip of his coffee. I tab the window button and it rolls down.

"You know"—he laughs—"I'm not complaining, because you're really making my Monday mornings a lot more interesting. But we've got to stop meeting like this."

What the fuck? I look around and realize I'm in my truck, parked over at the medical offices in Granby again.

"Rock?" Chancer asks.

"Yeah," I croak out, looking back up at him.

"Did we have an appointment today? I haven't checked my schedule since Friday, so maybe—"

"No," I say. "No. I'm fine. Well…"

"Hmm," he says. "Did you… black out?"

I think back. "It's Monday?"

"I'll take that as a yes. Where do you last remember being?"

I look down at my clothes. Rock pants again. I move a little so I can see my shoes. Rock shoes. I hold my hands in front of my face. They are crisscrossed with white climbing tape.

"Are you wearing a harness?"

I look down at my chest, bare. And a climbing harness around my hips. "Um."

"Hmm," Chancer says again. "Looks like you had a good time at least." He laughs. "And you're alive so you must've done well."

I don't know what to say.

"Well, Rock. I think you probably need to go talk to Margie Sanderson again."

I look up at him, squinting into a glare shining between a crack in the pine trees. "Maybe."

He opens my door, like he's not giving me an alternative option, and says, "Last thing you remember?"

"Saturday night," I say. "At my house with Melissa."

He nods as I turn the truck off, pocket my keys, get out, and close the door. "Go talk to her. You can stop by my office if you need me to check your throat, but I can already tell you're getting better there. Your voice sounds good. Much better than the first time I saw you."

I nod.

"You probably need a shirt?"

I look down at myself again, then inside the truck. There are ropes and a t-shirt sitting on the passenger seat. I reach in through the open window and grab the shirt, slipping it over my head. It's the same Something Corporate shirt I was wearing on Saturday.

I finger the harness around my hips, considering taking it off, realize I don't even know how and then forget it. I just follow Chancer into the building, calling out a, "Thanks," as I go up the stairs and he heads to his office on the first level.

I slowly walk down the hallway and stop outside the door, reading the plaque that says, *Dr. Margie Sanderson, PhD, LP*.

What the fuck is happening?

The door opens and Margie is there. She smiles. "Dr. Chancer just called. Said you might try to make a run for it." She smiles bigger. "I'm here to make sure that doesn't happen."

I let out a long breath as she stands aside and beckons me in.

"Well," she says, admiring my climbing gear. "Looks like you did something fun recently."

"I think I already told you, I'm not a rock climber. I have no idea what the fuck is going on."

"Take a seat, Rock."

"RK," I say, annoyed. "Don't fucking call me Rock."

"Why not?" she asks, sitting in the second of two chairs. "Sit," she says again.

I sit, resting my elbows on my knees and scrubbing my face with my taped hands.

"Why do you hate it when people call you Rock?"

"I don't hate it. I'm just not Rock here."

"Who is Rock?" she asks. "What does that mean? You're not Rock here? Lots of people must call you that. Your manager? Does she call you that?"

"Yeah, but that's all she knows. She only knows Rock. You guys all know RK. I'm not Rock to you guys."

"Is there a difference between the two people? Is Rock someone different than RK?"

I roll my eyes. "No. Not really. If you're saying I've got like… split personality or whatever, I don't. I'm Rock, lead singer of Son of a Jack. But that guy is not who I am in Grand Lake. Here I'm just me. Rowan Kyle Saber."

"So," she says, crossing her legs like she's getting comfortable. "So, there's Rowan Kyle. RK. And Rock. Three different…" She hesitates. "For lack of a better word, and don't take it literally, three different people."

"Whatever. Lots of people have nicknames. Lots of people have stage names. I just don't want my friends and family calling me by my stage name. I don't think that's unusual. P!nk's family calls her Alecia, not P!nk. Slash's family calls him Saul, not Slash. So you guys should call me RK, not Rock." I throw up my hands. "It's not rocket science. And it doesn't mean anything."

"Well, it might mean something." I go to object, but she continues talking. "You know what I find interesting, RK?"

"What?" I growl.

"That you didn't ask me what's going on."

"When?"

"The last time you were here. Did you come to Grand Lake thinking it was Melissa who died on prom night? Or Melanie?"

"Why?"

"Because," she huffs, "everyone knows you thought it was Melissa who died. You made quite a scene at the funeral."

I think back to the funeral and oddly find most of it blank. I played the song. I do remember that.

"And then you just took off, never to be heard from again until a couple weeks ago when the Grand County Sheriff escorted you down from Steamboat Springs. How did you get to Steamboat Springs?"

"What? What kind of question is that? I was in a fucking accident, right? I was in the hospital where they repaired my throat and then they sent me up to Steamboat for rehab." I stare at her for a long second. "Right?"

She nods and then quietly asks, "What kind of accident were you in, RK?"

I rub the heels of my hands into my eyes, the frayed and dirty tape biting into the skin.

"RK? What kind of accident was it?"

"The car went off the road. Just like on prom night."

"Do you remember prom night?"

"How could I forget?"

"Then why did you think Melissa was the one who died?"

"Because…" I clear my throat and look her in the face. "Because Melanie was the one I took to prom, not Melissa. But I didn't know that at the time."

"I think everyone told you that the night Melanie died. I know Melissa did. She told you it was Melanie who died, not her. I was there, RK."

"I didn't believe her. Melanie had a bad habit of tricking me into thinking she was Melissa when we were kids. I just didn't believe her, I guess."

"Do you remember talking to me the night Melanie died?"

I shake my head. "No."

"Well, you did."

"So?"

"We were in this office, RK. Do you remember that? I was here, you were here, Melissa Vetti was here. It was all very dramatic. Tears and yelling. Not something most people forget."

"OK," I huff. "Well, I don't recall."

"My real point is, you were not in the hospital. So if the car went off the road on prom night, how did you survive without injury?"

I just stare at her. For like, a whole minute at least.

"How could you be in a car that careens off the side of a mountain and not get injured?"

I still have nothing. I wait to see if she will say something else, but she just looks at me. Waiting. "How?" I ask. "Tell me then. How did it happen?"

She shakes her head. "Nope. I'm not going to be the one to tell you that. You're not even trying, RK. You're not even trying to figure this out. But you know what?"

"What?" I growl again.

"There's a library in Grand Lake. They keep digital copies of all the newspapers. One trip down there will make a world of difference for you."

"Is that right?"

"That's right. It's closed Mondays, but I have it on good authority that Mrs. Schaffer is down there today preparing for the summer reading program." She smiles. A beeping noise sounds as someone enters the outer office. "Now, if you'll excuse me, I have an appointment. But RK?"

I look at her as she stands up, dismissing me.

"I think you need to start asking more questions. I think it will really help if you actually *participate* in your recovery. And I think you owe your friends and family an apology for taking off again. For being a clueless fuckup, as the kids today say. The whole town has been looking for you. I'm sure they'll be relieved to learn that you were off climbing sheer mountain cliffs."

She looks down at my harness and then says, "Have a nice day."

I stand up and walk through the open inner door, trying not to look the waiting patient in the face.

"And RK," Sanderson calls after me. "No more walk-ins. Schedule ahead if you need to talk again."

Chapter Twenty-Three

There's a library in Granby but I drive to the one
in Grand Village instead. It's right next to the town park,
two blocks off the lake, because I have this
overwhelming desire to be home. The hours on the door
do in fact say it's closed on Monday, but the lights are on
inside and when I cup my hands to my face and press my
forehead against the glass I can see Mrs. Schaffer
bustling around.

I knock, because it's locked.

Mrs. Schaffer smiles and waves. I don't wave back
even though I know it's gonna come off as rude. She
twists a key in the lock and pushes the door open.
"Hello, RK," she says in her old-lady librarian voice.
"Margie said you might come by. Come on in."

I walk in without a word and stand there while she locks the door back up.

"Now what can I help you with?" She clasps her hands together in front of her floor-length dress. Her eyes, which might once have been bright and blue, are now dull and gray, kind of like her hair. She has the proverbial reading glasses on a gold chain hanging around her neck.

I clear my throat. "I wanted to read about… that… night." I want to say 'Melanie's death' or 'the prom night crash'. But I'm fucking spinning right now. I'm afraid to say anything. I'm afraid everything I think is true… is wrong.

"A newspaper?" she asks, her thumb and index fingers coming up to her chin as she thinks about my request. "We have them of course."

Her thinking makes me nervous. Does she not want to show it to me? Is she afraid of what I might read? "Can you point me in the right direction?"

"I'll find it for you. Come on." I follow her into the main part of the library and we veer off to the left where the computers are. "In the old days you'd have to search and search for things like this. But now, RK, we can pull it up with a few clicks. Oh." She looks over her shoulder at me as she bends forward to type on a keyboard. "If you have internet at your house you can probably do this at home."

I just stare at her.

"Do you have internet, RK?"

I want to say, *Hell, yes. What kind of hillbilly mountain man do you take me for?* But the truth is, I have no clue. "My phone works."

"Well, that's probably sufficient." And then she goes on to explain whatever the fuck she's explaining that probably any three-year-old could figure out these days, but apparently I'm as dumb as a bag of hammers and require an entire course on accessing periodicals online.

Can I blame her for thinking I'm an idiot? Does the whole town know I don't remember that night?

"Here we go." Mrs. Schaffer straightens up again, beaming a smile at me. "This is the first day. If you click forward you can look for all the updates." And then she places a hand on my shoulder and gives it a squeeze. "I'm so sorry about what happened to your rock band friends, RK."

I nod. "Thanks."

She walks off and leaves me to it. I force myself to stare at the headline.

Melissa Vetti dies from

I stop reading and turn around, trying my best to unsee it.

"RK?" Mrs. Schaffer asks still only a few feet away. "Are you all right?"

I turn back to the computer screen.

Melissa Vetti dies from

But then the word goes blurry. It's not Melissa. *Melanie Vetti dies.* It says Melanie. I turn around to look for help. "Mrs. Schaffer," I call in a hoarse voice. "Can you read this headline to me and tell me what it says?"

She walks back over and puts her hand back on my shoulder, squeezing again. What's with this town and their sympathetic shoulder squeezes? "It says Melanie, RK. Melanie. Not Melissa."

I take a deep breath and nod. "OK, that's all I needed for now."

"Would you like me to print it for you? So you can read it later?"

"No," I say, shaking my head.

"It will just take a moment." And then she clicks the print button on the screen and walks off to find the printer, which must be behind the main desk, because I can hear it whirring to life.

I walk to the front door and try to leave, but it's locked. I twist the key to unlock it, but that Mrs. Schaffer is quick. She's already pressing the printout into my hand. "Take care, RK. Margie already called the sheriff to let them know we found you. But I'll call again and tell them you're on your way home. And if you need any more help with research, just let me know."

I pull the door open, give her a cursory wave over my shoulder, fold the article up into quarters, and stick it in my back pocket as I walk to my truck.

I get in and take a deep breath. What the fuck was that? I knew that headline said Melanie, but I swear, my eyes saw Melissa. It's like… I couldn't help myself. Like I was forcing myself to see Melissa's name.

Like you're delusional, RK.

I start the truck and back out onto the street, hoping like fuck no one just saw me. I just want to go home. I turn onto Grand Avenue and head up into the mountains towards my house.

Participate in your recovery, RK.

I put it out of my mind as I wind my way up the road, looking at that fucking guard rail. My dad's words coming back to me. *They don't keep you safe, they only make you feel safe.*

That might be true, but I'm happy to settle for that little bit of double-galvanized steel when my other option is going over the side of a cliff.

There are two sheriff's cars at the bottom of my driveway. One guy gets out of his car as I approach, waving me over to the side of the road.

Fuck.

I pull over and lower my window, the hot mountain breeze of early summer blowing my hair back. "Hey," I say.

He eyes me with a mixture of anger and relief. "Mr. Saber. We've been looking for you since yesterday morning. Did you get our messages?"

"Ah…" I feel my pockets for my phone, take it out, and hold it up. "Sorry, no battery."

The deputy stares at me for a moment. "Do you mind telling me where you were? We've been ordered to keep an eye on you at all times, so deliberately slipping away to avoid—"

"Hey," I say, interrupting. "I didn't slip away, OK? It's not my fault you guys can't keep up."

The other deputy walks towards us, his hand on his side arm, his face tucked into his shoulder as he speaks into his radio. "Mr. Saber," he says, once he reaches us. "How you did you get your truck from town? Do you remember being driven home Saturday night by Gretchen Linnie?" He leans to the side a little, like he's trying to see all the climbing equipment piled up on my passenger seat.

"Yeah, of course." Shit. I have no idea how I got my truck back. "I just walked. It's only like five miles."

"Why would you walk, Mr. Saber?" the first cop asks. "Why wouldn't you ask Miss Vetti for a ride? Did you leave in the middle of the night?"

"Am I under arrest for something?"

"No, of course not," number two says.

"Then it's none of your fucking business." I pull away from the side of the road and continue up my driveway, parking in front of the garage once I get to the top of the hill. I sit in the truck and get myself together for a few seconds, and then get out.

My eyes flicker over to Missy's house and I see the curtains flutter for a second. I'm heading over there to see if she's mad when I hear her call out from behind me.

"RK?" Missy calls. I turn and find her standing in my front door. "Where are you going?"

Not, *Where have you been?*

I look back at her house and figure it's just the air conditioning making the curtains flutter like that, and then walk towards her. The two sheriff's cars pull up just as I make it to the walkway leading up to the front door. They even make that fucking berrrp-berrrp sound and flash the lights like they do when they are half-heartedly pulling someone over.

"Jesus Christ," I say, stopping halfway between Missy and the road. "Now what?"

Deputy One gets out of the car while Deputy Two talks on his radio. "Mr. Saber—" Deputy One starts.

But Missy is up next to me now, one hand up, like she's warding the deputy off. "Hey," she says. "What are you doing? You were told to observe, not confront."

I look at her. "What the fuck does that mean?"

"Miss Vetti, there was a county-wide search for Mr. Saber based on your information. Now I realize what our job is, but we have a lot of resources to account for and that means paperwork. So I'm going ask Mr. Saber questions whether you like it or not."

"I'm calling TJ," she says, like this is a threat he needs to be aware of.

"What the fuck is going on?" I ask again. Only this time I'm less polite that I was down the road. "I was rock climbing, asshole."

Both Deputy One and Missy turn to look at me.

"Is that against the law? Am I under house arrest? Because if so, that's news to me. I was told to stay in Grand County and I have. But no one said I wasn't allowed to leave my house without an escort."

"How did you get to town to pick your truck up? Did someone come get you?" Deputy Two asks, suddenly appearing on the scene.

"I walked," I growl back at him. "I just told you that."

"You did not walk, RK." I squint my eyes at the guy, recognizing him as Angelo Marzetti. "We had two cars down at the end of the driveway all night. So you wanna start being straight with us? Or should we take you in for questioning?"

"Questioning for *what?*" I snarl.

"TJ," Missy says in her phone. "Angelo is here asking RK questions."

"Just tell us where you were," Deputy One says.

"Rock climbing," I say, pointing to the harness around my hips. "And if you had any deductive skills at all, you'd conclude I rappelled down the cliff at the back of my house and then hiked through the canyon that leads to the Bighorn Trailhead, and came out right on the edge of town. One mile as the crow flies. No need to take the long way around."

As soon as the words leave my mouth I know it's true. I actually see myself doing this in my mind.

"Go check the other side of my back deck for the anchor bolts and cams in the rocks. There's gear and rope at the bottom. I put that shit in the second day I was home."

"Why?" Missy asks.

I look at her to answer, but… I don't know why.

"Go check it out," Angelo says to Deputy One.

"Can you take me to the back, Miss Vetti?" Deputy One asks Missy.

She sighs loudly and then says, "Whatever. TJ is just down the hill and he's on his way." She shoots Angelo a glare that might be a warning and then walks back into the house with One.

"Look, RK," Angelo says, like we're old friends. I knew him. Sort of. We never ran with the same crowd. He was never into music. He was more like Sean. A jock. Minus Sean's cool side that made us click back then. "I'm just trying to help you out, man. That's all."

"Appreciate it," I say. "But not necessary."

"Well." Angelo laughs. "Tell that to TJ. And my boss. Because they want you watched twenty-four seven." He waits to see if I'll say anything to that, but I don't. "So until I get new orders, I'm gonna track your every move. Whether you like it or not. Now, the sooner you tell me where you were, the sooner I'll go back down to my post at the bottom of the hill."

"I told you, I was climbing."

"Where?"

I shrug. "All over."

"Why didn't you just wait for Missy to take you into town to get your truck? You do realize your actions are a little crazy, right?"

"Why do I have to explain myself to you? I wanted to climb, so I did. End of story."

TJ's Jeep screeches into the driveway and he get out without turning the engine off. "What the fuck are you doing, Angelo? You better get your ass back down the hill right now if you want a job tomorrow."

Angelo shoots me a dirty look, complete with a growl of, "I'm going to figure you out, RK. You can bet your ass on that."

"You're not getting paid to figure shit out, Angelo," Teej says, following him back to his vehicle. I stop listening. I can't hear them anyway. Angelo gets in his car and TJ leans in the open door as they have some kind of whispered argument.

"We're all set, RK," Deputy One says, coming back around the side of the house with Missy. "Thanks for letting us know about the route. Maybe you should open that climb up to tourists." And then he mutters, "Crazy fucker," as he brushes past me and joins TJ and Angelo out in the street.

Missy wraps her hands around my bicep and I look over at her. "Hey, sorry about this," I say. "I didn't mean to make you worry."

She just sighs, and then lets go of me and turns towards my front door. "We need to talk, RK," she calls over her shoulder. "So when you're ready for that, you let me know."

I watch TJ finish up with the deputies and then they leave. Presumably to go back down to their posts at the bottom of my driveway.

TJ watches until they are out of sight and then looks at me, pointing his finger. "You," he says, "are an asshole."

"Sorry. Jesus. I'm a fucking grown-up, TJ. I don't need the babysitters. And I really don't get what this fucking county arrest is all about anyway. If they want to blame me for the crash, then fucking let them. I got a whole team of lawyers. I got enough money to take care of things. I'm not in need of help."

TJ just stares at me. Turns away. Rubs his hand down his unshaven face. Then turns back. I wait for his comeback. *You're a fuckup. You're a selfish asshole. You're on your own then.* All that kind of shit he's known for saying when he's feeling superior.

But he doesn't. He just shakes his head, gets back in his running Jeep, backs out, screeching his tires, and leaves me standing there.

Chapter Twenty-Four

I go inside, instantly thankful that Missy has the air conditioning on because I stink like a mountain climber. She's not in the front room. It's littered with all my boxed-up shit, so I stop and rifle through the clothes to find some shorts. I need a goddamned shower. I find a pair of tan cargos, then spy a few carabiners lying in a pile next to the box I taped up the other day.

Secret, a voice whispers in my head.

I walk over to it, slinging my shorts over my shoulder, and then pry the top of the box open. And this time I know the name for every piece of equipment.

Tons of gear. Cams and bolts. Nuts and quickdraws. Lockers and slings. Two more harnesses. Another entire box filled with carabiners. Climbing pants, climbing shorts. One, two, three, four, five, six, seven pairs of climbing shoes.

I step back and take a breath.

"Yeah," Missy says. "I found that too. I figured it was something you did in California, not something you were doing now. You could've told me you were leaving, you know. If you want to climb, climb, RK. I'm not going to stop you."

I stare out the window, my back to Missy. "I've been blacking out."

Silence.

"At least three times since I've been home. The first time no one probably even knew. But I ended up over in Granby to see the ENT doctor. Chancer?" I ask. "You heard of him?"

"No," Missy says. "Never had a reason to see the ENT guy in Granby."

I turn around to face her. She looks tired. Probably up all night wondering where the fuck I was. "Well, I showed up there in a lot of pain. I yelled at you that first night and then got drunk, I guess. Anyway, I just remembered what happened that weekend. Just now, when I was standing outside with the cops."

I pick up a bright yellow power drill from the climbing gear box. "I bolted the route down the cliff. Just for funsies, I guess? Just because I could? I don't know. It felt good. It felt... normal. I don't know why I blacked out the climbing. Weird. But fuck, my head's so messed up these days. Melanie, Ian, Elias, Mo, my dad. I have all these fucking people in my mind. Anyway, I screamed when I got to the bottom. I did on purpose even though my throat was sore. A victory scream, you know? And it fucking hurt all night, so I drove over to Granby to see that Chancer guy."

"We were mean to you that first night."

I huff out a laugh. "Bitches, you were." She smiles, and I do too, for a second. And then I stop. "I don't get it, Missy. You were acting like Melanie that night. TJ was such an asshole to me when I came to the bar."

"I know," she whispers. "We made things worse. Gretchen wanted to see if you remembered whether it was me or Mel who died. And pretending to be her for a second was the only way."

I shake my head. "It fucked with me. Pretty bad, Miss."

"I'm so sorry," she says. "I'm so sorry." She lets out a long breath of air. "And Margie ripped Gretchen a new asshole for that too. She was pissed off."

"Margie," I say. "I saw her this morning."

Missy nods. "She called us after you left." Missy stares at me for a moment. "Did you go to the library?"

I nod.

"Did you find the articles from when Mel died?"

I nod again.

"Did you read it?"

"No," I say, shaking my head. "I mean, I tried. But I swear to God, Missy, my head is playing tricks on me. I would've bet a million dollars that when I read that first headline it said Melissa, not Melanie. It took me a minute to realize I was seeing things. I had to call Mrs. Schaffer over to read it to me. To make sure it was real." I clear my throat. "And then I just couldn't read anymore."

Missy frowns at me.

"But Mrs. Schaffer printed it out and made me take it." I pull the folded-up piece of paper out of my pocket, stare at it for a few seconds, then thrust it out to Missy. "I can't read it."

"Why not?" Missy asks, her voice low and soft.

"Because…" I swallow hard. "Because I don't think it says what I think it says."

"It doesn't."

"I'm fucked up, aren't I?"

"No, RK." Missy comes over to me, taking the article out of my hand, and presses herself up to my chest. "You're not fucked up, OK? You're a goddamned rock star. You write the most beautiful music. You have friends. You laugh and have fun with us. You're not fucked up. You're just confused because of the way you left things after Melanie died. And that just built up and up and up over the years until it became real to you. But you're home now. And you're here with us, and we love you, and you're going to be fine. Everything is going to heal. Everything is going to get better now."

I take the paper out of her hand and unfold it. Missy never lets go of me. Her arms are wrapped tight around my middle. Her cheek is pressed against my chest. "Read it out loud, Rowan Kyle. Read it out loud and get it over with."

I stare at the headline. "'Melanie Vetti dies from… suicide.'"

Missy starts breathing funny and I know she's crying.

"'On the night of May seventh, Melanie Vetti killed herself by jumping off a cliff near Berthoud Pass on US Highway 40.'"

"Do you remember?" Missy asks. "Because I never got answers, RK. And I know it was all a mess of what-the-fucks that night because she was the one who went to prom with you in my place. So I told myself I just had to wait until you were ready. But Jesus. It's been killing me slowly ever since. If you remember, please tell me what happened."

I rub my whole face with both hands, the climbing tape rough and scratchy against my cheeks. I push Missy off me so I can look at her. She hides her face. But I know why she's hiding it. I tip her chin up and see the tears falling.

"I'm so sorry," I whisper.

"Do you remember?" she asks.

I think about it for a moment. The images of Melanie in my head. She was wearing Missy's dress, the one I couldn't fucking wait to see her in. She was wearing the flower thing I bought Missy too. And the little silver necklace I bought Miss for her thirteenth birthday.

I take Missy's hand and lead her towards the back of the house. "Sit down and I'll tell you what I remember."

Chapter Twenty-Five

Prom Night - Five Years Ago.

Missy has been acting weird all night. *Distant, distracted. She didn't want to dance. She didn't want to talk. This night is not going the way I imagined it.*

"Is there something on your mind, Miss?"

"Why?" she asks in a sweet voice.

"See, that's throwing me," I say as we walk to the car. "You're not talking like you're upset but you're acting like you're upset. Just tell me what's going on. Did I do something wrong?"

I open the door for her once we reach the car and she slips inside. I close it up and walk around the back of the car to get in, watching her fumble for her seatbelt.

"Just tell me, Miss," I say, getting in and closing my door.

She sighs, then looks down at her hands in her lap, biting her lip a little. "I don't…"

I wait, but she never finishes. "You don't… what?"

She looks me in the eye and blurts, "I don't want to sleep with you tonight, RK. I don't think we're ready."

I laugh. "Why would you think I'd pressure you into sex tonight? Jesus, Missy. We've waited for years. I'm not in a hurry. So if that's all it is, then—"

"That's not all," she says.

I get a very weird feeling in my gut.

"You're leaving for school in a couple months. And you know I don't want to go to college. I want to play music, sure. But I want to do it like our dads did. Juilliard isn't how they did it, RK. They just played, you know? Why can't we just play? Why can't we just be rock stars?"

I've heard this before, but I never thought she was serious. I mean, rock stars? I almost laugh. Who the fuck models their life on a couple of washed-up assholes like our dads? "You know I'm serious about the music, Missy. I don't even understand why you'd bring this up to me. What are you trying to say? I should stay home?"

She shakes her head and points to the car keys dangling in the ignition. "Let's go to the hotel."

"I thought you didn't want to sleep with me?"

"I don't," she snaps. "But I'd like to see the room. And enjoy the lake at Frisco. Do you want to go home?"

"No," I say, so fucking confused.

"Then drive, RK. Everyone is looking at us."

"Everyone," I mutter. That's a joke. "There's thirty-five people here tonight, Missy. It's hardly a mob."

"And they all know us. So now they think we're fighting."

"Are we fighting?"

"Just drive!"

I sigh and put the car in reverse, then back out and make my way out of the recreation center parking lot and head towards the Village so I can get on the two-lane road towards Winter Park.

We sit in silence as I make my way through the mountains. We pass through Granby, then Fraser, Winter Park. This is where the driving gets real. Thirty miles per hour through the switchbacks, no emergency lanes. And there's guard rails.

I hate the fucking guard rails. They only put them up to make people feel safe. They only put them up when they know, if you go over the side, you're dead. You're not living through that. I go slow as we get closer to Berthoud Pass. Eleven thousand feet in elevation means snow in May. Lots of it.

"God," Missy says. "This is taking forever."

"Sorry, Miss. Just trying to be careful with you."

"I think you're too drunk to drive this road, RK. Pull over."

"What?" I laugh. "I had two drinks over six hours. I'm not pulling over and letting you drive."

"Well, I didn't have any. Pull over."

"There's nowhere to pull over, Melissa." I'm annoyed now. "It's a fucking switchback. Just calm down, we're almost to the lookout and then we can stop and—"

"Pull over!" she yells. They don't keep you safe, they only make you feel safe.

The tires hit a slick spot and swerve. Melissa screams so loud, it scares the fuck out of me. I press the brake, keeping both hands on the wheel and both eyes on the road as I growl, "Knock it the fuck off, Missy!"

She grabs the wheel and I overcompensate, swerving towards a car coming up the mountain. It honks and flashes its headlights at us.

"What the fuck are you doing?" I yell.

"There's a turnout up here, now pull over and let me drive or I'll do it again!"

"For fuck's sake, Missy."

"Pull over now, RK. I swear to God."

I slow down and put on my blinker so the cars coming down behind me can figure out what the fuck I'm doing. There is a turnout ahead. Amazingly. So I break to almost a crawl and pull in, parallel to the guard rail and what is probably a hundred-and-fifty-foot drop down a fucking cliff.

Missy is out of the car before I even get it in park. "What the fuck are you—" I stop talking. Because she's climbing over the goddamned guard rail.

"Melissa!" I yell, getting out of the car. "Get your ass back here right the fuck now!"

She doesn't even turn, just continues scrambling, her long blue dress gathering snow and water on the edges as it drags. She stands up on one of the posts holding the guard rail together.

I'm losing my fucking mind. This is not happening.

"Tell me you'll stay with me in Grand Lake, RK. Tell me that or I'm going to jump off this cliff."

"Melissa! What the fuck—" But then I stop. This isn't Melissa. "Melanie," I say in a loud, clear voice.

"I'm not Melanie! You're such an asshole! You don't even know the difference between us! You never did. She tricked you over and over again. You fucked her, didn't you? That's why I won't sleep with you, RK! You fucked Melanie and you liked it!"

"No," I say, shaking my head. "No. You're not Missy. You're the crazy cunt of a twin. No wonder—"

"Won't you be sorry when you get home tonight and find out I was Missy?"

"Was?"

She looks down, teetering a little on the post.

"Melanie—"

"You better call me by my name, RK. Or I'll jump."

I take a deep breath. What if this is Melissa? "Missy," I say calmly. "Missy, get down—"

Lights pass behind me as another car pulls into the turnout. Blue and red lights flash, and when I look back at Melanie/Melissa's face, I know what's going to happen next. I know.

"She jumped," I tell Missy. I'm staring at the family photo of me, Teej, and my mom and dad on the front hallway wall. It was taken when I was about eight. We were fishing on the lake every day that summer. It was a good summer. Lots of laughing. Lots of happiness. Lots of love. We were whole back then. "She fucking jumped right in front of me. I can still see her face. The panic from the approaching deputy as he came towards us. There was snow that night. Not a lot, like maybe it was just blowing off the trees in the wind. But it was in her hair. That's the last thing I remember of Melanie Vetti. Standing on the post of a guard rail, that blue dress flapping in the wind and the snow."

Missy rubs my arm. "It wasn't your fault, RK. She was crazy. Cray-zee."

"I know that. I do," I say, taking a deep breath. "But I should've known it wasn't you. I should've known right away. Should've taken her home."

"I should've stood up to her, RK. Or at the very least, understood her sickness for what it was. Understood how serious the repercussions of letting her have her way all those years were. If I had, none of us would be here right now. But what happened, happened. We can't change it. We just have to deal. Forgive ourselves. Maybe even forgive her, although I will tell you, for me that hasn't happened yet. I hate her, RK. I hate her for so many things. Not just the things she did to me, but the things she did to this town. To you. She changed your whole life. She changed TJ's whole life. Mine too."

My mind is racing with the memories. The sheriff in the car, who saw the whole thing. My mind blanking out. So fucking confused as to what just happened. Melissa? Melanie? Which girl just killed herself in front of me?

I look down and realize I'm still wearing my climbing harness. That I stink like fucking sweat. That I'm as lost as ever because Mo, and Elias, and Ian are still dead. I got Missy back, but my best friends are still gone. My band is gone and I haven't talked to Kenner yet. Why the fuck haven't I talked to Kenner yet?

My life is a fucking nightmare I can't wake up from.

"I need to take a shower," I say, prying Missy's fingers off my arm. She stands still as I walk off to the front bathroom and close the door, everything about this day running together until it feels right and wrong at the same time.

There's a soft knock that jolts me out of my thoughts. "Yeah?" I ask.

"Are you hungry?" Missy asks from the other side of the door. "I promise not to burn it if you let me make you lunch."

"Yeah," I repeat. "That would be nice."

Chapter Twenty-Six

Missy is making me lunch when I finish up my shower. The climbing tape is so sticky, I leave it on so I don't have to shave the glue off my hands. I can't smell anything cooking in the kitchen yet, so when I pass by the music room on the opposite side of the foyer, I stop.

"Just a look," I say, creeping into the room where I spent all those years obsessed with music. "Not an intention," I mumble.

The center of the piano bench is worn from all the people who have sat on it over its hundred years of life. There's a small chip on the edge of the ivory of middle C. A torn edge from a sheet of music is peeking out from under the bench lid. I lift the lid up and take the music out. I smile. Minuet in D Minor. I'm not a fan of D minor, but there's another song stuck to this one, and I am a fan of Waltz by Clementi.

I look over my shoulder. Missy is still busy.

So I take a seat and once that first step is over, my fingers just play. The piano is slightly out of tune, but I don't care. I'm just fucking around.

The waltz is lively and fun, so not what I'm feeling right now. But soon enough I transition into Spinning Song by Ellmenreich. Another light one, but fuck it.

"Oh, my God." Missy laughs behind me.

I look over my shoulder to find her leaning against the wall with a giant smile. My fingers keep playing. "What's so funny?" I ask. But I smile too. "Should I play this instead?" I start the familiar parts of the Funeral Song by Chopin.

"Ack," she says, walking all the way into the room. "No." She bumps my shoulder with her hip, making me screw up the song, and then slides in next to me. "We played that duet once." Her fingers find the keys and music pours out. "Remember this?" The melody for Love Song. I jump in with the harmony and she laughs.

"I missed you," I say, my eyes down on the keys. "I missed this."

"I'm here now," she says, her fingers still picking out the notes. "You're here now. We can do this for the rest of our lives, RK."

"I feel like there's a catch," I say, picking up the tempo. She matches me, her fingers flying along the high notes while mine complement her on the low notes.

"There's not, RK. I promise," she says, slowing down the music so I have to match her now. "All we have to do is finish what we started."

I stop playing and it takes her a few notes to catch up. "Yeah," I say, giving her a sidelong glance. "But a lot of shit has happened between then and now, Miss."

She sighs and grabs hold of my bicep, leaning her body against mine. "I know it feels that way, RK, because you like to take the long way around. But if you just went in a straight line, we'd get there a lot faster."

I roll my eyes and then I sniff the air. "Something's burning."

"Ah, fuck!" Missy jumps up and runs to the kitchen.

I start playing Love Song again and call out, "I'll still eat it, don't worry." But then I stop playing and start thinking about what she said. The long away around is definitely the way I like to do things.

I mean, no. I don't *like* to take the long way. But it is typically the way I get places. Except for that climb down into Grand Lake the other day, I chuckle silently. One mile as the crow flies, quite literally.

Why do I climb? How do I know how to climb? Why did I place those bolts in the cliff that first weekend I was home? Why am I blacking out and driving myself over to the medical offices? Hell, maybe I wasn't there to see Chancer that first time at all? Maybe I knew Margie was the therapist who talked to me after Melanie jumped off that cliff? Maybe I was there to see her, but Chancer found me first?

I realize I've started playing something else while I was thinking. The song. Why did I write it if I never intended on finishing it? Why did I play it at the funeral if it was for Missy and I knew the girl in that casket was Melanie?

Maybe I wrote it to help me with the confusion? Take away the uncertainty of who died on the highway that night? Maybe I didn't write the lyrics because I knew Missy was still alive?

"RK?" Missy says, once again behind me.

"Yeah?" I answer, my fingers never stopping the music.

"You should finish the song. I think it might give you closure."

"I'm not sure what it means. I'm not sure I *can* finish it. I'm not sure it's relevant anymore."

"You didn't write the song for me, RK. Or Mel. You don't write songs for people or make music for people. You didn't start playing music because your dad wanted you to. You didn't write all those songs and play in front of hundreds of thousands of people because they wanted you to. You did because *you* wanted to, RK. You wrote the song for yourself. You write every piece for yourself. That's how art is made, RK. For the soul. Not my soul, or Melanie's soul. Not your dad's soul or the world's soul. Your soul, Rowan Kyle. Your soul."

God, she's right. I stop playing. I don't need to take the shortcut, but why do I always take the long way around?

"I want to show you something," Missy says. "Stay here for a second. Don't move."

It's so much quicker to just move forward in a straight line than it is to wind my way down the mountain like a switchback road, doubling back on itself to make the descent easier.

Missy comes back a few minutes later with a mirror I know she got off the wall in my dad's bedroom. She balances it on the piano where the sheet music should go, then sits back down and adjusts it so we can see our reflections.

"That's her," Missy says.

"Who?" I ask.

"Melanie. That's Melanie these days. Sometimes, RK, I look in the mirror and I don't know who I am. I look in there and say to myself, 'You're Melanie.'"

"You're not Melanie, Miss."

"I know," she says, smiling at herself. "I know I'm Melissa. But…" She lets the pause hang for a moment. "But she told me so many times that she was me and I was her, I might've lost track. And after she died, even after that horrible, heinous trick, I missed her, RK. I missed her every moment of the day. So I'd look into the mirror and talk to her. Ask her questions. And because we're twins, I could answer for her too. We were the same person at that point. All the good and all the bad. All the right and all the wrong. All the past and all the future."

"Miss," I say, putting my arm around her.

"I'm just saying. I know who I am, but when a person looks exactly like you, that person"—she points to herself in the mirror—"that person morphs into you, you know?"

I think about this a little. "That's kind of how I feel about Rock, now that you mention it. I mean, he's me, so it's different. But that's you too, Missy." I nod my head to her mirror image. "That's not Melanie."

"I know. I know that's me. And I know you know that Rock is you. But she was my clone, you know? In the very strictest sense of the word. We shared the same DNA. So why was she so hateful and angry? Did I do something wrong? Did I not love her enough? I asked myself these questions over and over after that night. And I blamed myself. She wanted to kill me that night, RK. Kill. Me. Like dead. And sometimes I wonder, when she jumped off that cliff… I wonder… did she say,

'Finally, that bitch is gone?' Did she really think she was killing me by killing herself?"

Fuck. That is some deep hate.

"Because she so truly believed she was Melissa and not Melanie?" Missy shakes her head. "God." She laughs. "Talk about the long way around."

I chuckle a little too. But it's freaky.

"You know what the saddest part of all this shit is, RK?"

I turn my body so I can see her head-on instead of the reflection. "What, Miss?"

"I don't think she ever loved me."

"Aw, Miss. She was just sick."

"I know," Missy says. "I know that. But I loved her so much. I worried about her so much. I wanted her to be happy and live a long life fulfilling her dreams. And I don't think she felt the same way about me. I think the day she decided to be me, back when we were six, she had already fostered a deep resentment and hate. Something that couldn't be undone. She hated me, RK. We came into this world equal in every way, and it wasn't enough. She wanted to destroy me just for being born. Just for taking up space. Just because I had your heart and she didn't. She ruined us that day, RK. But we have a second chance now. To put the past behind us, stop taking the long way around, and just move forward like the crow flies."

I sigh. "This is one fucked-up life we have up here on the mountain, Missy."

"I know, RK. But it's not the mountain's fault." She glances at me from of the corner of her eye. "It's not my fault and it's not your fault. It's her fault. You started something when you wrote the song, Rowan Kyle. But you never finished it. Not for real. It trapped you in the past. Somehow, some way, that song trapped you in the past and screwed you all up. And I think if you just did that, if you just finished the song, you'd feel a lot better."

All we have to do is finish what we started.

"Are you still hungry?" Missy asks after a few long silent minutes.

"Yeah," I reply, lost in thought.

"All right. I'll give the grilled cheese one more try." She laughs as she gets up and walks into the kitchen.

"I'll eat it no matter what," I whisper to my reflection in the mirror. "Because that's the kind of guy I am."

I get up off the bench, lift the lid, and then shuffle through the sheet music looking for a note book. Not much here. Just loose pages. Things from my childhood. If I want anything recent, this isn't where I'll find it.

"Come talk to me while I cook," Missy calls from the kitchen.

I do join her. If only to watch her attempt to be domestic.

"Don't laugh at me," she says, pointing the spatula in my direction.

"What else do you make, Miss? Tomato soup? PB and J?"

"My PB and J can win awards. And my can-opener skills make me the best tomato soup maker in Grand County."

"What kind of cheese is that?" I ask, looking at the white stuff bubbling down the bread and scalding on the pan. "Please don't say Swiss."

"Muenster!" she says. "Jesus, you give me no credit for knowing all your favorites."

I walk up and wrap my arms around her middle, my hands slipping into her front pockets. "You probably know more about me than I do," I whisper. "So, not true."

Missy takes a deep breath and then lets it out. "Will you finish the song?"

"Maybe," I say, kissing my way up her neck. "Will you come back to LA with me?"

Her body stiffens. "When?"

"I don't know," I say, continuing to work on her ear. "We can work out the details. But… would you ever? Come to LA, I mean?"

She flips the grilled cheese sandwiches over and they sizzle in the frying pan as she thinks. "I don't know," she finally says.

"Just a visit? See if you like it? Don't you ever get that old feeling, Missy? You used to want to go everywhere. Be a rock star. Tour the world. Play in front of stadiums filled with people."

"And I thought you were over your rock-star days. I thought you weren't going to play anymore. So if I go back to your rock-star life, what does that mean? Will you play? Will you look for new members? Keep the group going?"

I think about it as she gingerly lifts up one corner of a sandwich to check it. "I'm not there yet," I say after a long minute of silence. "And I haven't talked to Kenner, but I'm going to assume he's not there yet either. So no. I'm not going to worry about the music. I just want you."

"Then why do we have to leave Grand Lake? We're already here. If there's nothing there you want or need, then why go back to LA?"

She takes two plates out of the cabinet above her head, then slides a grilled cheese onto each one. I take my hands out of her pockets and grab two beers from the fridge, and then we walk over to the breakfast bar like we've done this a million times. Like this is a habit we made together.

"I know why," Missy says as I take a bite of my sandwich.

"Why?" I say with my mouth full.

"Because you think Grand Lake is a place to retire to. That's what your dad did. That's what my dad did. They were old, washed-up, assholes. They spent the last of their real money on these houses. This land. Those basements. The bar."

I shrug and take another bite, chewing before I speak this time. "Maybe I just don't want to be a one-hit wonder like they were."

"RK," Missy chastises. "That's not fair and you know it. So they only had one big hit as a band. They wrote and sold songs until they died. We both get the royalties from those songs, and we will for as long as our estates retain the copyright."

"Yeah, but—"

"No, no buts. They wanted to get out of the scene, RK. The one that poisoned them in the first place. The one that stole everything. The one that broke you too, even though you knew the risks."

"Look," I say, a little bit pissed off that she'd bring up my addiction. "You're the one who wanted to be the rock star, Missy. Not me. It just happened this way. I don't need the fans, or the accolades, or even the money. But this place is a poison. Grand Lake is the poison."

"No," she says, shaking her head before I'm done talking. "Nope. This is a good town. These are good people. If you were in LA and all this shit was happening, no one would give a fuck about you, RK. No one. Not the sheriff, not the librarian, not the therapist who lets you walk in every Monday morning after a blackout. You have no Sean in LA. You have no Gretchen in LA. You have no TJ in LA. And most importantly, you have no *me* in LA."

"Which is why I want you to come with me, Missy."

"What if you black out in LA and never come home?"

"Why would I do that?"

"Why do you black out now?"

"I didn't remember how Melanie died. I was trying to make myself forget. I probably blacked out every time I started to remember. This place reminds me of everything, Missy. All of it. I can't stand it."

She stares at me, her eyes darting back and forth, searching them the way she does. "I don't think that's why, RK. I don't think that's why. And until you figure it out, I'm not going to LA, or anywhere else, with you."

"You'll stay here?" I ask, annoyed with her. "In this dead-ass town? Nobody lives here, Missy. It's a dead end in every sense of the word. The world ends here in the winter. We have avalanches and moose. They fucking killed a wolf out near Kremmling last year, Missy. We have one road in, one road out. And that highway between us and civilization is a deathtrap."

"Oh, for fuck's sake! You didn't drive off a cliff, RK."

"It doesn't matter," I huff.

"It does matter." Missy gets up and takes her mostly uneaten sandwich over to the sink and drops it in with a clang. "If you leave," she says, her back to me, "I won't go looking for you, RK. I'm not going to chase you." She turns around, her palms grabbing the countertop as she leans back a little and studies my face. "If you leave, you're just running away again."

"Running away from what?"

She stares at me for a few seconds. "Did you black out in California?"

"No," I lie. *Why am I lying?*

"Never?"

"No," I say, digging in my heels.

"So why are you blacking out now?"

"If I knew I'd tell you. I'm not keeping secrets."

"What—" she starts, but stops short. She stares out the back window.

I wait, but nothing else comes out. "What, *what?*" I ask. "What were you going to ask?"

She hesitates, looking down at her feet. Then, just a I'm about to get frustrated, she says, "What's the name of the song?"

That wasn't what she was going to ask. But hey, if she wants to drop it, I'm gonna go along. Because I do not want to start thinking about the blackouts in LA. Not now. Maybe not ever. "Errr, well, it never really had one."

"How's the first verse go?" She takes a deep breath and then walks over to me, takes my hand, and places it over her heart. "Tell me how it goes. I've been dying to ask you that for five years."

I pull her in for a hug, thankful that our argument has passed. I don't want to fight with her. "I have to change it all now. I'm not going to use any of the verses I was thinking about."

"Ah-ha!" she says, laughing into my chest. "I knew you had words!"

"It's just a bunch of feelings, really, that's all. I never put it all together. So it hardly counts."

"You should go write it down. Right now, RK. And then play that song for me and sing those words. My life would be complete if you did that."

"The piano is a little out of tune. It'll drive me crazy."

Missy pulls away from me and walks over to the door next to the pantry, punching in the key code and pulling it open to reveal the blackness within. "You don't need a piano, RK. You've got your dad's studio in the basement." I stare at the dark stairwell for a long time before Missy can't take it anymore. "Just go down there. I stocked it all up for you, Rowan Kyle."

Margie was right. There is a big difference between Rowan Kyle, RK, and Rock. And there is a big difference in the way people use those names when they're talking to me.

"The fridge has food, soda, and beer. The bathroom has fresh towels. There's even cigarettes if you need them."

I scowl at her.

She shrugs. "Rock stars smoke, right? I didn't know how many bad habits you picked up in the City of Fallen Angels."

"So dramatic," I say. "I don't smoke. Anymore, anyway." My smile leaks out with the words. "My throat won't tolerate it." I haven't tried to smoke since the accident. But I don't want to either. It hurts just thinking about it.

"You filthy degenerate."

"I don't think I can sing."

"You can. Your dad completely remodeled the studio right after you left. State of the art, RK. All of it. My dad helped. They even mixed a few songs at the end."

I look up at her face. "I'm sorry," I say.

"What for?" She smiles, but it's weak. She knows why.

"For not being here when your dad died. For not coming home to help you say goodbye."

She pouts her lips a little, looks down, looks up at me. "Don't be sorry. We both had a lot of reasons to be mad at them, you know? They were total fuck-ups. Total." She smiles a little wider now. "In all ways but one. Your dad made you and my dad made me. So they did something right. Because I cannot imagine my life without you, RK. Never again. I'm expecting you to figure this out. I'm counting on you to do it. So"—she waves a hand at the open door—"go down there and make me proud. It's the next step. Maybe it's not the final step in your healing, but it's necessary."

I don't want to. I really don't. But I do want to make her happy. And proud. So I take a step across the kitchen. And then another and another. And before I can think twice about it, I flip on the light, step down, and close the door behind me.

Chapter Twenty-Seven

Some things never change and this studio, even with the recent upgrades, is one of them. It smells the same. Old smoke, because my dad did have a thing for cigarettes, hence the lung cancer. Old records, because this place is climate-controlled and he kept his album collection down here. And old books, because hey, if you've got perfect climate control and a thing for first-edition books, why not keep your library down here too?

But the remodel is apparent too. Mostly in the production room. Brand-new analog desk with a digital version off to the left with a bank of monitors. But the actual performance studio looks the way it did the day I left.

The drum set is tricked out in the center of the performance room, surrounded by acoustic panels. On the left side is the bass setup, the right side is the guitar setup. There are mics, and amps, and cords, and pedals. Music stands that still have music propped up on them. The keyboard set up is in the back, hidden by the drums.

The pictures on the walls haven't changed either. My dad when he was young, the single gold record they earned when their band had their first hit. Pictures of every friend he ever had in the business sitting down here on the couches, smoking, drinking, doing drugs. I don't remember anything about those days except being banned from the basement, but I've been looking at those same pictures all my life.

Bad influences, my mom used to say.

When I got older the famous people stopped coming. It was all phone calls and online meetings. Jack stopped recording and only wrote by the time I was eleven or twelve. So Teej and I would come down here and fuck off. We learned how to mix, how to record, how to do it all from scratch. Hell, we mixed tons of songs down here before we were in high school. It wasn't anything special. But it was good experience.

I flip the rest of the lights on, start up the computers and then the rest of the equipment in the production room. I check out the headphones and pull open drawers, just to see if they contain all the same stuff.

They do.

And then I walk out into the performance room and pick up the papers on the stand near the lead mic. I have never written down the notes for the song, but I can read music with the best of them. And I hear that melody tapping out on the piano in my head as I scan the notes in my hand.

My dad did this. My dad was the one who leaked that video of me at the funeral. He recorded it, wrote it down, and let it loose.

I sigh and put the sheet music back on the stand. Don't need it. I just head over to the keyboard and turn it on along with all its accompanying equipment.

I sit on the padded stool in front of the keys and a moment later, my fingers know what to do. I play it straight through one time, all nine minutes of it, and wipe the words I have been writing in my head away.

Starting over, Rock. Starting over.

From there it's a whirlwind of work. I find a notebook and a pencil and take them over to the couches at the front of the room. I drink a beer, then a water, then grab a snack from the fridge. Missy was right, she stocked it all up. Like she was expecting me to come home. Like she was waiting for me. There's even milk in there. And cereal in the kitchen cupboards. Nothing is expired. Nothing.

I scribble the words, counting the syllables to keep my rhythm. I count it all out, sing it in my head. Tap out the beat with my foot, or with my pencil, or my fingers on the old wooden coffee table.

And after six beers, eight sodas, two bowls of cereal, and one batch of microwave popcorn, I get up and walk to the guitar area. I choose a vintage 1959 natural-colored Gibson that graces dozens of framed pictures on the wall.

And I play.

I don't stop. Not like when I'm songwriting. When I'm composing I go until I'm done. And when I get that right, I lay the track down, mix it in with the keyboard, and move on to the bass.

I always knew the rhythm, and bass is not one of my specialties, so it's simple. It doesn't need to be overpowering and hard the way it was with Son of a Jack. Just simple.

I record that, mix it in with what I have, and move on to the drums. I excel at the drums. Not as much as the guitar and the piano, but I'm really good. And since this is primarily a keyboard piece, it's subtle and soft.

I do it all backwards of course. Melody, harmony, rhythm instead of rhythm, harmony, melody. But that's the way I like it, right? The long way around.

I mix it, then put the headphones on, and stand in front of the mic, controlling the production with a laptop.

My heart beats so fucking fast.

My throat aches so fucking bad by the third take.

My head pounds from lack of food, and lack of sleep, and lack of sunlight.

I have no idea how long I've been down here.

But I don't care. Because when I'm satisfied and play it all back, I feel different.

I feel whole. And satisfied. And ready.

For what? I'm not sure. But I'm ready.

I shower down here, then wrap a towel around my waist and go upstairs. The sun is just peeking up over the mountains when I look out the window. I don't even know what day it is. The air is cool as a gentle wind blows through the house, making the curtains shudder and wave.

I find Missy asleep in my bedroom, her legs all wrapped up in the white sheets. I drop the towel and climb in next to her, exhausted.

"Did you finish?" she asks, sleepily turning to mold her body into mine.

"Mmmm," I say, unable to stay awake.

"I love you," is the last thing I hear before I drift off.

I say it back in my dreams. Over and over and over.

Chapter Twenty-Eight

The mattress bounces a little and I roll over to find Missy kneeling on the bed, wide grin on her face. "Good morning, sunshine."

I close my eyes and mumble, "What time is it?"

"Six," she says, easing down next to me. Her body is cool and mine is warm from being wrapped up in the blanket. "At night."

I laugh as I slip my arm under her back and pull her up to me. "What day is it?"

She giggles as my fingertips find their way under her shirt. "Wednesday."

"Jesus," I say, eyelids flying open. "How long was I down there?"

"Two days. Do you still want to go to the party with me tonight?"

"Party?"

"Yeah, for the opening bands this weekend at Float's."

I think about this for a moment. "Are you one of them?" I turn a little so I can see her face as my thumb traces a slow arc over her belly button.

She sneaks a smile out. "Headliner this year."

"Headliner?" My hand dips under the waistband of her shorts and slips between her legs. "You're turning me on, Melissa Vetti."

"Then my evil plan is working." Missy laughs. She shifts her body too, so we are face to face. "Did you finish the song?"

"Mmmm-hmmm," I say, one hand coming up to brush a stray hair out of her eye. "Recorded it, edited it, mixed it. Done."

"Done?" she asks. "Done as in I can sit down and listen to the finished product? How did you do that?"

I shrug, staring into one blue eye. God, she's pretty. "It's just how I roll, Miss. All manic, all the time, right?"

"Does it have a title? Can we stop calling it the song?"

I lean in and kiss her neck. "It's called the Show Me Your Tits Song."

She laughs and pushes me away. "Is not." She laughs again. "Asshole."

I grin and then lift her shirt up so she has to show me her tits. My mouth covers her peaked nipple and then I bite it. Not hard. It's not a push-me-away bite. It's a throw-back-her-head-and-let-out-a-moan bite. "It's called the Take Off Your Pants Song."

"RK," she lazily warns. "What's it really called?"

My hand is still between her legs, so I begin a slow circular motion over her clit. "It's called the Let Me Take You Any Way I Want Song."

"OK," she says, her hand reaching down for my dick. I'm hard as fuck right now. "I'll play along."

"Sucker." I laugh, taking a break from biting her nipple to peer up at her. She goes to pull back, the slap I probably deserve already in motion. But I scoot up, move over top of her, and pin that hand to the mattress. "Be patient, Miss Vetti."

"I was patient for two days," she says, her hand slowly pumping me up and down. "I want answers. I want inside info. I earned it."

"Are you going to sell this conversation to *Metal Notes Online*?" I laugh.

"I will," she says, shooting me a sly smile. "If you don't tell me what you're calling it."

"That was my dad, you know."

"What was?"

"The person who recorded the song at the funeral and leaked it. I found the evidence downstairs."

"Well, I'm glad he did. The world deserves to hear it. Now," she says, leaning up to give me a quick kiss before she finishes her thought.

But I don't want a quick kiss, so I open my mouth and kiss her thoroughly, my hand reaching behind her neck so I can control it.

"Tell me the name of the song, Rowan Kyle," she whispers into my mouth.

"It's called the Let Me Fuck You Hard First Song."

"RK!" she yells. But she's laughing. "Why do you torture me?"

"I'm horny," I chuckle back. "Give in, Miss. Just give in and your torture will go a lot easier."

"Maybe I don't want it to go easy?"

I sit up, lean back, pull her shorts down, and slip them over her feet. "Perfect," I say, throwing them on the floor. "Now for the pesky tank top. Sit up a little."

She sucks in a breath between her teeth, but she does as I ask. I ease the top over her head and it joins the shorts on the floor. "Now we're naked," she whispers.

"So we are."

"What do you have in mind?"

Both hands grab her under the knees and I lift her legs up and out, spreading them wide. "Lie back and relax, Miss. Enjoy the show." My face dips down to her warm pussy, inhaling her scent. And then my tongue darts out and begins the same lazy circles my thumb was doing earlier.

She fists my hair, grabbing it hard as her hips rise up, begging for more. "Hell, yes," she says. "That feels amazing."

"Hmmm," I murmur, taking her clit gently between my teeth. She hisses out a breath, so I pull back and lick her. I push a finger inside her wet pussy and this elicits another moan. Her legs tighten around my shoulders and I have to push them back down into compliance before inserting another finger and pumping her harder. "Do you want to come like this?" I ask.

"No," she says, her eyes closing. "But I want to enjoy it a little longer."

"Don't worry," I breathe between sucking and licking. "I'm not in a hurry to stop." I flick my tongue back and forth a few times, then lean in to suck her. This makes her back arch again, and her knees are pushing against my ears. I reach up with one hand and squeeze her nipple, then palm her whole breast and start kneading it. I pull my fingers out and my tongue replaces them.

"Oh, yeah," she says in a low voice.

My fingers are still dripping and wet when I reach up and slip them into her mouth. She begins to suck. That makes my dick even harder. I peer up at her face between her legs and she's watching me.

We smile.

I ease up, licking and kissing her as I make my way up to her mouth and then replace my fingers with my tongue there too. She kisses me. And just the thought of her tasting herself drives me wild. I reach under her hips and roll over, placing her on top of me. We kiss a little more, our tongues twisting together until I taste her too.

She pulls back and kisses my throat. I realize her lips are on the scar I have from the tracheotomy the medics did the night of the accident. She looks up at me, frowning, but I shake my head. "Don't," I gently warn her. "Don't ruin this moment with that one."

She sighs, but continues kissing, moving down to my chest. She kisses my nipples, licks them, and then licks all the way down my abs.

I can't fucking wait anymore. All I want is her mouth on my dick. So I grab her hair and push. She responds by moving lower, the heat of her breath flowing over the tip of my head. But the moment she has my cock in her mouth I lose all sense of reality.

"Fuck," I say, gripping her hair tighter and pushing her down. She opens wider to take in my full thickness, and then her lips seal around my shaft and I'm the one closing my eyes.

I sit up so I can place my hands on her back and feel her soft skin. They ease down the length of her body and squeeze her ass cheeks. She pulls back, her tongue flat and sliding along my shaft, and then dives down again, trying to take me in as far as she can.

"'It would've been better,'" I whisper-sing. Missy's eyes dart up to mine. "'So much better if I had never let her,'" I continue, the words coming out without warning. She stops what she's doing and goes very still. Like she's afraid she'll spook me. "'Get to me the way she did.'"

Missy sits up a little and frowns, realizing that line is about Melanie.

"'It would've been better. If we lived through it together. It's always better to do it together,'" I finish.

"RK," she whispers back.

"That's the name of the song, Missy. It's the Better Together Song."

She crawls up my body, her eyes all glassy with the threat of tears, and then she cups my face in her hands and kisses me. "I love you," she says into my mouth. "I love you so much and we're going to get through this."

"And be better than ever on the other side," I say back.

She lifts her hips up and reaches down for my cock, placing it at her entrance. She slowly eases down, filling herself up with me. I wrap my arms around her back and pull her to my chest until she lies flat and relaxes.

And then we really begin.

This isn't the hate fuck of that first night. This isn't the manic fuck in the back room of Float's. This isn't even the first real fuck when we got home that night.

This is starting over.

This is making love by making good.

This is finishing what we started.

This is getting there the way the crow flies.

We come at the same time and the only thing on my mind is how much I want to do this again. Not fuck her. Love her.

And then I gently turn, letting her body fall to my side, and I hold her tight. I hold her like a man who is drowning in his past and she is the only person around with a life jacket.

Chapter Twenty-Nine

*"**We don't have to go to the party,**"* Missy says a few minutes later. We're just relaxing. Enjoying each other in silence.

"Fuck that," I say. "I want to go. You're headlining opening day at Float's. You gotta soak it all up, Missy. Enjoy it. I never did, ya know? It was all fucking rushed when I did it. Kenner and I worried about everything. Bills. Making enough to cover the beer we drank on show nights. Making enough to pay the rent on that crappy studio apartment we were sharing. It was stressful when we started playing clubs. This is the perfect way to make your entrance."

"Entrance to what?" She laughs.

"Rock stardom, Melissa Vetti. It's your destiny."

"No. It's just a stupid festival at the end of the world."

"Ack," I say. "It's not. It's a huge deal."

"You play in front of a hundred thousand people, I bet."

"Shit. Stadium shows are nothing compared to Float's. I'd rather play Float's, to be honest. I'm a little jealous of you right now."

She sits up and smiles down at me, her long mahogany hair draping over her shoulder and tickling my chest. "You can play if you want."

"No," I say, pulling her back down to my chest. "This is your gig, Missy. Not mine. Like you said, nobody wants me there upstaging their big day."

"I'd want you there, Rowan Kyle. I'd love it if you played."

"I'm pretty sure your show has no room for me. Besides," I say, kissing her mouth. "I'm not ready."

She stares into my eyes and nods. "I get it. Don't worry. I get it."

"Do you want to hear the song before we go?"

"Oh, my God. Are you kidding?" She chuckles into my chest, those little vibrations making me so happy, I have no words to describe it. "Yes. Right now."

She jumps up and walks out of the bedroom, coming back a few minutes later after using the bathroom. "Come on," she says, taking my hand and pulling me up. "Get dressed and take me down there."

She starts putting her shorts and tank back on and I reluctantly go to the front bathroom, clean up, and then rifle through my boxes in the living room for a pair of jeans. When I come back into the kitchen Missy is leaning against the basement door, grinning like a kid on Christmas Day.

She takes a deep breath and lets it out. "I'm nervous."

"Why?" I laugh, pulling the door open. It's not dark this time, I left the lights on when I came upstairs. "It's just a song."

"It's not," Missy says, taking my hand. "It's so much more than that."

We walk down the stairs and go into the production room. I take a seat in front of the monitor and wake it up. I have everything inside a folder, and in that folder are all the other folders for each track.

I click the master file and it opens up in the player. The mouse pointer hovers over the start button and I look over at Miss. "Ready?"

She takes in a breath and holds it. Then nods. "Yeah," she says softly. "I've been ready for five years."

One click. That's all it takes to change everything.

I've never watched Melissa Vetti as she listens to one of my songs. It's a big deal to watch her now.

It's nothing but piano in the beginning. Thirty seconds of soft music before my new voice enters. It's deeper now, and it's not bad. Not as bad as I feared. But it's definitely not the same either.

I think I'm OK with that.

Missy leans in, listening intently to the words. I close my eyes and picture the imagery going through my head. *I grew up seeing double, like a mirror, same as you. Never knowing if it's true. Never knowing what you'll do. Because the truth is hard. And the truth is leaving. And the truth is tricking me into believing. I'm always the one believing.*

She looks at me as the last line of that verse ends and the piano picks up a little.

It's sneaking out and slipping down. The rabbit hole of lies and silencing the sounds. It's an innocent kiss from me. Not for her, just you. Leaning up against that tree. Can't you see me? Drowning in your beauty?

She lets out another long breath. Like she's nervous and can't remember how to inhale and exhale. "You," I say, before the next verse starts. "Are my life jacket."

I'm seeing double so how am I to know? Which of you is real to me and which of you is putting on a show? Because she hurts you when she lies. And I hurt you when I'm blind. When knowing better is the only way to. Keep our love. And let it go.

Missy comes and sits on my lap, wrapping her arms around me and leaning her head against mine.

The bridge starts and I smile. It's a good song.

Your eyes are not her eyes. And I don't even have to try. I can pick you out and pull you in. Your soul string always pulls me in.

There is no chorus or refrain in this song until the very end. So the verses are merely separated by the bridges. And since the song is long, it's got a three of these transitions.

And then that night the shattered dream won't let me go. Tightens its fist and delivers one last blow. And so I did it alone. And I left you here. Because how will I. Ever get over all the things she made me do. When I should've known better...

Another bridge and this is where it all gets deep.

It would've been better. So much better. If I had never let her. Get to me the way she did and. Made me live with I did.

So there I was that night, twisted and confused. Nowhere else to turn but classic self-abuse. And even though I did it alone. It's never better to do it alone. But I'm a sucker for abuse.

It would've been better. So much better if I had never let her. Get to me the way she did. It would've been better. If we lived through it together. It's always better to do it together.

Another sigh from Missy as the piano dominates again and I repeat the last part three times. All the other instruments fade away and then it's over.

"It's an apology song," Missy says, wiping her eyes.

"I'm sorry," I say. "I'm just sorry."

She leans in and kisses me on the cheek. "Me too," she says, sniffling. I didn't want to make her cry. "Me too."

I reach over for the mouse and highlight all the folders inside the main and press delete.

"What are you doing?" Missy asks, getting up off my lap. "RK? What are you doing?"

I highlight the final render of the song and press delete again.

"What are you doing?" Missy says, louder now. "Get it back!"

I shake my head as I go into the trash bin and hover over the empty button. "No," I say. "I did this for you because you said we needed it to move forward. This was only for you, Miss." I look up into her shocked face. "I love this song and I'll do it again. But not without Kenner. No one but you will ever hear this version without Kenner. He's all I have left of that life. I don't want to make music alone, Missy. And I did this alone. But that's the whole point of the song, right? It's better together. So if this song ever gets released, we're all going to do it together."

And then I click the mouse and empty the trash.

Chapter Thirty

Where is Kenner? That's all I've been thinking about since Missy and I left the house, escorts behind us, and headed down to Float's in town for the party. The town is alive now that summer has officially started and there are tourists walking down Grand Avenue. Families mostly. Here for a week of fishing probably. The bar is at the western edge of town, so we only get a glimpse of what's really happening as we pull into the parking lot.

"How many people invited?" I ask Missy as I park the truck. The sheriff's car pulls up to their usual space in front of the door.

"Fifty or so. There's five bands. Each of us get two tickets. And Teej and the staff, of course."

I turn the truck off and watch the deputy get out of his car. He's got a buddy with him tonight. Why double up? They don't usually have a partner. "Why do we need tickets anyway?" I look over at Missy who is checking her makeup in the visor mirror.

She shoots me a sardonic glare. "Please."

"What?"

"People know you're here. Everyone is trying to get in the bar since it got out you're home."

"So put a 'private party' sign on the door and get a bouncer. Why spend money on tickets?"

Missy looks away nervously and then opens her door and gets out of the truck before I can ask any more questions. I'm not done though. Something is going on. "Miss," I say, walking around the truck and taking her hand. "Just why the fuck? Why does he need tickets? There's not even a show."

Missy sighs, avoids my gaze, looks out the water, then at the bar, and gives in by slumping her shoulders a little. "OK, we just want to know who's here. That's all. Everyone had to fill out a form online to print their ticket."

"That makes no sense." I gave it a second. I didn't just write it off. But it makes no sense.

"Not everybody likes you, *Rock*." Missy enunciates my name in that sentence, making a point.

"So?" I laugh. "What are you trying to say? People have been making death threats or something?" She doesn't look me in the eye, but instead stares over at the deputies, who are each leaning up against a post, arms crossed. Both are glaring over at me like I'm wasting their time. "Missy?"

She lets out a long breath of air. "Not exactly. I mean, no. No death threats. But weird shit, RK. Some really weird shit is happening. We almost canceled the opening weekend show. In fact, I told TJ we should cancel the whole summer, but he said no. We'll just get more security and we'll handle it. You can come see me play on Saturday, RK, but you're going to have to watch from the office window above Float's."

What? "What kind of threats?" I ask.

She rubs my shoulder and smiles. "There's no threats, RK. I swear. It's just everything that happened with the… accident, you know? People are upset. No one really understands what happened. You're not talking about it and we just feel like… extra security is necessary."

"Is this why I was sentenced to Grand Lake?" My mind spins a little at the shift in my reality. "So people could keep an eye on me?"

"Sentenced?" Missy laughs. "You make it sound like a punishment."

"Well," I say, "it was. Kinda. You have to remember what my state of mind was that first night. I was all kinds of fucked up, you know? Why didn't they just tell me this in the first place? I thought they were trying to accuse me of killing my friends that night." I shake my head. "That is not cool."

Missy looks at me with a pained, sympathetic expression. "I know. I'm sorry. It was TJ's call. He wanted you home until we knew what was going on. He's got a lot of pull in this town, RK. The money your dad left him is mostly donated to the community. He's probably going to run for mayor next election cycle."

I laugh so loud it makes Missy jump. "I don't even know what to say to that." She frowns, so I switch gears. "OK, sorry. It's just, TJ?" I laugh again. "Mayor?"

"You don't even know him anymore, RK. He's not the same guy you remember." She pauses, then adds,

"He's good, you know? He's good for this place. He loves this town, even if you don't—"

"I never really said that, Missy."

"You don't need to, RK. We all know how you feel about it. We read your interviews. And you called it poison. More than once."

It's my turn to frown. I've only been asked about my personal life a few times, but yeah. If people bring up Grand Lake I typically have a lot to say, and none of it is good. "Well," I say, letting out a long breath. "It's a good place. You know I was only reacting to the way things were when I left."

Missy squeezes my arm again, then leans in and kisses me on the cheek. "We know that, RK. We know that was the sadness and confusion talking. And that's why we're being extra careful now. Everyone fills out a form to get a ticket so we know who they are."

"And I get to watch you, not from the cool VIP boulders in front of the dock, but way the hell up there." I point to the office window on the second floor.

"It's only because we love you. Now, come on. Let's go inside and forget about all this. Just have a good time."

I let her take my hand and urge me towards the front door. I nod to each of the deputies, which makes their eyebrows shoot up in surprise, and follow her through the front door.

Inside the bar I have to stop and do a double-take. It's like it was on Saturday morning. White linen tablecloths, fresh flowers on each table, and that godawful piano guy on the stage.

Not the kind of party I expected for rock bands.

"Fancy," I mumble as Missy starts greeting people. Sean and Gretchen both come up to me with big smiles.

"RK!" Sean says.

"Hey, didn't know you were part of the band."

"Dock manager," Sean says, puffing out his chest. "I'm always invited to the pre-season party."

That makes sense. But Gretchen? She smiles as I look at her. "Head usher for the VIP section."

We laugh. It's ridiculous. But fuck it. I let it go.

TJ comes over and starts talking to Missy, and then a few guys wander up and they chat too. The band. I recognize them from the other night. Missy lets them pull her away.

"So," TJ says, coming up to me. "Things have changed, huh?"

I nod. "I guess they have." I point to the piano guy. "You hire a swank chef, get a new menu, pull out all the stops with the white tablecloths and flowers. Yet this is the best guy you can get to pound on the piano?"

"Like I said, you're welcome to—"

"Yeah, yeah. That's not happening. So what's all this about security and tickets? Missy says there's been threats?"

"She did?" TJ asks, throwing me a sidelong glance.

"Well, not exactly. But she said you're the reason I've been corralled up here on the edge of civilization and why my best friends all wear badges."

TJ stares at me for a few seconds like he's trying to figure me out. "Do you really want to have this conversation tonight? Because it's a party and what's happened to you this year is not exactly party conversation."

Kenner. His name runs through my mind again. Where the fuck is Kenner? "Hey," I say, leaning into TJ's ear, the whole ticket and security thing forgotten. "Do you know where my drummer is?"

TJ pulls back. "What do you mean?"

"I mean, I haven't heard from him. He texted and called, but it was bad timing, you know? Couldn't talk. And then Jayce called and told me to give him space. Like he wasn't ready to talk to me."

TJ stares at some distant point in the back of the bar, silent. "Let's talk about all that tomorrow." He refocuses his gaze on me. "How about that? Let's just have some fun tonight. Eat some good food, celebrate Missy, and relax. There's time for all that stuff tomorrow." And before I can answer he's got me by the arm and he's tugging me to the back table. Which seems to be the only place I'm allowed to sit in this bar these days.

It's not me who's not talking about the accident, I realize. It's everyone else.

I sit in my assigned seat and watch Missy work the room. There's a lot of people here. Fifty doesn't even come close when you add in the staff. Probably more like a hundred with the waitresses and the busboys. The bartenders, the stage guys, who I recognize from that day I helped Sean with the dock. Lots of staff at this party. And bouncers. Two guys at the front door, two guys at the public back door, and two guys at the door marked private that leads to the employee break room and the stairs to the office. All looking like they moonlight here between WWE gigs.

And two deputies out front.

That's quite the security setup for a bar in a town this size.

Sean and Gretchen are busy drinking and talking in the booth with me, and TJ and Missy are busy working the room. So I pull out my phone.

Because Kenner.

I find that last message stream and read it again.

Kenner: dude help me man tell me what the fuck is happening

Kenner: what the hell is happening

Kenner: come see me

Rock: I can't I'm not allowed

Kenner: don't leave me here man they r telling me things rock I don't know what's happening

What is happening with Kenner?

I text Jayce.

Rock: Hey, where is Kenner?

I get that little notification that says delivered. Then read. I wait for the little animated dots to tell me she's replying, but nothing.

Rock: Jayce?

Delivered. Read. Nothing.

I look around and spot the deputies coming through the front door. TJ makes his way over there quickly and they talk, leaning into each other like they have a secret. Then all three look over at me. The moment they realize I'm watching them, they all look away.

What the fuck?

TJ urges them back outside, but he follows. I'm just about to get up and ask what the fuck is going on when Missy comes back. "Hey," she says, making herself comfortable in my lap. "You doing shots?" She asks Sean and Gretchen. "Pour us two each!"

Sean huffs. "Not shots, you wench!"

I laugh.

"This is fine whiskey. You don't down it like a shot. You sip it in a glass."

I sigh, then push the little secret meeting out of my mind and smile over at Sean. "I'll take one."

Sean obliges. "What kind of Macallan you have at your bar, RK?"

"What's this?" I ask, turning the bottle. "1997? Shit. Dude, when you come to my house in LA, I'll treat you to some fine Macallan 62."

Sean whistles as he pours each of us two fingers in the glasses. He gives Gretchen and Missy each a sideways glance and says, "You girls don't get any. I might not have a 62 here, but Macallan isn't for dabblers."

"Pfft," Gretch says, blowing her hair up her face. "I've got margaritas to keep me happy. You can keep your stuffy old Scotch."

"You're sexist, Sean," Missy says, taking the glass he just poured for me. "Bottoms up," she says, downing it all, then grimacing from the burn as she slams the glass down with a *thunk*.

I laugh and tap the table, asking him to refill. He looks pained at the way Missy just downed his prize drink. But it's an act. I think he secretly loves her double for that. He looks at me as Missy and Gretchen talk. "How much does that bottle you have go for, RK? Ballpark?"

"You do not want to know. And I'm too embarrassed to say. But it was a gift from our label the day *Living the Dream* went platinum."

"Jesus Christ," Sean says, filling my glass up two fingers. "They bought one for each of you?"

I nod. "Wasteful. Since neither Ian or Elias drink Scotch. They sold their bottles at auction a few months later. Ian bought a boat with that money and Elias put his in the bank." I smile thinking about it. I miss them. I miss them a lot.

"Did you drink any of it yet?" Sean asks.

"Yeah, about half. So you better come visit me quick, because when I get home, I'm hitting that shit first."

"I'm there, man," Sean says, lifting his glass up to toast. "To more Scotch."

I clink him, then take a sip. "It's good shit," I say. "No matter the year."

After that we get loud. And drunk. And even though it's a fancy fucking party with dinner served under silver domes, Missy sits in my lap, the rockers all end up on stage badgering that pianist—which makes me happier than it should—and TJ and I laugh about our prick of a dad and all the bullshit that came along with being a son of a Jack.

I don't hate this town and I certainly don't hate these people. I just needed this vacation, I guess. I just needed to be reminded what it feels like to belong somewhere.

Chapter Thirty-One

I wander through the door marked private to find the bathroom a few hours later. "I'm not wasted," I tell the image looking back from the mirror as I wash my hands. "Nope." I smile at my reflection and take it in for a moment. My eyes are a little red, but other than that, I don't look too bad. I've got a little color in me, probably from my unauthorized climbing days. That thought lingers in my brain for a few moments before I have the good sense to shake it away. *Not tonight, Rock. Tomorrow, Teej said. We can think about all that shit tomorrow.*

I dry my hands and pull the door open, almost smashing into one of the waitresses. "Sorry," I say, backing up with my hands in the air.

She holds a hand over her chest like she's startled, but when I look up at her face, I get the impression fear isn't what's on her mind. She stares at me for a second, squinting, like she's confused about something.

"You OK?" I ask. "Didn't mean to scare you."

"Rock?" she asks, her look getting more and more puzzled as time ticks off.

"Yeah," I say. And then I recognize her. "Hey, you're the girl who asked me to sign her ticket stub last week, right?"

She says nothing.

"Um…" I get this sometimes. People are starstruck, can't talk. Shit like that. So I do what I always do in those situations. Make a break for it. "OK, well, sorry for bumping into you." I shoot her a drunk rock-star smile and turn to leave. But she grabs my arm.

I jerk away real quick, probably an overreaction, and say in my most friendly drunk voice, "Hey there, don't grab me."

"Sorry," she says, letting go of my arm. "It's just…" Her eyes dart to the door that leads out to the bar. "It's just I have these three magazines with you on the cover. Could you please sign them for me?"

I look at the door too, but only because I hate being ambushed by fans and I want to find an excuse to say no, but can't think of one that won't end up with her calling me a dick on Facebook tonight. Probably complete with pics. So I say, "Sure," instead.

She smiles and backs away, feeling the wall to guide herself back to the break room where the magazines must be. Her eyes never leave mine. "You remember me?" she asks just as she reaches the doorway.

"Yeah," I say struggling to figure out what's got her acting so weird. "You're the one who asked me to sign the ticket stub. I just said that."

She nods, then holds up one finger, telling me to wait a second.

I look back at the door leading to the bar, wishing I'd just pretended to be wasted and walked away. I'm about to take my chances with bad PR when she reappears, magazines in one hand and a Sharpie in the other. "Sorry," she says, smiling bright now.

Yeah, this one is weird. I smile back anyway. Giving her what she wants is the easiest way out of this now. I take the Sharpie and she hands me the first magazine.

I smile down, ready to scratch out my name, but then I notice the headline for *Metal Notes*. "'Where in the World is Rock?'" I say, reading it. It's got one of those Where's Waldo kind of images on the front with hundreds of people all crowded together at a rock concert. I try to find Rock for a second, but I'm not even sure what cartoon Rock should look like. "Where'd you get this?" I ask.

"That was the April issue. After you disappeared." She says 'disappeared' like she took it personally.

"Hmm," I say, signing my name and handing it back. "Never saw it before."

"No," she says, handing me the next one. "I bet they're not showing you anything. This one is from May."

"Who?" I ask, looking down at the next magazine. I've never seen that cover either. This headline, also *Metal Notes Magazine*, says, *It's a Rock Hunt. Where is Rock and what really happened that night?* And there's a picture of me on the cover from some shoot I did a few years back. I sign it and hand it back, starting to feel very uncomfortable.

But the third magazine she hands over stops me dead. "That's June," she says. "Just came out today."

Never mind the fact that I've been on three covers for *Metal Notes* in three months and never knew about it, the picture is what tips my world. My head actually spins a little and it's not from the drinks. On the front is a picture from the very first photoshoot we did for the *Living the Dream* album. All five of us.

I stare at us and get lost in it. We were painted up to look like an American flag for that shoot. Ian, Elias, and Mo are mostly blue with white stars on their chests. Kenner and I are the red and white stripes. The headline for this one is *Living the Nightmare*.

I look at my friends for a moment and let myself smile at the memory. Ian with his pale skin and dark red hair. He was sunburned that day because he fell asleep lying on a raft in the pool at our new house. Elias with that asshole look on his face that says, *Talk to me and I'll throat-chop you*. Mo, looking a little bit like a Buddy Holly terrorist crossbreed in my mind, because his only hobby, aside from music, was blowing things up with illegally obtained M-80 firecrackers.

God, I really fucking miss them.

We didn't end up using that photo for the cover art because the band decided it was stupid and Ian was mad about having to scrub that paint off his peeling skin. The real photo was Photoshopped. The flag was added in afterward.

"It's a terrible, terrible story, Rock," the girl says. Alice, I remember TJ calling her. "I'm sorry it ended like that."

I sign my name and thrust the magazine back. "Thanks." I'm just turning away when she grabs hold of my arm again.

I stare at her fingers for a second, not as amicable about it as I was a few minutes ago, and then I look back into her eyes. "What?" I snap.

She pulls out a handful of multicolored pieces of paper, which I recognize immediately as more ticket stubs. "Do you even remember me?" she asks, her eyes filling up with tears. "I've been to all your shows, Rock. You have to remember me. I was—"

The door to the bar swings open so hard, it slams against the wall and bounces back, revealing TJ in the entrance. "What the fuck are you doing, Alice?" he roars. His eyes dart to her handful of magazines and stubs and I swear to God, I have never seen my brother so pissed off. "You're fired, bitch. Get the hell out of here. I warned you last time—"

I make a break for it, not even remotely interested in hanging out for that meltdown. One thing I have enjoyed about this town is the peacefulness. I guess that's about to change now that I've been found. I bet the July issue of *Metal Notes* is all about my mini-vacation in the Rockies while my ex-bandmates rot in the ground.

"Where have you been?" Missy asks, panic on her face as I approach the booth. "You've been gone for like fifteen minutes!"

"Not fifteen minutes?" I laugh, pulling her close and kissing her on the cheek. "I was in the bathroom. Some girl cornered me—"

"What?" Missy asks. "Who?"

"No one. A waitress. TJ is firing her right now for talking to me. So no big deal. Are you ready to go? Because I am all partied out. Hey, Gretch, are you driver tonight?"

Gretchen and Sean both laugh from across the table, like I'm out of my mind.

"I am," TJ says, appearing behind me.

"What the fuck, TJ?" Missy asks him. I look over my shoulder just in time to see him shake his head at Missy.

"I'll drive you guys home," he says, as soon as I catch him.

"I'm not even interested in that little secret look the two of you shared, so let's go." I start walking, my arm still around Missy's waist, but TJ redirects me.

"Back door, stud," he says, turning me in the other direction and moving in front of us. I laugh and follow him to the back door where the two bouncers part to let us through.

I fuck with the radio all the way home and every time I look over my shoulder at Missy, she's chewing on her fingernails. "What's up, buttercup?" I ask.

"Nothing," she insists, as Teej turns onto our road, flashing a wave at the deputy parked there. I look behind us and see the other sheriff's vehicle that followed us home flip a bitch and park next to him, their driver's side windows facing each other so they can talk.

"Fucking cops, man," I sigh.

TJ and Missy say nothing in reply. Teej just pulls into the driveway and looks over at me. "You gonna be around tomorrow? I could use some help down at the bar. Get ready for the show this weekend."

I'm too drunk to even think about this right now, so I just nod and say, "Sure," as I open my door. Missy gets out too, giving TJ a long glance before exiting. I take her hand and pull her away, closing the door as I turn with Miss and walk up the drive.

Missy is quiet as we go into the house and I disarm the alarm. "Did you have a good time?" I ask her.

"I did," she says, wrapping her arms around my middle and smiling into my chest. "I just worry about you when there's crowds."

"I'm fine," I say, walking us both into the kitchen. "I can take care of myself. And besides, this is Grand Lake, right?" I laugh a little as I pull open the fridge and grab two waters. I twist off a cap for Missy and hand it over. She takes a long sip as I twist open another and guzzle until half the bottle is gone.

"Thirsty?" Missy laughs.

"Yeah." I smile my half-drunken smile at her. "I haven't had this much to drink in a while."

Missy shifts her feet and then looks over at the patio door that leads out to the deck. "You're not planning on some midnight rock climbing, are you?"

"No." I laugh. "Why?"

She takes a deep breath. "Well, you always seem to disappear after you drink."

I squint my eyes as I think about this. "Do I?" I shake my head. "No, I don't think that's it."

Missy comes closer, taking my water and setting it down on the counter with hers so she can take my hand. "If not drinking, then what's the trigger?"

I shrug. "I dunno. But I got drunk a lot with the band and woke up to a normal hangover the next day. So it's not drinking."

"Where do you go, RK? Do you remember?"

"No," I say, shaking my head. "Not really. Climbing, I guess. People saw me that first time. And I had the harness on that one time."

"Did you climb in LA?"

I think about this a little bit. Because the obvious answer is yes. I know this is the correct answer or how else would I have had all that climbing gear? How would

I know how to use it? How would I not kill myself climbing down the cliff? And how the hell did I know how to drill holes and hammer bolts into the rock if I haven't done it before? "I guess," is the best answer I can come up with. "But I really do not remember."

"Doesn't that scare you, RK?" She slips her hands under my shirt and holds tight to the muscles just above my hips. "Because it scares the shit out of me. What if you go climbing and never come back? And we don't know where you went, or how to find you? What if you get hurt and need help—"

"I don't climb alone, Missy." It comes out before I even realize what I'm saying.

"What? Then who were you climbing with?"

"I mean—" Shit. "I don't know. I just know," I say, tapping on my heart, "in here, that I don't. I have a partner every time. And Margie said that I was with a bunch of people that first time, so that confirms it."

"Yeah, TJ talked to them. They didn't know you, RK. They said you just showed up on that climb. Like, uninvited, or something. So how did you know people would be up there?"

"I don't know, Missy." It comes out a little irritated and I'm sorry for that, but why is she pressing me? "I don't want to talk about it, OK? Besides," I say, shooting her my best charming rock-star smile, "it's not Saturday night yet." She does not laugh, but I do. "Apparently I only black out and climb on Sundays."

"That's not funny." She pouts.

"I know, but I'm sorta drunk, Miss. I just want to go to bed and hold you tight, OK?" I take her hand and lead her to the bedroom. "Come on, let's go to bed. We have three days to talk about it before the rock climbing urge takes over."

"I'm getting security to start sleeping in the house tomorrow, RK. I'm not kidding. I'm going to handcuff you to the bed on Saturday night."

I lead her into the bedroom, flick on the light, and start taking her clothes off. "I don't care," I say, whipping her shirt over her head. "As long as they don't mind listening to some rock-star fucking."

"Oh, my God," she says. But a little giggle escapes from her mouth and I can't help myself. I grab her by the hair and kiss that mouth. Our tongues twist together as we forget about rock climbing, and blackouts, and security.

I unbutton her jeans and wiggle them down her hips. Her hands reach down, our mouths still busy with the kiss, and help, until she gets them all the way off and she's just standing in her barely-there panties. My forearm swipes all the shit piled up on the dresser, making it crash to the floor, and then I lift her up and sit her on top of the smooth wooden surface and press my fingers up against her pussy.

She breathes heavy, and I can almost hear her heart start to beat faster as she reaches for the hem of my shirt and works it up my chest. Her lips go there, kissing and licking. And then her hand is grabbing my dick through my pants.

"Unbutton them," I whisper into her hair.

Her fingers fumble for a second as she releases the button, and then she drags the zipper down. Her hand is frantic to pull my cock out, and when she does that, I watch her look down and smile.

"The rock-star dick," she laughs, "is huge."

"Hey," I say, reaching behind her back to unclasp her bra. "Only the best for you, Melissa Vetti." Her breasts fall free as I ease it down her arms, making her release her hold on my cock. I throw the bra on the floor and then push her back against the dresser mirror, opening her legs and lifting them up, so her knees are pressed against the soft fleshy sides of her tits.

I bite one, making her squeal softly, and then kiss her mouth before making my way back down her body, kissing her every inch of the way. Her nipples, where my tongue swirls around the bunched-up peaks. Her flat stomach, rippled with the small muscles of a girl who is fit. Her hip bones, the ones my hands always seem to gravitate to. And then I get to her sheer panties. They are pink mesh with white lace.

I lick her pussy through the panties and she runs her fingers through my hair, grabbing it as I bury my face. I slip her panties aside and rub her clit. She automatically clasps her knees together, squeezing my shoulders, as she squirms.

I push her legs open and continue licking her until she's arching her back and writhing underneath me. My dick is hard as fuck, and I want her hands on me. So I stand up and redirect her attention by placing her palm around it. She immediately begins to pump as I watch. She grips it firmly, stroking me up and down. Slow. Way too fucking slow. It's driving me crazy. Her small fist eclipses the tip of my head, then slides back down, stretching the skin, before releasing.

I want her mouth on it. I want to see her lips wrap around me, her tongue licking and flicking, and then my cock disappearing down her throat.

"RK," she moans, trying to sit up, trying to reach me better.

I push her back against the mirror and whisper, "Be still. You first." I bend down again. She protests with a small moan as she is forced to let go of my cock, and then I resume my licking. I insert two fingers in her pussy and swirl my tongue around her clit until her legs are wrapped around my neck and no matter how hard I urge her to ease up, she doesn't.

She locks her ankles together behind my back and thrusts her hips up towards my mouth, soft rocking motions adding to her pleasure. I lick, then take her clit between my lips and suck her as I pump my fingers in and out.

"I'm gonna come," she whispers. "Just so I can have my turn to make you feel like this."

I laugh a little as I keep going, reaching up to grab her tit and knead her nipple.

That's all it takes. I look up between her legs and watch her come. She throws her head back against the mirror, twisting her neck back and forth, like she's overcome with the ecstasy. Her hips writhe, her back buckles, and then she lets out a long, soft moan as she fists my hair, pushing my face farther into her pussy.

I taste her release. It's sweet and tangy and pours into my mouth. And after about a minute of this, she stills and I kiss her body all the way back up to her mouth. Her tongue meets mine eagerly. Like she can't get enough.

Her voice is husky from the climax when she whispers, "Your turn now."

I lift her whole body up, her legs automatically wrapping around my middle as I walk us over to the bed. I sit down, placing Missy in my lap, and hold her tight for a few seconds. "Thank you for being here when I came home," I say.

"I was waiting for you, Rowan Kyle. There was never a time in my life that I didn't know you were the only guy for me."

"I'm sorry it took me so long to come back."

"It doesn't matter," she says, pulling away and placing her palms on the stubble of my face. "It doesn't matter now. This moment," she says, "all these precious moments we've had since you came home wipe all those missing years away."

She eases herself out of my lap and kneels on the floor in front of me. Her eyes never leave mine as she does this, her hands firmly gripping my cock as she slides them up and down my shaft.

And then… she gives me everything I ever wanted. I stare in awe as she places her mouth over my dick. Still, her eyes never leave mine. She looks up at me through a few stray strands of hair that I automatically tuck behind her ear, and pushes her face into my cock like she's dying for it.

It's my turn to throw my head back. I place my hands on her head, urging her to take me deeper. She gags a little, but doesn't pull back. I ease up to make her more comfortable, and then guide her more gently.

She sucks hard and flattens her tongue against my shaft as she draws up. I almost want to die. I force myself to watch her, even though my eyes want to close and my body wants to sink back into the soft comforter. Her eyes are watering a little, making her dark makeup smudge.

"Fuck, yes," I mumble as she dives down on my dick again. And then I come down her throat without even asking first.

She gags for a second, but recovers quickly, her gaze still locked with mine. She swallows until I'm done and I can't hold my eyes open for another second. I flop back on the bed, my fingers running through her hair. She climbs on top of me, her breasts flattening against my chest, and kisses my neck, then my ear, then the scruff of my cheek and finally my mouth.

"I love you so fucking much," I say.

"Don't leave me again, Rowan Kyle. Because if you do, I might die."

I roll us over and pull her into my chest, her head resting on my upper arm, her face buried in my hair, and make a promise. "I won't. I swear, I'm not going anywhere."

She sighs a little and then whispers, "Wake me up when you want to go again. Because I'm not ready to be done."

The last thing I recall is chuckling before sleep overtakes us and we are out.

Chapter Thirty-Two

"Rowan Kyle," a female voice says as my shoulder shakes. "Rowan Kyle? Wake up, dear."

I pull myself awake and blink, trying to make my eyes focus. When I manage that, an older woman is leaning down, looking at me with a worried expression. "What?" I ask, sitting up in the bed and looking wildly around, trying to figure out where the fuck I am.

"You fell asleep," the woman says. She smiles and lets out a breath, like she was worried about me. "I was able to dig up a little bit, but not much." She thrusts a folder at me and I accept it without thinking as I take in my surroundings.

I'm in a hospital room.

My heart begins to beat like crazy and the first thing that runs through my mind isn't, *How the fuck did I get here?* It's—"Missy is gonna kill me."

"Who's Missy, Rowan Kyle? A friend of yours?" She smiles one of those patient smiles. She's wearing pink scrubs and she has eyeglasses that remind me of the Grand Lake librarian.

What the hell is happening?

I look around the room again and take it in. The bed is still made and I'm fully clothed, so I'm not a patient. I can hear a lot of voices and yelling beyond a sheet pulled closed for privacy and stare at it for a second.

"I know," the nurse says. "They need the room, Rowan Kyle. So I only have a minute. They're bringing a patient up right now from the ER. I looked up the info on your friend," she says, her hand resting on my shoulder to refocus my attention on her. "I found out a little bit, but not much. It's all very hush-hush. VIP's have a lot of extra security afforded to their records. But he was here."

"He was?" I ask, my mind still trying to catch up with the situation. "Kenner?"

The nurse nods and I read her name tag. Alice Gooding.

Alice. Why do I know that name?

"He was flown here after he was stabilized and put into an induced coma at Cedars-Sinai."

"LA? Why was he in LA?" I'm so fucking confused.

"I guess…" Alice Gooding shrugs. "I guess that's where they take rock stars when they need immediate medical attention. He was life-flighted from Big Bear on February twenty-ninth—"

"Big Bear?"

She stops talking and stares at me. "Are you OK?"

"No," I say quickly. "Yes. I mean, yes. I'm OK, just confused after that… nap."

"Nap." She smiles again. "You looked pretty tired when you came up to the nurse's station. Which is why I brought you in here. And to keep prying ears and eyes off you while I looked." She gives me a conspiratorial wink.

I have no fucking clue where I am, other than in a hospital room. "What's the day?" I get another concerned look, so I quickly add, "I lost track, sorry. Recovery mode and all."

"Thursday, Rowan Kyle."

"Thursday," I repeat. So I can't be too far from home. Unless I somehow have a private plane stashed away I don't know about. But no hospital in Grand County has the kind of activity I can hear out beyond that sheet.

"Life-flighted here to Denver on February twenty-ninth in an induced coma as they assessed his brain recovery."

"I feel sick," I say.

"Just take deep breaths, Rowan Kyle. Do you want me to call someone?"

"No," I snap. "No. Don't call anyone. I just need a second to deal, OK?" There's more activity on the other side of the sheet, more shouting, some kind of medical alarm going off and the thud of footsteps.

Alice is looking at the sheet as well. *Alice the nurse, not Alice the fan*, I hear myself thinking.

"Like I said, we don't have much time. Kenner McConnell was flown here and taken to the VIP wing. He stayed there for three weeks."

"Then what happened?" I'm trying really hard to focus on her words.

"They took him up somewhere up in Routt County. That's Steamboat, I think. Well…" She considers thoughtfully. "I guess it could be one of the other towns. But I do know there's a VIP medical center up in Steamboat. It's heavily guarded. They take people there who need specialized care but also high security."

I'm afraid to ask, but I hear the words coming out of my mouth anyway. "Why did he need so much security?"

"You still don't remember, do you?" She pulls back. "I'm sorry, but when you came in you were lucid and asking all the right questions." She shakes her head at me. "But now… I didn't know you hadn't remembered yet. I'm sorry, I can't tell you—"

I grab her by the wrist and grip tight, not letting her move away. And then I stare into her eyes and plead. "I need to know, Alice Gooding. I need to know what the fuck happened to me. And I'm gonna beg here. I'm not too proud to beg, OK? Just please, tell me what the fuck is going on."

She hesitates for a moment, looks at the sheet again, then nods. "OK, come with me." I don't let go of her wrist. I hold on like my life depends on it. So when she moves towards the sheets, I follow her. She peeks out, and it's fucking chaos. People rushing by, family members crying. Some kind of very big emergency is happening. It's an intensive care unit, I realize. *Where you were, Rock*, a voice in my head says. *That's why you came here*. Someone is dying. Right now. That's what all the activity is in the hallway. Alice the nurse drags me towards a stairwell and we slip inside. We walk down several flights of stairs and come out into a semi-lit basement. She stops in the hallway and takes a deep breath, then peeks into a door window, nods and leads me into a small empty break room. There are a few tables with chairs in the center, littered with magazines and newspapers, and paper cups. Several cots line the walls.

"This is for ER docs," she explains. "When they need to crash after double shifts."

There's no one in here now, but I get what she's saying. We don't have much time.

"Do you remember me?" she asks. "I took care of you when you first got to Denver. They brought you in first, since your injuries weren't as serious as your friend's. And when they transferred you, they never told us where you went. The FBI were here and they had you drugged pretty good to stop you from…" She hesitates. "I don't know if I should be telling you this. It could make things worse."

"Alice," I say, dead fucking serious. "This *is* worse, OK? Not knowing. Blacking out and waking up in strange places. I can't keep doing this. I need to know what the fuck is going on."

"You went a little crazy, Rowan Kyle. Once you realized what happened."

"But I don't remember what happened." Obviously I was mixing up Melanie's death up in the mountains with whatever happened to the band. My band did not drive off a cliff any more than the car I was driving on prom night. "How could I know what happened and then forget?"

She puts her hands up, like she's helpless to answer that. "The mind is a tricky beast."

"I promise, OK? I'm not interested in doing something stupid. I just need to know what's going on now."

"Now?" She says it hesitantly, but then exhales and gives in. "Three of your friends died that night. You and your friend Kenner survived, although he was touch-and-go for a few weeks. You were the least injured. Whoever did this tried to smash your throat with some kind of blunt object. All the others were shot. I can only assume when Kenner McConnell didn't die from the gunshot wound, they took the same blunt object to his arms as well. Or maybe that happened first? I'm just not sure."

Welcome to RK's insane delusions.

"Who?" I whisper, unable to recognize my voice anymore.

"No one knows. *You* know, Rowan Kyle. You know and then you made yourself forget." She starts grabbing at the magazines and newspapers on the table closest to us. Not finding what she's looking for, she searches the other tables until she comes up with a *Metal Notes Magazine*, thrusting it out at me. Son of a Jack is painted up to look like the American flag and the headline reads, *Living the Nightmare*.

"It's all in here," she says.

I take the magazine and stare at it. There's a subheading that I didn't see last night. It says, *Who killed Ian, Elias, and Mo? Only one man knows, and he's not talking.*

"We have to go before anyone sees you. Unless..." She looks at me. "Unless you want them to come get you. I can call them—"

"No," I say, rolling the magazine and the folder up and heading towards the door. "Don't call them, Alice." She follows me to the door and I hold it open for her. "I swear, I'm OK. I'm OK now. I just need to get home."

We go out into the hall and enter the stairwell again, just as the elevator dings. I close the door and we both watch a weary ER doc make her way to the break room.

I have one last question for Alice the nurse. "Why did they move Kenner to Colorado? Do you know why?"

She swallows hard and nods. "Because the killers are still out there, Rowan Kyle. The FBI needed to get him somewhere safe to protect him."

Which explains the sheriff keeping such a close eye on me up in Grand Lake. Why they sent me there to begin with. People are easy to spot in a town that small. Strangers stick out.

Unless there's a music festival coming up. Unless it's tourist season and people come from all over to boat and fish on the lake.

Am I bait?

I bet they didn't expect me to take so long to tell them something useful and now that the town is filling up with people, they are desperate to get me talking.

"Thank you, Alice. Really, I'm OK." We walk up a flight of stairs and then she points to an emergency exit, keys in a code in the alarm system, and then holds the door to the back parking lot open for me.

"Be careful," she says as I walk through.

I nod. But I have no intention of being careful.

I'm gonna make myself remember and then I'm going to kill the motherfuckers who killed my friends.

Chapter Thirty-Three

I half expect them to be waiting for me when I get to my truck. Not the... killers. But TJ and Missy. The Grand County Sheriff. Someone. But the parking is full and busy and no one is there to confront me when I get in the truck and stare at the magazine in my hand.

I study at the cover again, reading the headline. *Living the Nightmare?* Yeah. I think that about sums it up.

I'm not sure I want to read this article, but I am sure that whatever the fuck made me forget what happened that night won't go away unless I face reality. So I open it, flip through about a dozen pages of ads, until I see my photo.

Not a pretty one. Not one in a studio with great lighting, making me look the rock-star part.

No.

It's a picture of me outside the ambulance that picked me up in Big Bear, lying in a stretcher, about a dozen people working on me. There's another stretcher, which I can only assume is Kenner, because the person, while not really visible, must not be dead or he'd have a sheet over his head. I can just make out the Life Flight helicopter in the upper right corner.

I can't tell if I'm awake or not in that picture. I can't remember any of it, but I'm not sure that counts for much right now. There's blood everywhere. I can see my hands, strapped down. And they are covered in it.

I involuntarily place my fingers over the tracheotomy scar at the base of my throat and find it difficult to breathe for a moment.

And then I start reading.

Son of a Jack never thought their first night in the resort town of Big Bear, California would end up being the last night they ever spent together as a band.

I have to stop for a moment and ask myself if this is really the best idea. But what choice do I have? Whoever did this is still out there. And if there's a chance that facing the truth will help me remember, well, I have to take that chance. I probably saw the killers. If I could just remember their faces I might be able to identify them.

It was a night of partying and celebration as the band wrapped up their second album and got their gear ready for a private day of skiing on the slopes of Bear Mountain. Two hours after arrival Ian Malone, Elias Chestro, and Mo Darzi would be dead, lying in a pool of blood. All three were shot.

Fuck. I close my eyes and try to stop myself from throwing up.

Was someone waiting in the house? Did they come to the door? Were the killers known to the boys? No one knows. Kenner McConnell and Rock Saber both survived, but either they don't remember—or they aren't talking.

I spoke with Jayce Willington, the band's manager, for a brief update and interview last week and while she didn't give me a straight answer, she did hint that Kenner, who only recently woke up from a coma after he was shot twice—once in the side of the head, which Ms. Willington assures me was only a graze, and a more serious bullet wound to his left side, would recover.

"He was in bad shape. We think he fell over at some point and knocked himself unconscious. Possibly from the bullet wound. He didn't wake up after they stabilized him after emergency surgery for the gunshot wound and dislocated elbows. Then his brain started to swell with blood and they needed to put him in a medically induced coma for surgery," Willington said last week on the phone.

She also relayed information about the extent of his arm injuries and when asked if he'll ever drum again, she hesitated for several seconds before finally admitting "his long-term prognosis remains to be seen."

Rock Saber, the charismatic lead singer, came out of the attack better than the rest because he was not shot. But Willington did say, "We think someone hit him in the neck with a blunt object. A baton or a bat. It's a miracle they didn't break it. The doctors are assuming he fought back pretty hard, but the larynx was fractured. The soft-tissue trauma was extensive."

At a press conference in early March, Rock's doctors relayed the successful outcome of the surgery to repair his voice box and said he was breathing on his own. But that he had "suffered severe emotional stress and isn't able to communicate at the moment."

And that's when the two surviving members of Son of a Jack disappeared. No new information came for almost eight weeks when Willington called us up and asked if we wanted an update.

The timing of the update is suspicious. Just one week after the FBI admitted they had no leads and were asking for help from the general public.

That was less than twenty-four hours after Rock was seen mountain-climbing up near Rocky Mountain National Park, just a stone's throw from his home town of Grand Lake. He's been spotted several times since then at a local bar owned by his brother.

People were both relieved that he looked well and outraged that he was off having fun while Kenner McConnell was still under heavy guard at some unnamed rehabilitation facility.

Well, I sigh. I don't really blame them for that.

When I asked Willington about his sudden reappearance, looking happy and healthy, she only replied, "He's suffering an enormous loss and hasn't quite come to terms with what has really happened. He has family and friends—and law enforcement— watching over him and guiding him back to the present."

And when pressed for more information about that statement, Willington refused to offer any more explanation other than, "[He] needs time."

Since then dozens of pictures of Rock have surfaced from the town of Grand Lake, a tiny resort community on the edge of civilization, deep in the Rocky Mountains of Colorado.

I study the picture on that page for a moment. It's a collage of me trolling around Grand Lake. One of me that first night I was drinking at Float's, tucked between Missy and Sean in TJ's back booth. You can't really see my face. But they got a good one of me walking out, takeout container in hand. The caption reads, *Getting food at Float's before disappearing back into the mountains, heavily guarded by the Grand County sheriff's department and more plain-clothes security than people can count.*

Well, I guess those ex-military guys were there all along. I turn to page seventy-nine, where the article continues with a picture of all five of us at the last photoshoot for the second album.

The FBI is interested in any information leading to the identification and capture of those responsible...

It goes on like that. Asking for help to identify the killers. But, if what they say is true about Kenner being knocked out after he was shot, I might be the only person who would recognize them.

Where the fuck is he? I pull out my phone, ready to text again. But it's dead.

No. When I press the power button it starts up. And when my home screen comes on, there's not a single message. Not Missy, not TJ, not Jayce, and not the sheriff.

Why haven't they called?

Bait, my mind whispers. *You're bait, Rock. They're here.* There's no way I got out of town again without people noticing. Even if I did climb down that cliff and walk down the trail to get my truck at Float's, they had to have been watching it. Expecting it.

Unless they were waiting for Saturday night again. I haven't taken off on a Wednesday night before.

I look around warily. I'm in the middle of Denver, obviously. And Grand Lake is hours away. I start the truck up and make my way out of the parking lot before heading west.

The whole drive up into the mountains I search and search for the memories I need. How did I let things get this fucked up in my head?

Melanie, I decide. It has to be Melanie. Watching someone jump off a cliff isn't something you forget, but it's not exactly something you want to think about either. And when you add in the fact that she was pretending to be Missy that night, well, that's a whole mindfuck. But what does it have to do with the band?

Maybe I'm just crazy? I am delusional. Even if I do remember, how would a lawyer for the defense see it?

I shake my head. I'm not crazy. These things that happened to me are crazy and maybe my reaction wasn't typical, but it's not crazy.

My head is spinning with the implications of my mental state. So much so, I almost pull over at Margie's office in Granby. But I don't. Her warning last time was pretty clear. *Do not walk in without an appointment.*

So I continue on the winding road until I reach Grand Lake. I pull down the little road that leads to Float's but the parking lot is empty and there's a sign on the door that says, *Closed.*

I get a very sick feeling in my stomach and the approaching darkness does nothing to quell it.

But just when I think I have that under control, the flashing red and blue lights outside my house almost shut me down.

I pull over on the side of the road because two unmarked cars are in my driveway. TJ's Jeep is there. Gretchen and Sean are standing outside, and as soon as they see my truck, they start running towards me.

A pair of vehicles pull up behind me and I realize I've had security on me the whole way home. Probably since the moment I left here last night.

Bait, Rock. You're bait.

I get out of the car and Sean is on his phone talking as Gretchen throws her arms around me. "Oh, my God, RK. I'm so glad you're back."

"What the fuck is happening?"

"Missy's gone," TJ says, walking out of my front door, coming towards me like he means business. "She's fucking gone." And then he throws a punch, hitting me square in the face.

I throw back. Because fuck that. I get him around the middle and tackle him to the ground. Everyone starts screaming. Hands are pulling at us, people yelling. TJ is livid.

"What the fuck is your problem?" I yell, letting Sean and some cop drag me away from TJ as two more guys do the same to him.

"She's gone and you fucking did it! Where the fuck have you been?"

"What do you mean? I was in Denver looking for Kenner! Your thugs were following me the whole time, right?"

TJ shoots a glance over at the guys who pulled in behind me.

"Hey," one guy says. "He never left our sight, TJ. It's not him."

The other guy agrees. "We didn't see him the whole time he was inside at the hospital, but Missy was gone by then."

I look at TJ, seeing red. "You better fucking explain, asshole."

TJ grabs me by my shirt and drags me down the driveway towards Missy's house. And that's when I notice there are even more cars parked in Missy's driveway. "Look for yourself, RK." He pushes me through the Vetti front door, making a deputy sidestep to get out of my way. "Do you see this shit? What the fuck is this?"

I look at the wall. Covered with pictures of Missy. Or Melanie. Or maybe both. The other wall says Lying Cunt, spray-painted in red letters. There's pictures of Missy undressing at night. The printouts are digitally dated the night I got home.

More pictures of her line another wall. Sleeping in my bed. Taking a shower, her body clearly visible through the glass shower doors of the hallway bathroom. Dated the second time I disappeared one week later.

More. And more. And more. Damning evidence that I didn't do much rock climbing on those days. Because I was secretly stalking Missy and taking pictures of her. Very busy writing threats on the wall.

"I didn't do this," I say. "No way. Someone is setting me up." *The curtains*, I think. The curtains fluttering when I looked over at Missy's house that first night I was home. And then again when I came home from the second blackout.

"Who?" TJ says, shaking me. "Who the fuck hates you so much they kidnapped your girlfriend, RK? We need answers, dammit. Now."

I let him shake me for a second as I put the pieces together. "I saw the article in this month's issue of *Metal Notes*. Whoever killed Ian, Elias and Mo. That's who did this."

"You killed Ian, Elias, and Mo, *Rock*." My brother seethes my stage name at me. "You did it."

Chapter Thirty-Four

I charge TJ like a bull this time. Straight in the chest. He goes flying backwards into the two security guys, setting them off balance and sending all of us to the floor. My arm is back, ready to crash a fist into his face when they pull me up.

I can't even hear the screaming. My mind is nothing but rage. "Fuck you!" I yell at my brother. "Is that what you assholes think?" I look around at all the faces, familiar and unfamiliar alike. "You think I killed Ian, Elias, and Mo? Fuck you!"

"RK," Gretchen says, one hand on my shoulder. "It's not—"

But TJ interrupts her. "You're fucked up, RK. In the head," he says, shaking off the people who are still holding him so he can point to his own head. "What are we supposed to think?"

"Not," I growl, "that I'm a killer." I'm breathing heavy now, the air coming out in long exhales. Sucking it back in like I can't get enough.

"We don't think that, RK," Gretchen tries again. My eyes are on TJ's face. Locked. "We don't think you did it. TJ is wrong. That's not why you're here and he knows that."

TJ glances over to Gretchen and she must be glaring at him, because he looks down at his feet. "You need to talk then, RK." His breathing matches mine, huffing and panting. "Now."

"We just need answers," Gretchen continues. "That's all. And you and Kenner are the only ones who have them and he's not talking until he sees you."

"Where is he?" I stop looking at TJ and look down at Gretchen. "Where is he? Because I just came back from Denver and they said they took him up to Steamboat. Did you know he was there when I was?"

I look around and see nothing but guilt.

"And what the fuck happened to Missy? How long has she been gone?"

A man steps forward. Suit, tie, air of authority. "A few hours at least, RK. We just noticed she was missing. So if you know anything about who attacked the band—"

"But what"—I stop him with a hand—"does that have to do with Missy?"

"We think they came after her," he replies. "So if you could just talk to Kenner and try to remember what the hell happened that night, it might go a long way to saving your girlfriend's life."

She's gone. It hits me then. She's gone and might be dead. And it might be my fault.

"RK?" Gretchen says, shaking my shoulder. "Are you listening?"

I drag my gaze over to her. "Where. Is. Kenner?"

"Across the fucking street," TJ says, wiping some blood from his mouth. "He's across the fucking street. And whatever the fuck you two are hiding about what happened that night in Big Bear, you better get over it. Because if Missy dies because of—" He stops short.

But I know what he was going to say. "If Missy dies because of what?" I ask him. "Because of me, just like Melanie?"

"RK," Gretchen says. "Get out of here, TJ, you're not helping!" I've never heard Gretchen yell, but she yells now. "Get out and leave him alone."

TJ punches a wall on his way out of the house and then Gretchen is right up in my face again. "Go talk to Kenner, RK. He's in your house. We *need* you two right now. You need to figure out what happened. You had to have seen something, RK. Anything might help."

I realize the two security guys are still holding me, so I shrug them off and walk down the hallway and exit the house. TJ is leaning up against his Jeep, arms crossed, glaring at me. We lock eyes, see the rage like we're looking in a mirror, and then I refocus on the front window of my house.

It takes me a minute to realize what I'm seeing.

Kenner. Sitting at my piano.

I feel happy and sad at the same time. I have to close my eyes for a second before getting myself together and walking through my open front door.

I round the corner into the music room and stare at his back. "Kenner," I breathe out the word. It's not a hello, or a question. It's just… relief.

He nods his head slowly, but doesn't turn around to look at me. His light brown hair is longer than normal and I can see the massive scar alongside of his ear where the bullet barely missed his brain. It's mostly healed now. And his arms are bent, his hand balled up into fists and resting on the cover over the keys.

"Rock," he says, standing up and turning around to face me.

He's wearing a faded black Metallica t-shirt and a pair of jeans. But the only thing I see are his arms. Elias was the only Son of a Jack member with tattoos. He only had one and it was on his stomach. Kenner always said they were a way to hide who you were and become someone else, so he swore up and down he'd never get one.

But his arms are tatted up now. The beginnings of two full sleeves are outlined in black. He's inked up from wrist to shoulder. Kenner shrugs, reading my mind. "I'm done, Rock." He has to swallow hard to get the rest of the words out. "That guy is gone."

I want to hug him—shit, kiss the fucker on the mouth, that's how happy I am to see him here. Standing. Arms working. Talking. Whole. But I get the feeling that Kenner is not interested in my affection right now. So I have to swallow all that shit down and force myself to stand still. "I'm so fucking sorry, man."

He frowns and lifts his hands up in a little shrug gesture that doesn't reach his shoulders. "What are you sorry for?" He studies me just as carefully as I did him, his eyes resting on the scar at the base of my throat. "Living?"

I realize he's asking me that because that's what he's sorry for. I know this guy so well. My best friend. Ever.

So I nod. I nod and say, "Yeah." Because I am. I'm sorry I lived. I'm sorry I'm standing here and Elias, Mo, and Ian aren't.

Kenner lets out a breath that might be relief and says the words so I don't have to. "I'd rather be dead."

Movement outside catches my attention. The whole crowd of people—cops, friends, brother—all stand there in front of the house waiting for answers. "Do you remember what happened? Did you see who it was?"

He nods. Slowly. So very, very slowly.

"Who?" My heart starts racing.

Kenner looks over his shoulder, a quick glance to check where everyone is at outside, then brings his gaze back to me. "Do you have somewhere private we can talk in here? They said they found cameras in every room. She was watching you."

"What? Who? She?"

Kenner glances over his shoulder again. "Private, Rock. We need to have this talk in private because obviously, this bitch is not fucking around. Your girlfriend is dead if we do this wrong."

Those words reverberate through my head like the music when we play in a stadium. I have a flash of a face. Blonde hair. Blue eyes. Skin tanned from days spent in the sun.

But looks are deceiving. I actually picture her mouth moving as she tells me that. We are hanging off the side of a mountain. Swinging and taking pictures of the things we dare to do. Things most people will never do. The only thing between us and death are the harnesses attached to a toprope anchor bolted right into the sheer rock face of a cliff.

"Rock?" Kenner says, bringing me back to him. "We don't have much time. She'll kill her, Rock. Just like she killed us. We don't have much time. And if your friends think they can stop her from doing that, they're wrong." He hesitates, once again shooting a sideways glance over his shoulder. "She's insane. And she's been ten steps ahead of everyone since this started. They're all wrong."

I look around the room, then glance down the hallway to the kitchen. "The studio. It was locked until a few days ago. I doubt anyone got in there."

"Take me," Kenner says.

I turn and walk down the hall, Kenner's boots thudding on the tiles as he follows. I key in the code and open the door once the lock releases. The lights are still on from the last time I was down here with Missy.

Missy. I can't lose her. And if Kenner has an idea of how to get her back and what the fuck we're up against, well…

I wave him forward and he grips the rail hard as he descends, an indication that he's not quite whole yet. I follow him down and we end up in the production room. He sits in the long, brown leather couch and I perch on the stool in front of the monitor, my nerves frayed with everything that's happened today.

"Hook my phone up," Kenner says, tossing it to me. I catch it, then find a white cord in a drawer to connect it to the computers. "My lock code is three four eight seven." I look over at him, so many questions. "I'd do it myself but…" He hesitates. "But my fingers are still trying to figure shit out."

I glance down at his hands, bunched up into fists, and understand. He only looks whole on the outside, just like I did when I came home. But he's not. As fucked as it sounds, I'm the one who's got his shit together right now.

That scares me a little. I've never been that guy. Not since Melanie died. I've always been the fuckup. The partier. The addict. Kenner was the responsible one. He was the rock, not me.

I tap in the code and his phone unlocks.

"Go to the photo album." He waits as I do that. "No one got into my phone, Rock. No one has my code and even though they asked, and the cops wanted it, there was no good reason for a judge to let them. I wasn't a suspect and they thought it was random."

I look over at him again. "It wasn't, was it?"

He shakes his head. "But I don't blame you for forgetting her. I really don't, dude." I'm about to ask who, but I see the warning on his face. "Open the album dated March last year."

I take a deep breath and double-click. I know what March last year was. That's when the band forced me into rehab.

Pictures pop open, hundreds of them. But none of them are of rehab.

It's me. And Kenner. And the blonde girl.

Everything slips into place as Kenner starts talking.

Chapter Thirty-Five

"It was a nice day," Kenner says, his voice devoid of emotion. "Hot, but not too hot. Blue sky to match that girl's eyes, you know?"

I nod, my eyes glued to the girl as I flash the pictures on the screen one by one.

"And I knew you were in a bad place, man. I knew it for months. Maybe since the day I met you, ya know? All the baggage you left behind up here. And I knew you weren't right. The blackouts. The disappearances. But you always came home. And it didn't take us long to figure out you were out rock climbing."

"Yeah," I whisper, remembering back to those days.

"We thought it was doing you good. So we let you go. That was our first mistake. The second was trusting that beautiful psychopath."

He's talking about the girl. "Alice," I say, picturing her at the bar the other night handing me those magazines. Her expression. The way it pleaded with me to remember her.

"You know what?" Kenner asks.

"What?" I say, tearing my gaze away from the screen and focusing on him.

"You should never trust a girl named Alice. It's just all wrong. And everything about this girl was wrong."

"Except her deceiving looks," I finish for him.

He nods. "Mo met her that day," Kenner says, pointing to the pictures. "I'd met her a while back. And I did trust her. We climbed together for seven… eight months? I trusted her with my fucking life out there on those cliffs." He looks down at his hands, wringing them together. "I'm so fucking sorry, dude. I'm the one who needs to apologize to you, because this is all my fault."

Memories start flashing through my head as I click through the images.

You're mine, Rock.

Forget about the past, Rock. It's just me and you now.

Try some of this, Rock. It'll make you feel better.

I did try those pills. Just little white pills that made the whole world smaller. Made everything inside me feel better. Made the past melt away.

Until it didn't. But she was there. She was always there with something else to make it better. More pills, then needles. Then I was addicted.

"Mo knew immediately. Like…" Kenner exhales out a long breath. "Like instantaneously. And he came to me that day." Kenner nods at the screen of the climbing pics. I start flipping through them faster, searching for Mo. "And he said, 'Dude, this girl is psycho. She knows everything about me. Everything about *us*.'"

"And she did," Kenner continues. "She did. You know, you hear about stalkers, right? And we'd laugh. Because…" Kenner and I both grimace. Because we had no idea how crazy people can get. "Because they're fans, right? They love us. Who are we to complain when people love us?"

We are silent for a few moments. I picture that image I just saw in the magazine a few hours ago. "That's not love," I say. "What she did to us wasn't love."

He agrees with a slight nod. "So that night, after we packed shit up and headed home, you went with Alice and Mo and I were in another car. We decided on rehab. I mean, we knew you were using, but we also knew this girl, somehow, some way, was the one responsible for that."

"And you forced me to go away and never talk to her again."

"This is all our fault. We didn't know how sick this bitch was until she showed up in Big Bear and started shooting."

I see the danger now. I see it very, very fucking clearly. "If she has Missy—"

"She's dead, dude. If we do this wrong, she's dead. She knows you love this girl. Jayce filled me in on what's been happening up here and hell, man. I'm surprised Alice hasn't killed you both yet."

"Do you know where she is?" I ask, just as the panic starts to kick in. "Kenner? Do you know?"

He gets up from the couch and takes his phone, unplugging it from the computer, and starts awkwardly fumbling with the touchscreen to pull up email. "She's been sending me these for about a week now. I can only assume when they reported I was awake she got antsy."

He hands the phone to me. "But I have no clue what it means."

I take the phone and read the messages. They are short sentences. About fifteen of them. I scroll up and start reading them from start to finish. "They're verses," I say. "Like a song."

"Bitch is crazy, Rock. Straight-up crazy. But I think it's like, one of those psycho clues killers send to their victims. Or cops, you know? I think there's a message in there. And I think you are the only one who can figure it out."

Kissing her, not me? the first message says. *So young and innocent, up against that tree.*

"Do you know what that means?"

I know it. I know it immediately. "I did that interview with *Metal Notes*, way back when we first started releasing music on the internet. Remember? Mo was brand new, just barely with us. And no one thought it was a good idea. We were too new. We didn't want to paint ourselves into a corner with contracts and shit. We wanted to be a mystery, hold our cards close. But I wanted to do it."

To piss off my father, I realize now. So he'd see it. We must have a hundred *Metal Notes Magazines* down here in the studio. Packed away in boxes. He read that fucking magazine every month and I knew he'd see this too.

"The Valentine's Day interview. What was the best kiss of your life?"

We stare at each other for a few seconds.

And then I say, "She took Missy there."

"Where?"

"That waterfall in the woods. It's not far from here. She fucking took her there." I get up to tell TJ and the cops. But Kenner is suddenly agile and quick, because he grabs me before I get to the stairs.

"Don't tell them, Rock. If they get there and spook this bitch, she will do crazy shit. And I don't mean to be a dick, but if your girlfriend is even still alive, she won't be once they storm that place with cops."

He's right. Alice is not sane. She will shoot first just like she did up in Big Bear. I see it now, for real. In my head I play that night out just the way it happened. Mo answering the door. Bang. He flies backwards, blood spattering everywhere. Ian was next, bits and pieces of Mo blasted him in the face and then she shot him too. Elias and Kenner lunged at her. I was on the other side of the room, looking out the window. Looking at the side the mountain we were gonna ski the next day. Elias took a bullet to the chest, and Kenner ducked…

"Alice has been in town for weeks, Kenner. She knows everyone is looking for the killer. I saw her at Float's. Fucking TJ hired her as a waitress." And then I get a sick feeling in my stomach as I picture him yelling at her in the hallway the other night. "And he fired her when she approached me on Monday."

"How far is this place? We have to go, Rock. The only chance you have of getting your girlfriend back alive is to take her. Talk Alice into letting her go. Lie, dude. Just flat out fucking lie. We cannot threaten her or she will shoot us all." He points to the scar on the side of his head as proof.

Yeah, I think in my head. *He's right.* She already killed Ian, Mo, and Elias and took her best shot at Kenner. "But how do we get there? There's like two dozen cops outside."

Kenner shrugs. "I guess we'll have to explain and hope to God they understand."

"Wait," I say. "I have bolts on the cliff at the back of the house. That place is only about two miles away if we cut through the woods. We could hike up there." I walk to a door that looks like a closet on the wall opposite of the stairs. But it's not a closet. I pull the door open to reveal the gun safe and Kenner is right up next to me, the Kentucky boy in him already understanding. We shoot each other a look and then we both nod as I punch in the code and open it up.

We take two high-powered mountain rifles and two Glocks. We're just checking the barrels and looking for some ammo when I hear TJ yelling upstairs.

Kenner and I shoot a quick look up at the door to the kitchen, then each other. "Get rid of him," Kenner says.

I grab the bullets and cartridges we'll need and shove them into his open hands. "My climbing racks are in the front room. Grab them. I'll meet you out on the back deck."

I take the stairs two at a time and burst through the door just as TJ is opening it. I push him back into the kitchen, closing the door behind me.

"What the fuck is going on down there, RK? Do you not understand how serious this situation is?"

I drag him through the kitchen towards the front door. "I just need a few more minutes, Teej. He's fucking traumatized, OK? He needs a minute."

"We don't have a minute, Rock." He sneers the stage name and even though it pisses me off, I focus on Missy. If Alice really has her, and she's still alive, she won't be for long.

"Ten minutes," I say. "I think he might be able to remember who did it, OK? But he's having a hard time, TJ. Just give me ten goddamned minutes!"

There's a whole crowd of people in the front room and I know Kenner needs to be here to get our gear to go down the cliff, so I stick my fingers on my tongue and whistle to get everyone's attention. "Out!" I say. "I need everyone out. You have no warrant, so get the fuck out and give me a few minutes to get this shit straight."

There's a roar of protest from everyone... except Jayce. I realize she knows more than the rest. Kenner must've told her something. Maybe not everything, but something. When I look at her she gives me a little nod. "Out," Jayce says. "He's right. Kenner needs a minute to get himself together. I won't have you guys forcing him into something that will affect his mental state afterward. Everyone out."

Say what you will about Jayce, but she knows how to command a room. They call her all kinds of names in LA. Bitch, mostly. But formidable is also at the top of the list. She stands toe to toe with the guy I can only assume is the lead detective, yelling up into his face until he's so worked up, his partner drags him outside to calm him down. TJ is the last to leave, so I follow him out, shutting the door behind me so Kenner can get to the gear.

"Ten minutes, TJ," I tell him as I lead him down the driveway. Jayce is talking to Gretchen and Sean, who both look over at me with frantic looks. "He knows what happened. Maybe even who did it. He just needs to let it out in his own way. Just like I needed to come up here and see all you guys before I could remember."

"Do you remember?" TJ asks, whirling around to look at me.

"Some of it," I say. "But not who did it," I lie. "Ten minutes. Please." I beg. I beg for real. "Because if I lose Missy..." I have to look away and take a deep breath.

TJ huffs out an exasperated breath of air. "I'm timing you, RK. Ten minutes and then we're taking his ass down to City Hall for questioning."

I nod. "Be right back." And then I run back into the house, slam the door, and head to the back deck. Kenner is there, looking over the railing at the sheer cliff below.

"Can you rappel?" I ask him. "I know you can't climb, Kenner. But can you rappel down?"

He looks at his hands like he doesn't recognize them, but nods. "I can do it."

We slip the harnesses up over our hips and buckle them tight. Then I hand him a sling with gear on it, and start snapping on carabiners and cams just in case. I swing a leg over the edge, clip myself in to the ropes that are bolted to the rock just below the deck, and then stare at Kenner. "I've got it, OK? We'll go down together."

"Hey," Kenner says, trying to smile as he adjusts his rifle strap over his shoulder. "That's the way we came up, right?" And then he swings his leg over, grasping for the rope as he clips himself in too. "I trust you, Rock. With my life, dude. The only reason that bitch didn't shoot me straight through my brain was because you took her down."

"Damn," I say, fucking with the rope as I get us ready. "I wish I could remember that part. It sucks when your most heroic deed gets lost in your fucked-up head."

We lean back and start our walk down the cliff and a few seconds later we are jumping down long stretches until we land on the ground. We unhook ourselves, and then I grab Kenner by the shoulder and point into the woods. "This way."

Please, God, I pray as I run. *Don't let that psychopath get the rest of the people I love.*

Chapter Thirty-Six

Less than a mile into the run we hear them calling our names. I am ahead, even though before the bloodbath of Big Bear, Kenner could outrun me any time of day. But I've been in recovery longer than him. He just woke up a few weeks ago and it doesn't take a genius to figure he didn't have the access to the gym like I did.

He looks at me with a question on his mind and I can tell we're both thinking the same thing. What will they think of this little turn of events?

Guilty, is how I read it. Maybe they don't all think I killed the band, but TJ planted that thought in their heads. They can't *not* think it. Not really. I might've been the one in the dark a few hours ago, but now I am infinitely better informed.

They have no idea who Alice is. Aside from a waitress who broke TJ's strict rule to leave me alone at the bar. But with each pounding step over the rough mountain terrain, I remember bits and pieces of our time together. Climbing partners.

I'm not an elite climber. My God-given gifts come in the form of music and songwriting. But I'm good. She's good. And together, at least on the side of a mountain, we were much better than good. We took risks, and we only took risks knowing the other was equipped to react if the need arose.

I put my life in her hands.

It makes me sick to think about it.

The sun is not yet over the western mountains, but in here, under the thick canopy of evergreen trees, it might as well be night. The shadows creep in around us and Kenner's breathing becomes more and more labored.

"I can't see shit," he whisper-yells.

"Don't panic yet," I say. "We're still a mile out."

"What if that crazy bitch has booby traps or something?"

I look at him funny as I slow down so he can keep pace.

"What?" he asks, reading my mind.

"She's not the Viet Cong, Kenner. She's a psycho girl. And there's two of us. We have weapons this time."

"I'm just saying, she's got to know I talked to you. And she's got to know I showed you the texts. So she's got to know we're on our way. Especially since those dumbasses back at your house are out there calling our fucking names."

"We'll get her," I tell him.

"I'm gonna shoot that bitch in the head. What comes around, goes around."

I nod. I can't disagree. But all I care about is Missy. If she's hurt… if she's dead, please God, don't let her be dead… I'll make sure Alice never comes out of these woods.

A half a mile later Kenner is wasted. He's gasping, so we slow to a walk so he can catch his breath.

"Sorry," he whispers into the night.

"Don't be," I say back. "We go in ready. It's no good rushing in spent."

"How the fuck do you know your way around here in the dark?" he asks.

"This was my playground, Kenner. Less than five hundred people live in my town and my house might as well be another world away. You don't get into town on your feet using a road. I had my brother, I had the Vetti twins, and we had these woods. I shot my first deer about fifty yards that way," I say, pointing off to the left. "There's trail access about half a mile up the road from our house."

"If there's trail access—"

But his words are cut off by the sound of dirt bikes off in the distance.

"—then TJ knows where to start looking for us," I finish for him.

We break into a slow jog and suddenly the sound of the rack of gear clanging at our hips makes way too much noise.

"We should take them off," Kenner says, pointing to our harnesses.

But I shake my head. "There's a cliff where we're going. Alice might have something up her sleeve. Besides, I'm not going in stealth mode."

"What the fuck do you mean? We're gonna look through these rifle scopes, get her fucking brain in our sights, and then pull the goddamned trigger."

"No," I say, coming to a stop and thrusting my arm out in front of his chest to make him do the same. "I'm walking in there racked up and making noise. You stay behind and cover me."

I feel like we're playing war games or something. Invincible. And it's wrong for some reason. Because Alice has already shown everybody involved, this is no game for her.

"Do you hear it?" I ask Kenner as I stare straight ahead.

He squints his eyes, like he's straining his ears.

"The waterfall," I whisper. "It's right up there."

He nods. He hears it.

"That's where she is. I'll go—"

"Wait," Kenner whispers, creeping forward. "I think I see a light."

We both walk as softly and as carefully as we can, until there's a break in the aspen leaves.

"What the fuck is that?" Kenner asks, looking up at the glow on the side of a cliff.

My stomach sinks. No. No. No.

"Rock," he says again. "What the fuck *is* that?"

"A portaledge tent."

"A what?" But then it must sink in. "She's crazy. She's fucking crazy."

And she is. Because about a hundred feet up the side of the cliff, just off to the left of the waterfall, is a hanging tent. There's a lantern on inside, so we have a pretty clear view of the person moving around within.

"Let's shoot her from here," Kenner says.

"No," I whisper-yell back. "That might not be her. What if it's just some local climber—" But I stop talking mid-sentence. Because it's not some local climber. Anyone with intermediate skill could climb that wall. No one needs to spend the night on a portaledge to get to the top. "It might be Missy," I say instead.

We know it's not Missy. It's Alice. But if it's Alice, then where *is* Missy?

Adrenaline rushes through my body and the panic is back. *Don't let her be dead. Don't let her be dead.*

"I got you, Rock. But if the bitch even blinks wrong, you shoot her, Rock. You shoot her." Kenner is grabbing me by the shoulders and shaking that into me.

I nod. "I will, don't worry." I tuck the Glock into my sock and pull my pant leg over it, then drop the rope and adjust the rifle on my shoulder. "No matter what happens," I tell Kenner, staring into his shadow-covered face, "do not come out. You shoot from here, you understand? Do not come out until she's dead."

He nods yes, but I know he doesn't mean it.

"Kenner," I say firmly. "I mean it. I need you, man. I need you to live." But it's the wrong thing to say. I can read his fucking mind. I can practically hear him saying the same thing back to me. We need each other. There's no telling how far we will fall if we don't both come back tonight. So I amend. "I need you to stay alive and get me out of here if she tries to kill us."

We both look over our shoulders as the sound of dirt bikes once again comes from the distance. If TJ comes in the middle of this, we're all dead.

"Be careful," Kenner says as I start walking forward.

I will, I think in my head as I find the real trail that leads up here and make my way out into the clearing, thankful that the sound of the waterfall blocks any chance of Alice hearing us coming.

Chapter Thirty-Seven

I make it all the way to the waterfall with no notice or movement from the person inside the tent.

What if this isn't Alice? What if she has Missy somewhere else?

"Rock," her now-familiar voice calls down to me. "I knew you'd come back to me."

I look up and see her blonde hair in the golden light of the lantern inside the portaledge. "Come down and talk to me, Alice," I yell up.

She laughs. It sends a chill up my spine and the tiny hairs on the back of my neck bristle to attention. Spooks me the same way a bear might spook a dog out on the trail. "Who did you come here for?"

"You," I lie. "I came for you. I just got my memory back—" I stop talking because she's out of the portaledge and climbing on the ropes. In one swift move she cuts a tether keeping the tent stable on the side of the cliff with a knife, and it dips downward.

I am in shock as I watch. But the muffled scream and the tipping of the other body inside the tent shuts me the fuck up. *Missy.* "Alice!" I yell. "What the fuck are you doing?"

She glares down at me and I'm secretly wishing I had told Kenner to shoot first. But Alice is not even in his line of sight. He can't shoot her from the spot where I left him.

There are a lot of redundant tethers used to keep the cliff tent stable, but it doesn't *look* very stable. It looks like she's deliberately missing a few key straps.

"I know who you came for," Alice yells down. "And you're not going to save her. She's going to jump, Rock. Just like her twin. Do you remember telling me about it?"

No. I shake my head. No. I did not tell her anything. Did I? Jesus Christ. Is that why I was blacking out in LA? Every time I remembered prom night I took off and found... this psycho girl to share my crazy with?

Keep calm, Rock. Keep calm and just tell her what she wants to hear. "Alice, please—" I start again.

"Drop your rifle." It's a nonnegotiable command because she's got her knife pressed against the nylon strap holding another part of the portaledge in place.

I drop the rifle.

"Climb up," she says. "Climb up and see me." Her expression softens. She's stunningly beautiful when the psycho isn't leaking through. "It's been so fucking long, Rock. I can't believe they took you away from me and you never looked back. Why, Rock? Why?" Her voice cracks like she's about to cry. But I don't trust her. Not one bit.

"I was sick—"

"Climb!" she shouts. It echoes off the walls of the mountain and I have a moment of panic that TJ will hear her and come at just the wrong moment.

I walk over to the wall of rock and look up. It's not a difficult climb. Not really. There are plenty of foot and hand holds. But even so, it's practically dark now. I have no toprope to save me if I make a mistake. A fall from twenty feet could kill someone if they land the wrong way.

And climbing is the last thing on my mind. My head is filled with possibilities. Endings. Bad endings and worst possible outcomes.

I kick off my boots because I've got fucking boots on. There's no way I can climb this wall with boots on.

"You better hurry if you want to save your girlfriend," Alice snarls down at me.

Shoot her, I think. *Please, Kenner, shoot this bitch.*

There's a crack of a gun, but it doesn't come from behind me. I look up and find Alice grinning into the woods. "I got him," she yells. "I got him!" Her cackling laugh echoes through the canyon.

No, Rock, I tell myself. *She didn't.* I need to hold on to that. I can't lose Kenner. He's still there, he's got to be.

"Climb, Rock," she sings from above me. "Or I'll shoot you next."

I reach up, find a hand hold, then another, and bring my foot up. Do I really know how to climb?

I have my doubts.

But I let instinct take over. I remember the days in the sun, hanging off cliffs by ropes. I saw the pictures on Kenner's phone.

I know I can do this. I have to do this.

My hand goes up again. Then a foot, and a hand, and a foot. I repeat it, then hesitate when I lose my footing and small rocks go sliding down the cliff wall.

I look up, and see the tent moving. Not because it's swinging. It's not quite swinging. Yet. But because there's someone inside all right. Missy is squirming around like her hands are tied behind her back. And she's probably got some kind of gag in her mouth, otherwise she'd be calling out for me.

I keep going. One hand, one foot. Pull myself up and do it again. When I'm about six feet underneath Alice, I look up. Her foot is raised, her knee bent, like she's about to stomp on my face and kick me off the rock.

"Alice," I say, breathless. Her face is only illuminated on one side now, all sunlight gone. It is night.

The sound of my voice must change her mind, because she plants her foot into a loop of rope tethered to the rock by an anchor. "I like your new voice."

I don't know that I can actually hear her say the words. The waterfall is so close and the thunder of the water crashing down below is deafening. But I see her lips move. Very clearly.

She did this to my voice.

A memory flashes through my mind. Her distorted face. Not beautiful. Not at all beautiful. She bares her teeth at me like an animal as she swings a baton...

I wheeze in the present, gasping a little at the memory.

But then I see her with the gun.

Kenner ducks, the bullet grazing the side of his head, leaving behind an angry red gash in his scalp. I am running before he hits the ground. Alice turns towards me, smiling as she pulls the trigger again. She misses me, because I don't go down, but my foot catches on a bunched up rug and I go sailing towards the floor. Alice is laughing as she points the gun back at Kenner and shoots. Blood goes splattering, some of it hitting me in the face.

"What the fuck," I yell. "What the fuck are you doing!"

Alice pulls out a black metal wand from her coat pocket. She flicks it open, making the wand extend and lock into its fully open position, and then she brings it crashing down on my neck. My whole world blacks out from the pain. It takes whole seconds to come back to reality, choking and gasping for air through the damage to my throat.

Kenner is absolutely still. And maybe Alice doesn't like that? Maybe she wants a fight out of him. Maybe she was counting on Kenner to beg.

My eyes go fuzzy for a second and then refocus, zeroing in on her foot, just a few feet away. I realize I can stop her. Maybe even save Kenner if he's not dead. I lunge forward, grab at her ankle with both hands, and pull. She falls to the side, the gun going off.

"Kenner?" I try to say it, but I can't.

Sirens sound off in the distance and Alice gets to her feet, the black baton still in her hand. She brings it down on Kenner's arm, right in the crook of the elbow.

He's not dead. I know this because he screams. The scream turns into a wail the second, and third, and fourth times.

The sirens get louder and Alice looks down at me and smiles. She aims the gun at my head and pulls the trigger.

But I hear nothing but the deafening sound of a click.

She looks at the gun like it betrayed her. And the sirens are so close now, I almost dare to hope.

That's when her foot comes crashing down on my throat one last time and everything goes black. This time it stays that way.

"I'm glad you like it," I tell Alice, back on the side of this cliff in the woods. "I'm glad you like the new voice."

She smiles. Like I said just the right thing.

I reach down, lift my pant leg up, and pull the gun out. She shoots, misses. I shoot, miss, but I hit the rock behind her head and a little gash appears on the side of her face, her hands immediately flying up to shield herself. Her gun drops to the ground, but I can still see the knife, attached to a cord around her wrist. She gets it in her grip, lashes out at me, but I lunge for the drooping fabric of the portaledge, making it swing and sway as I grab a hold. My gun is forgotten in that moment and it goes crashing to the ground with hers.

Missy's muffled screams inside the tent stop me cold. Her body rolls, bumping into me. One of my hands loses its grip, and I swing again, taking Missy with me as the portaledge jostles a hundred feet up in the air.

"You're not going to live through this, Rock."

"Neither are you, bitch," I say. "How do you like the sound of those words? If we go, we're taking you with us."

She's climbing, making the portaledge rock and sway. Missy is panting hard inside the tent. I can hear her desperate nose breathing even over the sound of the waterfall. She is inches from me. And a whole other world away. Separated by the micro-thin fabric of the nylon tent.

The tent dips, making Missy crash against me. I grab hold of the tent and swing a leg up over an aluminum pole meant to stabilize it on the side of the cliff. When I am secure, I look up. Alice is grinning down at me, her knife poised to cut through one of three remaining straps anchored to the cliff.

"Shoot her!" I yell. I yell it so loud my throat is on fire. "Shoot this fucking bitch, Kenner!"

"He's dead," Alice says, spitting the words out from above. She starts sawing the knife across the strap. The woven nylon strands begin to unravel from the sharp edge. "He's dead—"

Her head splatters against the cliff and then her limp body falls. Stops, because she's clipped into the ropes by her harness. But her weight jerks the tent, placing more tension on the tethers.

The strap she was cutting when Kenner shot her comes apart and we fall together.

Chapter Thirty-Eight

We all snap back up, all our collective body weight pulling on the last two remaining tethers. One attached to the edge of the portaledge and one attached to the middle.

Alice hangs almost upside down by her harness, her sky-blue eyes still open, still haunting me from the other side of death, the entire side of her head is just… gone.

"Cut her down," Kenner yells from below. "Cut her body down, Rock! Before that fucking tent comes apart from her weight!"

I grab her knife, slip it off her wrist, and then start sawing the rope attached to each of the carabiners attached to her harness. She falls to the ground with a sickening thud. It almost sounds like a smashing watermelon.

A gunshot goes off and I chance a look below. Kenner is standing over Alice screaming. "This is for Ian, cunt!" Another shot goes off. "And this one is for Mo. Fuck you, bitch! One more for Elias. One for each of them!"

"Missy," I say.

She's crying. Sobbing. And that's not good. I swing the rest of my body onto what's left of the portaledge and frantically feel around for the tent opening through all the loose fabric.

When I find the opening, I pull myself in and scramble over to her. The portaledge swings wildly with the weight and Missy starts screaming behind her duct-taped mouth.

"Shh," I say, ripping the tape off. She gasps for air and I hold her face tight, looking into her eyes. "Shh," I say, kissing her nose. "I've got you. Shh, take deep, deep breaths."

I give her a second to follow, then flip her over and cut the tape off her wrists. There's blood, my hands are shaking, but a few shallow scratches are better than the alternative.

"Be still," I tell Missy. "I'm going to make you a harness. OK?"

She's still gasping for air. In shock. I can only imagine what she went through to get up into the portaledge. Alice had to have hoisted her. She was probably bound and gagged at the time. How fucking terrifying.

I grab all four double shoulder-length slings from around my neck and start making a harness for Missy. She's crying hysterically. "RK," she says. "RK, don't move! You're going to tip us over!"

She's panicking. "Missy," I say, taking her face in my hands again. "Trust me, baby. I know what I'm doing. You're not going to fall, OK? We are not going to fall. That psycho bitch is not going to win. You understand me?"

She nods and I go back to fastening the slings together with carabiners until I have the length I need. I fold the entire length of strap in half, tuck a loop into the waistband of her jeans, then pass both ends between her legs. I bring that around her thighs and finish it up by threading it through the loop still in her jeans and wrapping it around her waist until I'm almost out of length. I secure the ends with a knot, then clip a locking carabiner around the waist straps and the loop in her jeans.

"OK," I say, looking down at her. "Missy?" She's looking at the harness like she's living through a nightmare.

And she is. My nightmare.

"I'm so sorry, baby. But we're gonna have to get off this thing, OK? It's not stable enough."

"We could fall," she screams. "We're going to fall, RK!"

"No," I say, shaking my head at her. "We're not. This is how it's done, babe. This is how it's done." I take her hand. "Now follow me. Crawl to the edge. Let me get out first—"

"No," Missy says, her fingers clamping around my arm. "RK, please," she whines. "Please don't leave me up here."

"I'm not, Miss. I'm not. I'm going to hook myself into a cam and then you're going to clip yourself to me. Understand?"

She shakes her head no, but I nod at her. "You do understand and this is how we're getting off the side of this cliff. Now calm down and let me save you."

"We're going to fall, RK. Just like Melanie!"

I grab her face. Firmly. And stare into her eyes. "We are not going to fall. Do you hear me? And Melanie didn't fall. She jumped. We're not going to jump either." She just looks at me like a deer in the headlights. "Do you hear me?" I growl.

Her eyes dart back and forth, looking into my eyes for truth. And trust. She finds what she's looking for, because she takes a deep breath and finally nods her head.

"Stay here," I say. "I'm going to crawl out, then you follow when I'm secure. Stay on the ledge, OK? It's still connected. These things are fucking tough, Missy. We're only leaving it because we have to stack the odds in our favor. Once I get us anchored we can stay there all night, baby. All night. We won't fall. I promise."

"OK," she says. "OK."

I crawl over to the exit, get another carabiner off my harness and secure the tent flap to a rope, so it's out of my way, and then I swing out onto what's left of the rope Alice was using as her anchor.

"RK!" Missy screams.

I didn't tell her about this part on purpose. But I've got the rope, and it's still got a carabiner attached to the foot loop she was using, so I take a shoulder-length sling from around my neck and clip myself to it. Alice is a good climber, but I don't trust what's left of her rigging, so I shove a cam into a crack in the rock and release the spring. That creates another anchor point for us. I clip myself to that too, then reach my hand out for Missy. She moves forward and the portaledge straps creak.

When I look up, one of the last two tethers is swiftly unraveling. "Missy," I say, my hands furiously connecting two more shoulder-length slings together. "Quick," I say, looking up at the compromised tether. "Clamp that strap to your waist."

She hears the panic in my voice and her fingers fumble.

"Quick!" I shout. "Quick, quick!"

The last of the nylon fibers come apart just as she manages to get the clamp on and the whole tent goes sliding away. The tent opening flaps back down, and then the weight of her body is pulling on my harness, letting me know the only thing between her and the ground is… me.

She's crying now. Full-on sobbing. I don't blame her one bit. But I need her calm. "Missy," I yell. "You're OK. I've got you, baby. I've still got you." But my harness could slip over my hips from her tugging weight. It's not there yet, but it could happen and I do not want that to happen. I need her up here, in my arms. Safe.

"Claw your way free of the tent, Missy. I need you to see my face."

Her arms start frantically swiping at the tent fabric until she finally peeks through.

I laugh. "You're OK," I say. Now that I can see her, everything is OK. "I need you to reach for my hand and let me pull you up. I'm not going to be happy until I've got you clamped to me." I pat my chest, my hand over my heart. "Right up here, Missy. I need your cheek right here."

She takes a deep, deep breath and her foot finds a temporary place in one of the aluminum frame parts. She steps up, making the collapsed portaledge sway and swing. It dips a little, but it's enough to give her the crucial few inches.

Our fingers touch. My hand grabs hers, and I pull. She climbs up my body like a monkey and I have slings ready to clip her in.

"I got you," I say. "I told you, we're not going to fall here tonight. We're just fine."

"Hey!" a voice shouts from below. Then more voices.

I look down and see Kenner, his hands gripping his hair like he wants to pull it out. And a small crowd of people, who look like hikers, but I can't be sure from this distance. They are all clapping and shouting.

"We're good," I yell. "We're good."

Missy wraps her arms around me and cries.

I hear people from above. Then faces leaning down over the cliff. Sean and TJ. A few of the deputies from the house. They are yelling too, but the sound doesn't carry this way, so I can't make it out.

"Thank you, RK," Missy whispers in my ear.

My fingers dig into her hair as we swing there, a hundred feet in the air, suspended by ropes. "I told you, we're going to do this together, baby. And I meant it. You're stuck with me now."

Lots of people appear after that. No helicopters. *Please.* This is Grand Lake. Everyone up top stands around and tries to figure it out the old-fashioned way.

Jayce eventually makes her way down to the canyon below and lies down on the ground next to Kenner. He refused to leave until Missy and I are back on terra firma. He even had a little chest-pounding fight with a few of the deputies when they tried to make him.

His face is turned up to me. He's too far away to really see his expression. But I think it's one of peace. He shot Alice so many times in the head, she's unrecognizable. I can't fault him for that. Not one bit. She deserved to die today. And we deserved to live.

Jayce leans over and says something into his ear. I can see that smile for sure. They laugh. And I feel like this is a turning point for us. The period at the end of a sentence. Or maybe just the first word of a new chapter.

Hours later we are rescued, lowered down slowly after setting up some top ropes. Not by authorities, but by hikers. Because that's how we roll out here on the edge of the civilized world. We don't have rescue teams. We have friends. And family. And strangers who are more than willing to pull us out of a tight spot when we need it.

"I think I'll stay a while," I tell Missy, once we are finally home, freshly showered, and crawling into my childhood bed. "Grand Lake isn't so bad, I guess."

She says nothing, just snuggles her face into my neck. I'm not in a hurry to push her into reality. She can take her time dealing. I just want her to know I'm gonna be here for as long as that takes.

And maybe, I think, as her breathing deepens and she finally falls into a steady state of utter exhaustion, *maybe I'll put the band back together.*

Epilogue

We approach Float's by boat because we wanted to keep the last act on the down low for the music festival. Missy's band is just finishing up when Sean pulls up to the back of the dock. Kenner is squinting his eyes into the sun, but when I look up to follow his gaze I see nothing but blue sky.

"Endless," Kenner says, just as Sean cuts the engine and a few people in the shops next to the bar start pointing at us. "That sky is endless."

Sean gives me a funny look but just ties the boat up and jumps out onto the dock backstage where a few people are waiting to help us get ready.

"We don't have to do this," Kenner says. He drags his eyes off the sky and looks at me. "Not yet."

I know what he's feeling. I know he's got more doubts than me right now, and that's saying something. But we do. We do have to do this. "Well," I say back. "We don't have to do anything, I guess. But there's going to be a first time again eventually, Kenner. Let's make it today and get it over with. One song and we're outta here. One song and you can stop thinking about it. One song and we can start again."

He looks down at his hands, like he's not sure he recognizes them. They look fine to me. But I know it's what on the inside that matters.

"You remember what it was like? Back in Hollywood when we first got Mo?"

Kenner smiles at his hands and then looks up at me. "I want to go back there, Rock. I really do. But I'm not sure we'll ever find that sense of... destiny again, you know?"

I understand that too. And even though it feels natural to have TJ and Missy on stage with us for this song today, it's not that way for Kenner. He doesn't know them. He has no connection at all. Two days isn't enough time to get sense of anything.

"OK," I say. "Let's cancel." Kenner shoots me a look. "What?" I laugh.

"We're not cancelling, you dick. Do you see all those people?"

I look over at the shops and there's fans on the roof now. They are screaming and yelling at us. Mostly nice things, but... "You know, this town will probably bill us if anyone falls off that roof."

Kenner smiles.

"So..." I say. "You want to play or not?"

"Of course I *want* to play. I'm just not sure if I *can* play."

"You can."

"You don't know that. I should've tried it out last night like you said. Then I'd know what to expect."

"Expectations are over-rated, Kenner. What you need is a win. And I think today is a guaranteed win. For all of us, man. We cannot lose. It won't matter what my voice sounds like, what your beats sound like, or if people even like the song. It's just a symbol, ya know? We lived. We made it. We're still here and we're not going anywhere. This song today is more of a goodbye than anything. That life, yeah, it's over. But there's nothing we can do about that. They're gone. We have to move on."

Kenner's eyes shoot to mine. He shrugs, and that shrug says everything. The fear, the sadness, the loss. "I don't want it to be over," he says. "I don't want them to be gone and I don't want to move on."

"I know," I whisper, grabbing him by the shoulder and giving him a shake. "I know. I don't either. But they are. And we're still here. We have to find a way to get past this."

He sighs loudly, but stays silent as he pushes me aside and climbs out onto the dock. TJ is the one who stops him. "Dude, I haven't played bass in like eight years. So I'm just gonna apologize ahead of time for sucking ass."

Kenner rolls his eyes, but Missy is there next, pulling him into a hug. "And for reals, Kenner, I've tried my best to learn this song, but I just can't get the fingering, you know? Fucking, Rock," she says, shooting me a wink. "Had to go and make this shit all tricky. So if the show blows, it's my fault, OK?"

I step out onto the dock next to Kenner and say, "I don't know all the lyrics yet, man. So if I just start making shit up, well…"

"You guys are assholes," he says, taking a pair of sticks from Sean. "Fuck it. If we suck, then fuck it." He shrugs us all off him and then pushes his way towards the open flap in the stage backdrop and disappears. The crowd cheers and whistles when they recognize him.

"Ready?" TJ asks me and Miss.

We nod. I go next, then Missy, then TJ. I don't even look at the crowd, just sit down at the piano and adjust the mic. I know the lawn is packed. The festival is a closed event but there was no way to stop the influx of people, so about ten this morning the sheriff called TJ and told him to open it all up so no one got hurt. That's what we did. We never told anyone we were going to do a song, they just assumed. Correctly. Because how can we not?

We're not playing a concert. These people aren't here to *hear* us. They're here to experience us.

I said I'd never do this again and I'm sure Kenner's been telling himself the same thing since he woke up a few weeks ago. But we need this. There's no way forward without music. Not if we want to do more than exist. And life's not worth living if you're just existing.

"Hey," Kenner says into his mic. The crowd goes wild and I turn in my stool to look at him. He's not looking at the crowd, he's looking at me. "Rock," he says, pointing a stick at me. People try their best to quiet down to hear what he's got to say. "I just want you to know, you're it, dude. You're all I got left. And that's the only reason I'm here. You, man. You."

The cheering is so out of control it actually hurts my ears.

I nod, understanding. Everyone has a story, and not many people know Kenner's. But I do. So I nod. And then I look up at the crowd for the first time and say, "He's wrong though. He's got all of you too. Son of a Jack never got to play this one…"

I can't hear anything after that. They know what's coming. Kenner counts off the beats and my fingers find the way forward on the keys. My voice is deeper than it was. Softer too, since I'm not really one hundred percent yet.

I think I sound like shit, but hey, this is what I have left. And it's more than enough for now. Besides, no one cares what we sound like. No one cares. All they want is to be here with us. Support us. Love the fuck out of us. I smile the whole way through that song and that's the only thing that matters.

I am Son of a Jack's resurrection. I am Elias, I am Mo, and I am Ian. I am Kenner's win. I am Missy's other half. I am TJ's missing brother.

I am RK's new life.

Later that night, long after the festival is over and everyone has gone home or is sleeping, I swing my feet out of bed.

"Where the fuck are you going?" Missy asks, her hand clutching my arm. "Rowan Kyle Saber, if you think you're climbing down that cliff tonight, I've got news for you."

I look over my shoulder and then beckon her with a finger. "Follow me," I say. I get up without waiting. Her soft footfalls echo behind me out to the music room and

I can barely contain my excitement as I take a seat on the bench. "Sit," I say.

She sits. "What are you doing?" She's smiling big though. Big. Big. Big.

"That wasn't your song, you know."

"What?" Missy laughs. "What do you mean?"

"That song I played? That wasn't it. You think I'm going to share that with the world? No, way, babe." I grin just as big as my fingers begin to play.

"Wait," Miss says. "The Better Together song wasn't my song?"

"Please," I say. "Better Together is good. But I wrote you another song."

"When?" she giggles.

"Today, on stage. I thought up a new one."

"Just thought it up, huh?" She shakes her head. "RK—"

"You know what it's called?" I ask.

She pauses and then winks. "The Fuck Me Song?"

I have to look away to hide the grin.

"The Let Me Lick You Song?"

"Crass, Melissa Vetti. Crass."

"You started it," she says. And even in the moonlight, I can see her flush pink.

"No," I whisper, as I play the soft notes to the new song. "It's called the You're My Soulmate song." I get a big, big, big smile. "It's called the Spend the Rest of Your Life With Me song. It's called the Never Leave My Side song." I stop playing and then reach for a box on the top of the piano and open it up. "It's called the Marry Me, Melissa Vetti song."

"RK," she whispers. "Is that your mom's ring?"

"Yeah," I nod, taking it out of the box and picking up her hand. "Maybe Jack was a total fuck up most of the time, but he took me aside one day when I was about sixteen and he showed me this ring. And he said, 'This is for Melissa when you're ready. I know you're gonna marry her, so this is for Melissa.'"

She just stares at the ring in my hand for a few seconds before looking up at me. "You know what my song is called?"

"The Yes song?" I laugh. "The Absolutely song? The—"

Her fingertips touch my lips to quiet me. "The You're the Only One for Me song."

"I knew it," I say, grinning wildly. "I always knew it." I slip the ring on her finger and then place my palms on each side of her face, leaning in to kiss her mouth, whispering, "Be my wife."

"I will," she says back, just before her tongue twists with mine. "Now teach me this new song so I can play it with you." She snuggles into me, her head resting on my shoulder. Her hands around my bicep as I play the notes of our new song.

Because it really is better together.

Life is so much better when we do it together.

End of Book Shit

Welcome to the End of Book Shit where JA Huss gets to have her way with you. ;) Fans call this chapter the EOBS and they have somewhat of a cult status these days. Kind of like a Bruce Campbell B-movie. So... let me try and explain Rock...

It all started with a song.

I was writing Manic in the summer of 2013 and looking to make a new Spotify playlist. I had been playing Something Corporate pretty much on repeat for a while, mostly the song Konstantine because I just love it.

Konstantine a ten-minute piano-rock masterpiece that obtained cult-status for the band when lead singer

Andrew McMahon decided he wasn't going to play it at concerts anymore. Maybe just once a year. You see, he had this problem. That's the one song fans were demanding to hear in concert and it's ten minutes long. So it kind of interferes with the set, you know? Ten minutes is a big commitment when you're doing a show. You could probably play four songs instead of one.

And then I stumbled on this article… *("Something Corporate's "Konstantine" Has Been Haunting Us For A Decade" – "This nine-and-a-half-minute piano ballad has become something of a legend among emo fans in the decade since it was written. "Konstantine" is maligned by its writer, Andrew McMahon, but it's become something like an overwrought emo version of Bob Dylan's "Visions of Johanna," or a "Freebird" for suburban teenage romance. It was never released on an album, but it's become a favorite among fans of the band, and has arguably become their best-known song.")*

Andrew McMahon in 2009 on the legacy of "Konstantine":

"If I ever play it, I'll have to play it forever, every night. If it weren't such a big deal for me to play Konstantine, then I probably would play it. But the truth is, as soon as I bring that song out one time, I will never be able to walk through a venue, no matter what band I'm playing with or no matter where I'm at, and not have people chant and cheer for it." via Blast Magazine

I love the song. It's on like ten of my Spotify playlists. But wow. To have such a thing as an artist, right? Not many bands get a Konstantine and even though McMahon sorta comes off as disliking the song in that quote, there's a new interview I saw where he explains it better. The whole timing thing. I get that. It makes very logical sense.

But back to Rock. I was sorta in love with the piano ballads that summer (2013) and was really into Mayday Parade because they had two lead singers back when they first started, Derek Sanders and Jason Lancaster. I think it was too much talent for one band. I'm not kidding, and these two went their separate ways. Sanders and Lancaster can both sing (incredibly well) and play piano and guitar.

So I was sorta hooked on the piano rock back when I started putting this Rock plot together. I loved that these three guys I mention above are true artists and musicians. They make incredible music and they are way too talented. But what really drew me to them, especially McMahon, were their own personal back stories.

I stumbled across another song that summer called Swim by a band called Jack's Mannequin and after clicking over to read their bio on Spotify, guess who their front man was? Andrew McMahon. Now this song is really where the idea of Rock the character came from. You see, Andrew McMahon was filming a biopic for the band chronicling the album they were making and he had some health problems and ended up at the doctor's office in NYC.

Filming that same documentary that would become "Dear Jack".

As he was diagnosed with leukemia.

("Using a handheld video camera that his record label gave to him initially to document the process of recording his album, McMahon recorded everything from inside his hospital room and onward, from spinal taps to radiation and commentary on his deteriorating physical and mental state. The film follows him from diagnoses to recovery, including the stem cell transplant that saved his life and the first show he performed after being well again.") via Wikipedia

Andrew survived with help from his sister Katie's stem cells and a whole lot of support from his family and friends.

SWIM is the song he wrote afterward. That's what this is book is about. Rock isn't Andrew but Andrew and his personal story definitely inspired this book and this character. If you read the lyrics for that song you get chills and it's a beautiful, beautiful piano ballad.

So, as you can see, lots of things from Andrew's back story made it into the plot. From the name of the band, "Son of a Jack" to the song fans won't stop asking for, to the personal crisis (both physically and mentally) and the ultimate triumph that was a direct result of family and friends.

But that's not where Rock's story ends. Because when I finally did sit down to write ROCK on January 25th, 2016, two and a half years after I had the original idea, I stumbled onto something else.

A movie called Meru.

"I always wondered how I was going to die. And now… now I know."
~ Jimmy Chin, Meru

You have probably never heard of Meru. I had never heard of Meru. And I can tell you right now my only experience with rock climbing before this book was one friend I had back in like 2003 who took it up after her first child was born. She was in a bad place but rock climbing did something for her. Her eyes lit up and she got excited as she told me about how her and this guy she was semi-dating (who was much older than her) took her out to Utah and taught her to climb. And since I had decided Rock was from Grand Lake, Colorado way back in 2013, I decided maybe Rock could find solace in that sport too. It was just a whim, really. I had no idea how pivotal it would be to the plot until I saw Meru.

I have a thing for watching movies as I write. I tend to write in big chunks, like 8,000 words a day. And then I like to take a day off and think. Watch movies, mostly. They inspire me. So I was on one of these "off" days looking through on-demand movies on cable and came across Meru. It was a new title. I look for new movies all the time, so the fact that I'd never heard of it before was what caught my eye. And the minute I realized it was a documentary about rock climbers I knew I had to see it.

Meru is drama. Meru is personal triumph. Meru is a testament to friendship, trust, and the human spirit. And maybe no one reading this book cares that these three men climbed that mountain (the first ever to reach the top of that peak) but I do. And the reason it's personally relevant to my identity as an author is because all three of these men are bigger than life.

Rock is bigger than life too. All of the main characters in my books are bigger than life. They have unimaginable obstacles thrown at them and somehow they always pull through. I wrote in the Eighteen End of Book Shit about readers who were tired of the "drama" in books. Why does everything have to be so over-the-top dramatic? Why does everything have to be bigger than life?

Well, one, bigger than life makes for a good story. That's enough in and of itself. For me at least. But two, it's real. It's fucking real.

That movie isn't about the climb to the top of the Shark's Fin of Mount Meru. It's about the struggle it took to get there.

Three men—Conrad Anker, Renan Ozturk, and Jimmy Chin.

Their personal struggles go from losing best friends in avalanches and climbing accidents, to falling off a cliff and surviving with shattered vertebrae and a cranial fracture, to being swept up, and surviving, an avalanche in the Tetons.

If that's not over-the-top drama, well, I don't what is. And it's all true.

That was my thought as I was watching Meru. It's all true. Renan Ozturk climbed Meru less than six months after falling off the side of a cliff while skiing and cracking his head open. He had a fucking stroke on the side of Meru. Conrad and Jimmy didn't even know if he'd survive the night as they sat in their portaledge tent feeling helpless. They couldn't take him down the mountain, they were almost 22,000 feet up in the Himalayas. And they were tired from a full day of climbing. Even if they thought they could find Renan help in time, they couldn't do the descent until morning without risking everyone's life.

It was a long night but when Renan woke up the next day he said he felt better.

He said he wasn't going down—he was going up.

And he did.

All three of them went up and made it to the top. The first ever. Just watching Renan when he got there was enough to make me tear up. That mountain saved him. When he woke up in the hospital after that skiing accident and the doctors told him he'd probably never walk again, the only thing he thought of was, *Meru is in September and I'm not missing it.*

Conrad and Jimmy were like, *Dude, you know... I don't know.*

And all their friends and family were like, You shouldn't let him make that climb. He could get you all killed.

But Conrad and Jimmy were like, *Hey, if Renan says he can do it, if Renan is getting better after the accident because of this climb, we're not going to be the ones to crush his spirit. He's coming.*

Renan should not have been able to walk after that accident, let alone climb an unclimbable mountain.

But he did. He focused on it and made it happen.

The mind is a powerful thing.

Conrad was obsessed with climbing Meru after his mentor failed to do it back in the 80's. *"Meru is the culmination of all I've done. And all I've ever wanted to do was this climb."* It was also a kind of redemption for losing his best friend in an avalanche a few years later.

Jimmy got a second chance at life after surviving an avalanche in the Tetons just four days after Renan's almost-fatal fall from a cliff during that same ski trip. After Jimmy's mother died he figured it was now or never. He had promised his mom he wouldn't die before she did so every climb he did up until her death was with that in mind. Now he was free to take this risk. He says in the movie, *"If we go for it there's a probability that we're not going to come back."*

And Renan said, *"But it was worth the risk. It was worth possibly dying for."* Renan needed it to live. Renan needed that mountain to go on. It was his hope while he was in the hospital recovering from a cracked skull and shattered vertebrae. Meru was everything. It was the only thing that mattered. It was the answer to the "why" question after such a huge defeat. It was salvation.

This is what Rock finds in the climbing. It's a way forward. The only thing he has pushing him to live on.

Dramatic? Fuck yes. And I love it.

I spent the entire time watching Meru knowing full well all three guys were alive because the interviews were after the fact, but still wondering how it could possibly be so, because of what they all went through to get to the end. I had to stop watching and convince myself of this fact more than once, that's how thrilling this story was. They are all alive. I know this. But still, I asked myself, How could they possibly survive these unsurvivable things? So I watched that movie thinking, If I wrote this plot in a book people would call it unrealistic. They'd call it unnecessary drama. They'd call it over-the-top.

Well, it is, I guess. Rock is all those things too. I'd like to think the mountain saved Rock as well. If the mountain could save Renan than it could save Rock too.

I think Rock is probably the most suspenseful story I've ever written and while I was putting it all together I had some doubts about that. I won't lie. But this was the story from day one - way, way back in the summer of 2013 when I found the rock star named Andrew who learned he had cancer on what should've been one of the happiest days of his life. And fuck it, I was going to write my story, even if no one wanted to read it.

That's how I feel about each book I write. I get an idea and I see it through the eyes of the character until we get to the end. I don't write books for money, I write them because small ideas lead to big stories. And this book started with a song and ended with a movie.

In between I filled it with as much drama as possible. Rock is my story about this character, this town, and his friends through my eyes, as told by RK Saber. And I decided while I was watching Meru that I'd never again apologize for over-the-top drama in my books because Conrad, Jimmy, Renan, and Andrew are all real people who survived and triumphed through extraordinary circumstances.

If they can do it for real, surely my fictional characters can do it in a story.

So that's Rock. No, he's not real but his problems are. People experience trauma and handle it in different ways. I like exploring the psychology of that. I like exploring the recovery and what it means to overcome something. I like finding the happily ever after. Just like Andrew did. Just like Conrad, Renan, and Jimmy did.

Just like Rock did.

It's not fake, people. It's real life. And I love it.

So I hope you love it too, because I'm not going to stop writing about it.

If you enjoyed this book, please consider leaving me a review online. I'm an independent author and every bit of success I have is due to word of mouth from fans like you.

Thank you for reading, thank you for reviewing, and see you in the next book. If you'd like to chat with me and other JA Huss fans you can ask to join my private Facebook Group (Shrike Bikes) I hang out there every single day and I read every single post so if you've got a question or comment, I will be sure to see and answer it if you post in there.

~Julie

About the Author

JA Huss is the New York Times and USA Today bestselling author of more than twenty romances. She likes stories about family, loyalty, and extraordinary characters who struggle with basic human emotions while dealing with bigger than life problems. JA loves writing heroes who make you swoon, heroines who makes you jealous, and the perfect Happily Ever After ending.

You can chat with her on Facebook, Twitter, and her kick-ass romance blog, New Adult Addiction. If you're interested in getting your hands on an advanced release copy of her upcoming books, sneak peek teasers, or information on her upcoming personal appearances, you can join her newsletter list and get those details delivered right to your inbox.

JA Huss lives on a dirt road in Colorado thirty minutes from the nearest post office. So if she owes you a package from a giveaway, expect it to take forever. She has a small farm with two donkeys named Paris & Nicole, a ringneck parakeet named Bird, and a pack of dogs. She also has two grown children who have never read any of her books and do not plan on ever doing so. They do, however, plan on using her credit cards forever.

JA collects guns and likes to read science fiction and books that make her think. JA Huss used to write homeschool science textbooks under the name Simple Schooling and after publishing more than 200 of those, she ran out of shit to say. She started writing the I Am Just Junco science fiction series in 2012, but has since found the meaning of life writing erotic stories about antihero men that readers love to love.

JA has an undergraduate degree in equine science and fully planned on becoming a veterinarian until she heard what kind of hours they keep, so she decided to go to grad school and got a master's degree in Forensic Toxicology. Before she was a full-time writer she was smelling hog farms for the state of Colorado.

Even though JA is known to be testy and somewhat of a bitch, she loves her #fans dearly and if you want to talk to her, join her Facebook fan group where she posts daily bullshit about bullshit.

If you think she's kidding about this crazy autobiography, you don't know her very well.

Printed in Great Britain
by Amazon